No clergy were hurt during the writing of this book.

ALSO BY JANET BROWN

History, Mystery, Murder

From the series, *A Priest, A Rabbi, and a Baptist Minister:*
The Murders at Windy Meadows
The Murders at Thornhaven Manor

WHAT PEOPLE ARE SAYING ABOUT THIS SERIES

Janet's characters are wonderfully well-written—Brendan and his friends are adorable, and a great part of Maureen's mystery-solving team. The plot has a great many twists and turns leading you in different directions, not knowing who the real killer is until you masterfully decide to let them in on the secret. There's lots of humor, and everything gets tied up by the end.

–Stacey Goitia, Reedsy editor

A Priest, a Rabbi, and a Baptist Minister: The Murders at Windy Meadows *is a suspenseful and uniquely fun new mystery by author Janet A. Brown, and the title reveals the intriguing premise. I recommend it to readers of mysteries and thrillers, especially fans of more mature protagonists or sleuths from religious vocations.*

–Karen Siddall

I loved this story! Janet had me scratching my head all the way through, trying to figure out who the killer was. Well done. I hope the three main characters show up again soon.

–Richard Caldwell, Author of *The Empress*

A Priest, A Rabbi, A Baptist Minister

The Murders at Saint Charles Seminary

By
Janet A. Brown

Typesetting and Cover Design: Covered by Kerry LLC

Print ISBN: 979-8-218-89746-8
Ebook ISBN: 979-8-218-89747-5

This book is dedicated with love and deep gratitude to Father Michael Roach, my cherished parish priest and treasured friend, whose wisdom, humor, and encouragement helped bring this story to life.

Thank you for reminding me that God surely has a sense of humor — He gave you me as a parishioner.

CHAPTER 1

Saturday Evening

A biting wind howled through the skeletal branches of ancient oaks, their twisted forms casting long shadows across the historic Saint Charles Borromeo Seminary courtyard. The Maryland air that evening was thick with the scent of decaying leaves mingling with the faint aroma of incense that lingered in the drafty stone corridors. The chapel loomed ahead, its towering spires barely visible through the November fog. Dim light flickered from within, casting a pale, amber glow through the stained-glass windows that depicted solemn saints with watchful eyes. The chill of the evening seeped through every stone, and silence hung like a heavy shroud, broken only by the creak of the chapel's wooden doors.

Joseph Lin, a young third-year seminarian, paused at the entrance of the chapel, his breath forming delicate clouds in the cold air. His hands trembled slightly, not from the cold but from the gnawing anxiety that twisted in his gut. Something wasn't right. He had felt it all day—a mounting tension, a creeping sense of dread that clung to him like the fog. He crossed the threshold with hesitant steps, the echo of his footfalls swallowed by the oppressive quiet. His eyes darted nervously toward the shadows that pooled in the corners of the chapel, where the candlelight couldn't reach. He made his way to the confessional, the ancient wood groaning softly as he opened the door and stepped inside.

Sinking to his knees, Joseph clasped his hands tightly together, trying to steady his breathing. The confessional felt colder than the rest of the chapel, the worn wooden walls pressing in on him as though they carried the weight of centuries of whispered sins. He opened the sliding door that allowed him to speak, heart pounding in his chest as he heard the faint rustle of the priest's robes on the other side. Yet something felt...off. He couldn't shake the feeling that something unseen was lurking just beyond the veil of darkness.

Hesitantly, he whispered, "Bless me, Father, for I have sinned..." His voice trembled, more from fear than guilt, and he struggled to suppress the growing dread gnawing at the edges of his mind. In an embarrassed whisper, he related some of his sins of the past week, none more serious than choosing to sleep in one morning, making him late for his first class.

"We are all judged, Joseph," the voice intoned, its inflection slipping into something darker. "But tell me...who absolves the guilty?"

Joseph's breath hitched. Now sharp and biting, the voice seemed to slice through the thin wall between them. "Father, I don't—" His eyes narrowed in confusion, but before he could speak another word, he heard the confessional door crash open, and suddenly, a dark figure was on him, strong hands wrapped around his neck, cutting off his air. His vision blurred as he struggled against his attacker, the wood of the booth creaking under the violence.

Before Joseph's soul left his body, his eyes locked onto his assailant's. It was—no, it couldn't be! But why? What had he, Joseph Lin, the first-generation American of Chinese immigrant parents, done to deserve this? There was no mercy there, only cold resolve.

Resigned, Joseph ceased his struggle. His lips moved in silent prayer as his world faded to black, the last sound in his ears the haunting creak of the chapel doors closing in the distance before his soul left his body.

CHAPTER 2

Sunday Morning

The following morning, Aiden O'Clery, a first-year seminarian, headed off to the chapel to sweep the floors before the first Mass of the day. Aiden, a handsome, baby-faced young man with freckles scattered across his pale skin like faint brushstrokes, all hidden beneath a mop of unruly red hair, whistled as he swung his broom around, pretending to be leading a marching band.

As he stepped into the dimly lit chapel, the scent of incense from the previous night's prayer vigil still lingering in the air, his gaze fell upon something lying outside of the confessional. There, crumpled in a lifeless heap at its threshold, lay Joseph Lin. His face was frozen in a final, silent plea, and a rosary, tightly wound around his neck, gleamed under the flickering morning light like a sinister noose. The seminarian's normally caramel-colored skin was now a pale white with a purplish tinge to his lips.

Aiden dropped the broom and tried to catch his breath but found he had no breath in him. His first instinct was to run, but he then steeled himself and stepped forward, kneeling beside Joseph, feeling for a pulse, only to meet the chill of a lifeless limb.

Releasing Joseph's arm, he saw what appeared to be an old piece of parchment with something written in calligraphy pinned to Joseph's shirt. It read:

"When the shepherd is blind, the flock shall bleed.
A serpent coils within the house of God, its fangs in the hearts of the chosen.
Three shall fall before the dawn of reckoning.
One by the hand of judgment, one by the weight of sin.
Only the faithful shall see the light beyond the veil."

"My God," cried Aiden, crossing himself, offering a quick prayer for Joseph. He stood and ran out of the chapel to find help.

Father Vincent Gabriel, the rector of Saint Charles Borromeo Seminary, was a solid man in his early eighties, with thick, white hair atop a serious face. He carried himself with the quiet authority of a lifelong shepherd of young souls. He stood by the large leaded-glass window, his steely gray eyes staring out at the trees as the sharp wind stripped them of their leaves. Deep lines etched his face, not just from age but from years of listening, guiding, and keeping the confidences of others. To the seminarians, there was always the sense that he knew more than he let on, a keeper of mysteries both sacred and worldly.

A loud knock on his open office door startled him away from the window. He turned, smiling as he saw the young man at his door. "Aiden, my boy! What can I do for you?" He walked over to his desk and took a seat.

"Father, I was sweeping in the chapel and—and Joseph Lin is on the floor, dead." He raised a balled fist to his face and covered his mouth, not wanting to have to describe what he had seen. His gaze drifted to the office window, fixating on the world beyond—the swaying branches, the distant rooftops—anything but the piercing eyes of the rector. In a barely audible voice, he said, "I think he was murdered."

The rector shot up from his chair. "What? Joseph Lin? *Murdered?*" His eyes darted around until they rested on the landline, his hand poised to make the call. "What makes you say murdered?"

Aiden relayed how he had found the body and the rosary that had been cruelly twisted around his neck.

The rector's eyes darkened as he turned back to the window, his gaze distant, his mind racing. "Aiden," he began, turning to the boy, "you may go. I'll call for an ambulance and the sheriff's department." His eyes searched the face of the young seminarian. "I don't want you to say anything to any of the other students right now, is that clear? I need to be the one to tell them." His face grew serious. "And remember, there will be no need to discuss anything that happens within this seminary with the police, do you hear me? Only about what you witnessed related to finding Joseph. Say nothing more. I'll speak with the authorities." He began dialing. "You'll all likely be questioned, but the police need not be bothered with anything that goes on in here that does not relate to whatever happened to Joseph, is that clear?" His eyes narrowed.

Aiden nodded vigorously. "I understand, Father. You can trust me." He remained standing, awaiting further instruction.

Father Gabriel turned and looked at the boy. "You may go, Aiden. I'll go down to the chapel myself after I call this in, but remember my words."

"I will, Father," said Aiden, nodding again. He turned to go.

Father Gabriel pulled the chair from his desk and sat again, his shoulders sagging, as he waited for the 911 operator to answer his call. He removed his glasses and ran his hands through his hair.

"And so it begins," he mumbled to himself as he reached for the whiskey bottle in his desk drawer.

SUNDAY AFTERNOON

In the cool afternoon, Ezra Lieberman stood behind a long table in the community room of Beit Ahava, the synagogue where he served as rabbi. His short frame carried an energy that belied his stature, with a wild halo of tight, brown curls framing his face. Round glasses that were perpetually slipping down his nose were nudged back into place with a practiced push. He sported a stained white apron and an oversized chef's hat perched precariously over his yarmulke. He wielded a wooden spoon dripping with a blood-red liquid.

The Annual Beit Ahava Fall Chili Cook-Off brought people of all faiths together at the synagogue as soon as November rolled in, when the weather was perfect for comfort food.

A huge hulk of a man with skin the deep hue of roasted coffee stood off to the side of the table. Pastor Langdon Boothe of the Hallelujah House Baptist Church scratched at the strands of silver that weaved their way through his neatly trimmed Van Dyke beard. The soft creases around his eyes spoke of both hardship and kindness.

"Which one you think the little dude's gonna pick?" He turned to his friend.

"He'd better pick my Burning Bush chili or I'm banning him from our poker games," replied Father Brendan O'Clery in a thick Irish accent as he leaned on a decorative Celtic cane. He scratched at the stubble on his chin, where a close-cropped yet scraggly beard stubbornly clung—a wild thing always begging for a trim.

"Why they pick *him* for the judge?" groused Langdon as he looked over the many chili entrées on the table. "He don't know chili. I'm a Loosiana boy, an' back home, if you ate *my* chili, you'd swear you just heard Satan whisper, 'Welcome home, boy.' Your tongue be so hot it'd be *beggin'* for a divorce."

"Gee," said Brendan. "Your chili sounds like a controlled explosion in a spoon!"

"True dat."

"Well, I should win," Brendan began, "because I offered a prayer during Mass this morning for our judge, who may be underestimating the spice level of the ghost pepper right about now." He gave a knowing grin to his friend.

The rabbi, clearly relishing his role as judge, pushed his glasses high up onto his nose, then scooped up a generous spoonful and took an exaggerated bite, savoring the moment with theatrical flair.

Suddenly, he began fanning his face as he reached for a glass of water, gulping it down and gasping dramatically, "This is how I die, isn't it?"

Just then, a voice from the crowd yelled out, "I think that priest cheated and used divine intervention to make his chili taste better—and maybe some holy water."

The crowd laughed.

Ezra, enjoying the attention, continued after composing himself. "I think divine intervention should have prevented the burned beans," Ezra answered, continuing to choke on the spices.

The crowd roared again, and Langdon threw Brendan a grin before bursting into laughter himself, punctuating it with a hearty slap on Brendan's back

"Little dude gotcha, bro," he said.

Ezra, seeing the crowd's obvious reaction to humor, continued. "Okay, folks, I kid, but all of these chilis are excellent, and may I add, this is the only contest where fire and brimstone are actual ingredients."

Again, the people erupted into laughter.

Just then, Mary Magdalene, Brendan's little Yorkie, wrenched free from his grasp and shot forward, the leash whipping behind her like a banner in the wind. With a flying leap, she landed squarely on the chili table, setting off a catastrophic chain reaction as crockpots toppled like dominos, sending steaming chili in every direction.

Mary Magdalene licked furiously at as many of the chili entrées as she could before someone in the crowd rushed forward, shooing her away from the mess.

Brendan, appalled that the little dog had broken loose, lurched forward with an awkward limp, straining to catch her before she vanished into the melee. Someone in the crowd, seeing the tiny dog, yelled out, "It's a rat!" and pandemonium ensued, with folks screaming and running around and into each other. The ones closest to the tipped pots got splattered with chili.

Ezra stood there, watching the scene unfold. "I don't think this is kosher anymore," was all he could muster as he looked toward his two friends, who were trying to apprehend the little dog. "*Oy gevalt,*" he mumbled, covering his face with his hands.

"Dude, we gotta get outta here," hollered Langdon over the din as he watched the priest scoop up the Yorkie. He grabbed Brendan's sleeve and pulled him through the crowd, out of the community room, and into the cool fall air.

"Wait," cried Brendan, bending over, holding his stomach. "I need to catch my breath." With his free hand, he swept through his thick, black locks, the rich waves falling perfectly back into place, and looked at his friend, who was trying to stifle a laugh, but found he could not.

"Bro, that was hil-AR-ious! Little dude gonna be *steamin'* when all this be over."

Brendan, though trying to maintain a stoic facade, couldn't hide his shame at what his dog had perpetrated, but the growing amusement was starting to get the better of him like it had his friend.

"He's going to be *so* mad," agreed Brendan, leaning on his cane. He lifted Mary Magdalene to his face and gave her a mock scolding. Unfazed, the little dog simply licked a spot of chili from his beard.

Just then, Brendan felt his cell phone vibrating in his jacket pocket. He lowered the tiny dog to the ground and slipped a hand into his pocket, pulling out his phone. His eyes flicked to the screen, his brow furrowing in quiet concentration.

"It's my brother, Finn," said Brendan, looking at Langdon. "He and his wife, Mary Virginia, are out of town. I hope nothing's wrong." He answered the call. "Finn! *Conas atá tú?* How's the vaca—"

"Brendan, Aiden just called me from the seminary," came a voice sharp with panic, as though he couldn't get the words out fast enough. The accent was as thickly Irish as Brendan's. "There was a murder this morning at the seminary. One of the young men was killed last night. The wife's calling Maureen, but herself is getting ready to go on vacation, too, I hear, so she won't be handling the case—"

"Oh, dear Lord," interrupted Brendan, crossing himself. "I'll call Mo in a minute. You guys stay put. How's the lad faring?"

"Your nephew is beside himself, Brendan. He's a delicate boy and not made of the stuff you are, so. We're still at Mary Virginia's sister's place in North Carolina. That's why we're calling you and Maureen."

"Good. I'll grab Mo and get over there as soon as we can. We'll check on the boy." He paused. "I'll bet Father Gabriel will be over the moon to see me."

Finn gave a guarded laugh. "I'm sure he will. Thanks, Bren. And keep Mary Virginia and me posted, will you?"

"Sure thing, Finn. I'll call you later. Tell Mary Virginia not to worry." He ended the call and looked at Langdon, his face lost in a flurry of emotions.

"Hol' on now...did I hear right? A preacher boy done got hisself kilt?" Langdon put a meaty arm around Brendan, a bewildered look on his face. "Your brother's voice were loud, and I heard ev'ry word."

"You heard right. And I'm calling Mo. I know she's itching to start her vacation, but we need to get over there and see how her cousin Aiden's doing." He jabbed at his niece's number, urgency in his movements as Mary Magdalene danced around his ankles, tugging at her leash, the neon pink bow in her hair covered with chili. He looked down at the Yorkie. "Not right now, princess. I need to get you home."

"How can I help, bro?" asked Langdon as he watched the priest put the phone up to his ear. "You know me an' the little dude be here for you."

Brendan gave him a wan smile and gripped his upper arm. "You're a true friend, Pastor Boothe. A true friend. Let me find out what's happening and I'll catch up with you later." He turned to go but then remembered. "Hey, tell Ezra what's going on, okay?"

Langdon gave him a thumbs-up, and Brendan hobbled over to his beat-up Honda Civic, his leg, throbbing from an IED injury from his time in the Marines during the Gulf War, giving him a righteous pain as he moved as fast as he could.

What is going on at that seminary? he pondered as he turned the ignition on. The place had always been a mysterious and intimidating place when he was in attendance. So many secrets he had never been privy to, but now his nephew, a sweet boy who would make a wonderful parish priest, had witnessed something so horrific, so early in his priestly formation.

Brendan's tires crunched over the synagogue's gravel lot as he pulled out, heading for his old stomping grounds, hands tight on the wheel and a silent prayer on his lips for his sensitive nephew.

CHAPTER 3

Sunday Afternoon

Maureen McNeely sat on her sofa, bathed in the warm glow of the early afternoon sun. Her copper-gold hair caught the light from her living room window, transforming it into a cascade of shimmering flames. She was on her second cup of coffee, and scattered around her were various outfits, including a skimpy black bikini, one that she had starved herself for weeks just to be able to wear on the white beaches of the Bahamas with a troop of close girlfriends. She had two blessed weeks of leave so she'd be able to wake up when she wanted and sleep whenever she felt the urge. And food? All the rich island foods and alcohol she could partake in during her two weeks of heaven on earth.

She had just downloaded one of her favorite murder podcasts and began putting items in her suitcase when her cell rang to the tune of "Ave Maria." Letting out a primal *aargh*, she grabbed the cell and answered the call.

"You know I have two weeks of leave, don't you? Why are you bothering me?" She sat up and nibbled at a piece of cold toast, wincing. Cooking, she knew, began and ended with toast, and even that was hit or miss.

"Is that any way to speak to a priest? *Or* your favorite uncle?"

"Uncle Brendan, right now you've moved to the bottom of that list. What's up?"

"I guess Mary Virginia hasn't called you yet..." His voice trailed off. "This morning, Aiden found the body of one of the other seminarians in the chapel. He'd been murdered. I just got off the phone with Finn, and he says the kid is really upset."

Maureen put the toast down. "Oh my God, who was the seminarian?" She interrupted herself. "Hang on, Aunt Mary Virginia's calling."

"No need to answer, Mo. She's calling to tell you about Aiden and the murdered seminarian."

"So was he a friend of Aiden's? Do you know who got the case?"

She heard an exasperated sigh on the other end. "Whoa, slow down. I don't know anything yet, but I thought we'd both go over there to check on Aiden before you need to leave for your vacation. Finn and Mary Virginia are still out of town, so he wants us to look in on the boy."

Maureen frowned as her mind went into overdrive. "Okay," she sighed, resigned to giving up her frivolous afternoon activities. "Give me half an hour, and I'll meet you at your place, and we'll head up to the school."

She ended the call and stood, gazing sorrowfully at her array of shorts and sleeveless shirts.

"I'm so sorry," she said to the suitcases. "You'll all have to stay on the sofa for a while, but don't worry"—she picked up the remaining piece of toast—"I'll be back and we'll continue your journey into my luggage."

She gathered her empty coffee cup and plate and placed them in the kitchen sink. She shot a quick text to her aunt, letting her know she had received the disturbing news.

Changing into a pair of jeans and a thick cable-knit sweater, she grabbed her Glock, her badge, a heavy jacket, and the large canvas tote she always carried to crime scenes and headed out the door, mumbling to herself about how one Catholic priest could be so irritating.

SUNDAY AFTERNOON

Mary Magdalene wasn't happy about being left behind in the rectory, but Mrs. Morrison, Brendan's motherly housekeeper, lured her away from the door with a treat, giving him the chance to slip out unnoticed and meet his niece who had arrived in her ten-year-old Jeep Wrangler. Old and battered, it was a dependable, rugged, off-road vehicle, and the sun-faded, red exterior hinted at countless misadventures.

He threw his cane in the backseat of the Jeep and strapped the seatbelt around him.

"So, how do you feel about returning to Saint Charles?" asked Maureen as she left the rectory's driveway.

Brendan gave her a lopsided grin. "I'm okay with it. It was actually a grand experience. We had lots of late-night debates, and of course, the sports were always great competition moments. I mean, I came out with a boatload of friends and a heck of a good education. The studies were difficult sometimes, but I love learning, and I did get to read plenty of theological treatises!" His grin grew wider. "And look at me now. I'm a beloved parish priest."

Maureen flicked his thigh with her fingers. "Well, I hope you can behave when we get there. We're supposed to be helping Aiden, not solving any murders. One of the other guys will get this case since I'll be gone."

"Fine with me," replied Brendan, folding his arms across his chest.

Maureen frowned, glancing at him. "And when are you going to get that beard trimmed?" She reached a hand out toward his chin, but he ducked out of range. "You no longer look like Ewan McGregor with all that growth."

"Ewan McGregor," he spat. "I think you must have inhaled too many illegal drugs on some of those busts you went on years ago."

She wished she were in the mood to laugh, but her mind was on her cousin. She increased her speed, getting them to the seminary in record time.

As Maureen pulled into Saint Charles's driveway, Porter Mills Sheriff's cruisers' emergency lights were already flashing over the area.

Parking away from the police vehicles, Maureen and Brendan exited the Jeep. Maureen reached into the back, grabbed her uncle's cane, and handed it to him.

Maureen stood for a moment, perusing the old building, left to right.

"If you're looking for surveillance cameras, there won't be any," said Brendan.

"I was, and that's going to make it harder." She then spotted one of her fellow deputies. "I don't believe it."

"What?" asked Brendan, as he looked around.

"Looks like Caleb got the case. I would have thought Pollard would have given it to one of the more experienced guys." She shook her head. "Poor Caleb. Pollard's going to be merciless on him." She walked over to the detective, with Brendan tagging behind.

"Well, look who got stuck with this investigation," teased Maureen as she approached the man.

She saw the deputy's lips twist. "I don't know why Pollard handed this to me and not one of the seasoned guys. This is my first homicide, you know." He looked around. "A K-9 dog would be more experienced, and of course"—he managed a sad smile—"you're leaving us for warmer pastures."

"Not soon enough," said Maureen. She looked at her uncle. "Oh, by the way, you remember my uncle, Father Brendan from Saint Margaret Mary's? Anyway, he attended this seminary decades ago and might come in handy as a kind of unofficial liaison."

The two men shook hands and exchanged pleasantries.

"Well, Maureen, if I could solve this puppy, what a coup that would be, huh?"

Maureen whistled. "No pressure there, Caleb."

Brendan nodded amiably. "*Your* first wasn't all that long ago, Mo, remember?"

"But," Caleb said slowly, looking at Maureen, "I could sure use your help. Until you leave, that is." He leaned in toward her and in a low voice said, "Pollard doesn't have to know."

Maureen winced. She felt for her fellow deputy, but her mind was fixed on stretching out under a blazing sun, bronzing the ten pounds she'd just shed, and sipping something with an umbrella in it, not chasing a murder case that wasn't even hers. But, she opined, she had taken an oath, and she, of all people, understood what it felt like to have Captain Lamar Pollard, their toad-like supervisor with the feral breath of a dead animal, waiting for her to fail.

"Sure, Caleb. We can walk with you now, and no one will suspect a thing." She waved a hand toward Brendan. "His nephew—my cousin—is a first-year seminarian here. He found the victim, so we're here to check on him. But we can both help you, too."

Caleb smiled gratefully. "Perfect. Thanks so much, guys." He gave a mock salute, then the three began walking toward the seminary, entering the main building.

Gathered inside was a small group of young men wearing clerical black slacks and shirts, a few in cassocks. The first-year students were identifiable, as they were not allowed to wear the white clerical collar. Contrary to Father Gabriel's instructions, it hadn't taken long for word to spread, and now they were all chattering about Joseph Lin's death and who could have killed him.

Eugene Wingate, a tall, gaunt figure, stood alone. The first-year student fingered rosary beads in nervous hands, his lips moving silently.

Daniel Caruso, a handsome young man in his mid-twenties, left his group of friends and strolled over to where Eugene was standing. He ran a hand through his thick head of hair. "Praying for Joseph, huh, Eugene?" A smirk spread across his clean-shaven face as he turned to look back at his friends.

Eugene stopped praying and pocketed the beads. "I've been having nightmares, very disturbing nightmares. I had one the other night and"—he looked around to see if anyone was near—"someone was being strangled by a rosary, just like...just like Joseph." He stared at Daniel, his eyes wide with fright.

Daniel gave a disinterested grunt. "Another one of your wacky dreams? So what do you think it means? Did you kill Lin?"

"Oh no! Of course not!" cried Eugene. "Never! But it's like something, or someone, is trying to tell me something."

Daniel's head tilted as he put his face inches from Eugene's. "Dreams aren't divine. They're just guilt playing tricks," he said condescendingly. He laughed and walked away.

Eugene, trembling, reached for his rosary again and returned to his prayers.

Once inside, Maureen turned to Caleb. "You're resourceful, and you'll get this solved quickly." She gave Caleb a reassuring pat on the back and nodded. "We need to take a look at the body first, then we can start questioning the seminarians and staff. The uniformed deputies will keep prying eyes away, so let's head over to the chapel."

As the trio departed the main building, deputies who had been dancing from one foot to the other in the cold now gathered inside, grateful to be stepping into warmth.

After entering the chapel, Maureen and Caleb moved toward the mahogany confessional. Crime scene tape had already secured the scene. Maureen stopped her uncle from moving forward with them.

The small seminary had been built in 1845, and the majority of stone and woodwork, save for modern-day heating, electricity, and plumbing, had endured the decades. Ordinarily, the beautifully hand-carved confessional would have been an architectural wonder, but today, it was an object in a still-life tableau.

Crime scene techs moved with quiet efficiency, the murmur of their radios mixing with the faint scent of candle wax and incense lingering in the air. They crouched near the victim, a young seminarian in a black cassock now rumpled and smeared with dust from the floor. His hands had been carefully slipped into evidence bags to preserve any trace of skin cells or fibers he might have clawed from his attacker.

One tech photographed a narrow length of twisted cord lying half-hidden beneath the wooden confessional booth, its fibers frayed, as though yanked in desperation. Another collected a small scattering of pale wood splinters from the booth's side panel, likely broken during the struggle. A single scuffed loafer print had been marked with a yellow evidence tent, the faint tread outlined in church dust.

On the victim's collar, a dark smear was swabbed for DNA. A tech also plucked a few strands of hair caught in the victim's sleeve, the color a sharp contrast to his own.

The solemn hush of the church seemed deeper now, broken only by the click of a camera shutter and the whisper of latex gloves over evidence.

Maureen chatted with techs, watching as rosary beads were unwound from the young man's neck. Kneeling over the body, her eyes narrowed, and her lips moved as she read the strange prophecy-like note on what looked like an aged piece of parchment placed on the boy's chest. It made no sense to her, but maybe her uncle would understand it. He was good at puzzles and riddles, and this prophetic note was turning into quite a riddle.

"Can we take him now?" asked one of the techs, a pair of turquoise-blue eyes the only thing showing through the paper evidence suit and mask.

"Sure. Let me take a quick pic first." She pulled out her cell and clicked photos of the body from several angles, and then the cryptic note.

Maureen motioned to her uncle, allowing him to approach and view Joseph's body. He walked over, crossed himself, and sketched a cross over the boy's body, his lips silently moving in prayer.

Maureen noted Joseph's position as he lay slumped on the worn marble floor beside the confessional, his cassock twisted and bunched high on one shoulder, as if he'd fought to pull free. His face was a mottled, ugly shade of purple, lips parted and flecked with dried spittle, eyes glassy but still wide with the terror of his last moments. A raw ligature mark ringed his neck, the skin beneath it bruised and ridged in the exact pattern of the cord now sealed in an evidence bag. Although his hands had been sealed in the transparent evidence bags, Maureen could see the right hand curled inside, his knuckles scraped, while the left one was clenched tightly around a single thread of dark velvet, likely torn from the booth's curtain. The scent of candle wax and stale incense hung heavy in the air, mixing with the metallic tang of fear sweat.

Maureen's gaze swept the floor. No blood there, but the scuff marks told their own story of a struggle, quick and vicious, in the shadow of a place meant for confession, not killing.

Caleb left the body and went to speak with the techs, leaving Maureen with her uncle.

"Sad, isn't it?" she said, nodding toward the body.

"So what have you found out so far?"

"Well," she began slowly, "he must have come in here for confession and then was surprised by someone"—she pointed to the rosary that was now being lifted into the evidence bag—"who attacked him and overpowered him. It looked like the person wrapped the rosary around his neck and strangled him."

Brendan rubbed the stubble on his chin. "Can I have a look at that rosary?"

Maureen turned and motioned to one of the techs to bring the beads over. Reaching into the tote she always carried, she grabbed a pair of latex gloves and handed her uncle a pair.

Slipping them on, he took the beads from the tech and gingerly held them. He turned the gold crucifix over and held it up to the light. He showed the cross to Maureen. "Check this out. It looks like initials here." He watched as Maureen took in the writing. "M.M., written in what looks like an indelible marking pen."

A thin smile formed on Maureen's lips as she took the beads from Brendan. "Good catch, Unc. Should be easy to figure out who M.M. is if he's a seminarian." She handed the rosary back to the tech and asked for the other evidence bag with the note in it. "They found this on him." She held up the clear bag with the parchment note.

Brendan studied it, frowning. *"When the shepherd is blind, the flock shall bleed..."* he began reading in a hushed tone. He read the rest of it silently until he reached the end. "What's it mean?" he asked Maureen, snapping a picture of it on his own phone.

She shrugged. "You're the priest. You tell me."

He gave the note another glance. "Where's the rest of it?"

"Caleb said that's all there was. Maybe the killer ripped it on purpose, or maybe it got torn before the murder even happened."

Brendan nodded, then turned his attention to the chapel floor. Using his cane for support, he crouched, squinting at the floor beside Joseph's body. "Look at these areas here," he said, pointing to several dull, sticky smears.

Maureen knelt beside him, touching the end of a latex finger to it and pulling back a thin, tacky substance. "Something like an adhesive." She motioned for a tech. "Can you get some scrapings from these?"

The tech nodded and Maureen turned back to her uncle.

Brendan studied the substance. "Looks weird for the soles of a shoe, but where else would it have come from?"

Maureen stared at the markings, reaching down to feel them again as a smile began to grow on her face. "Hey, you know how you're always teasing me about listening to those murder podcasts?"

Her uncle nodded as he continued following the imprints.

"Well, there was this one murder where the killer wrapped duct tape around his shoes, so if he did leave any prints, which he knew he would, the cops wouldn't be able to trace them."

"Well, that's a good one, Lieutenant Columbo," said Brendan.

One of the techs walked over to Maureen. "We're finished here. The ambulance is here to take him to the medical examiner. Anything else you need before he goes?"

Maureen turned toward Caleb. "Caleb? You done here? It's your case."

When Caleb answered that he was finished, Maureen told the tech they were free to leave.

Two men began to lift Joseph Lin's corpse into a body bag, and as they did, something caught Brendan's eye.

"Hold on a minute," he cried. "Something just dropped from the body."

Caleb, who still had gloves on, picked up the piece of paper and read it. His brows formed a "V," and he showed it to Maureen and Brendan. "Is it part of that parchment?" asked Caleb.

Maureen and Brendan stared at the note: *Who absolves the guilty?*

Maureen reached for her cell phone and snapped a picture of the phrase. She looked at her uncle. "Doesn't look to be part of that first note. This is written on white paper, not old parchment. I'm forwarding all this to you, Caleb. And I'll help you as much as I can before I'm off." She turned and began walking back to the main building with the deputy and her uncle. "I'll help with some interviews, and if you want my uncle's help, I'm sure he'd be more than happy to stick his nose in—I mean, *help* you." She glared at Brendan.

"Okay, okay," he said, giving in, palms up. "No need to get ugly. I get it."

They walked back in silence.

Maureen watched Caleb gather the seminarians into the auditorium. Less than three dozen young men were currently enrolled. The old seminary had all but been forgotten, as a newer one had recently been built on the other side of Baltimore. The archdiocese had decided to keep Saint Charles for its historical value, and the staff was eternally grateful. Since some of the young men were still away on retreat, and the deacons preparing for ordination had been assigned to local parishes, the list of potential suspects narrowed.

"I'm Detective Caleb Martinez, and this is"—he glanced at Maureen briefly—"my partner, Detective McNeely."

Maureen sensed Caleb was uncomfortable stretching the truth, but she wanted to help in any way she could.

"We're just going to ask a few questions, and then you'll be free to go." He looked around and saw a small table surrounded by several chairs. He motioned for the young men to stay where they were, telling them they'd be called individually. He strode over to the table and took a chair, placing his notepad down on the table.

Maureen felt the tension in the room as she pulled up another chair. The sudden murder of a fellow seminarian had cast a long shadow over the school. She sensed the young men's paranoia and wondered what secrets they shared.

Caleb cleared his throat and called out to Aiden. "I'll start with you, son."

Maureen leaned over to the deputy. "Why are you questioning him? My cousin didn't murder anyone."

Caleb gave Maureen a stunned look. "He found the body, so he's the perfect one to start with. I can't discount him because he's your cousin." He shook his head. "Honestly, Maureen. You know better than that."

Maureen shot Caleb a sharp look but went silent as her cousin stood.

Aiden walked over, taking a seat opposite Caleb. The detective looked at the boy sitting in front of him and gave him a warm smile. He took out a notepad and began. "Start with your name and tell me about Joseph Lin and where you were last night between eight o'clock and seven this morning."

Aiden gave Caleb his personal information and where he had been until he had found Joseph's body. He then relayed how he had gone to the chapel and when he saw a fellow seminarian on the floor, went over to see if he could render aid.

"He looked so pale...so lifeless," he began, his voice low and tremulous. "He was my friend, and I thought he had a seizure maybe, or fell, but..." He pressed his palm to his chest, as if steadying his heart. "But he was cold and..." Aiden lowered his head, his eyes rimming with tears.

"So you had no beef with him?" asked Caleb.

Aiden jerked his head up. "No way! He was my friend, and I'd never hurt him or anyone. I want to be a priest and *help* people, not hurt them." He looked at his cousin, Maureen, his eyes pleading.

"Son, I'm not saying you had anything to do with this. I just need to get as many facts as I can." Caleb looked at Maureen then back at Aiden. He addressed the boy. "Look, do you of anyone who might have had it in for Joseph? Anyone at all? Fellow classmates or even any of the staff?"

"I'm telling you, sir, Joseph was a devout person, and I can't believe anyone in this seminary or elsewhere would have done something like this."

Caleb jotted down a few notes, then dismissed him.

Maureen gave her cousin a weak smile. "I'll talk with you later. So will Uncle Brendan. Go on now."

Aiden nodded and walked off.

Caleb turned to Maureen. "Sorry if that was rough. I know he's your cousin and all, but he was the one who found the body, and you know what they say about that. Until I interview the rest of these kids and see if somebody else steps up and proves they can kill, your cousin stays at the top of my list."

Maureen stiffened. "Trust me, my cousin did *not* kill that boy. You're barking up the wrong tree, Caleb. I suggest you look elsewhere."

Maureen watched the color drain from Caleb's face, but she didn't care if she was stepping on his investigation. She wanted to hear what the other seminarians had to say.

Caleb motioned for another young man in the group. A figure who had had his rosary beads in nervous hands earlier walked over, his lips moving silently in prayer.

He fidgeted for a few seconds and answered in a monotone voice. "I'm Eugene Wingate, and after dinner, I went back to my room to study. I always go back to my room after dinner. Then, around seven, we all went to prayers. And, as for Joseph, he was...intense, but we all are. This life isn't easy."

Caleb leaned in. "Intense? How?"

Eugene lifted one shoulder in a lopsided shrug. "Joseph held himself to impossible standards. Always in the chapel, always confessing, and he spent a lot of time in the library, studying. He was almost rigid in his beliefs, you know? And really opinionated. I mean"—he played with his rosary, running his fingers around the beads—"he always criticized others about the proper way to observe sacred tradition." He stopped fingering the beads and looked around. Leaning in, he said, "About a week before his death, he and one of the guys got into a heated debate about irreverent behavior in the chapel. We all heard this guy laughing during vespers, and Joseph started hollering at him and the two almost got into a fist fight, but one of our teachers broke it up."

Maureen watched as Caleb jotted furiously.

"And this person? Was it another seminarian? And do you think this argument could have festered into this person murdering Mr. Lin?"

Eugene squeezed his eyes tightly. "I'm a first-year seminarian, and I don't want to rat anyone out, Detective. It was probably nothing, just blowing off steam. I told you, life here can be stressful."

Caleb continued calmly. "I know, son, but don't you want to see justice for your friend? Please…just give me a name. No one will know the information came from you, you have my word."

Eugene opened his eyes. He found the crucifix at the end of the rosary and stared at it. "Judas did this…"

Caleb glanced in Maureen's direction. She read the frustration on his face.

"Okay, I'll tell you." He leaned in, conspiratorially. "It was…Matthew Mueller. He's always being disruptive. Joseph used to criticize him, a second-year student who should know better. Matthew always makes jokes during prayers and laughs, and he's always being fractious in class. Honestly, I don't know how he was able to return this year with that attitude." He continued. "He makes fun of some of the saints and some of our most beloved popes, and he mimics our holiest of traditions, like coughing excessively when incense is being burned." Maureen saw the boy's face darken. "Joseph was right for reprimanding him. I don't know how Matthew ever managed to get through the first year."

Caleb's eyes were wide. "Well," he said, "that's a lot to take in. Did Joseph exhibit any odd behavior when you last saw him at evening prayers?"

Eugene squirmed in his seat, but said, "No, he was himself. Nothing odd." He looked at Caleb. "Can I go now?"

Caleb gave a small shrug. "Go on, and thanks for your time."

Eugene slipped the rosary in his shirt pocket and walked off, his hands folded in prayers, muttering to himself.

"So how about that tall guy next?" asked Maureen, nodding toward a stocky, pasty-faced boy with thinning hair, then, after getting his attention, waved him over.

"Have a seat," urged Caleb, as the young man approached. "Tell us your name and where you were the night of Joseph Lin's murder, specifically between eight o'clock and seven this morning."

The boy gave his name as Nathan Silk, studying his hands as he went on to explain his whereabouts. "I went to the library to study until we had to go to the chapel for evening prayers. This is my first year here, and I want to work as hard as I can, so I can go on to be the best priest I can be." Maureen watched his face, waiting as he seemed to weigh his next words carefully. "Come to think of it, Joseph was always in that library, but he wasn't there last night."

"Was anyone in the library with you? Anyone who could give you an alibi?"

Nathan looked at Caleb and shrugged. "Sorry, I was the only one there. Most of the guys go back to their rooms after prayers, and that's what I did after leaving the chapel." He gave them a shy smile. "I like to get to bed early."

"So what was your take on Joseph Lin? Tell me about your relationship with him." Caleb leaned in, rubbing his back.

Nathan looked at the ceiling. "Well, let's see...he was quiet. Very solemn and reverent. I know his parents were Chinese, and that they were proud of him for wanting to become a priest." His face took on a thoughtful demeanor. "Other than that, I really don't have much time to socialize with the other guys." He looked from Maureen to Caleb. "Guess that doesn't help much, huh?"

"So you never argued with the deceased? Held no grudges against him?" Caleb's pen was poised over his notebook. "And don't know of anyone who did?"

"No, sir," he answered. "I'm a peace lover and, like Saint Francis, could never hurt a living thing, and can't imagine one of us students doing anything like that to one of our own."

Caleb looked at Maureen, then back at the seminarian. "Okay, thanks for your time, Mr. Silk."

Nathan extended his hand first to Caleb, then to Maureen, pumping their arms with the practiced enthusiasm of a seasoned politician.

After the handshaking, Nathan turned to go, then paused and turned back. "I forgot to ask," he said slowly. "What did you all make of that riddle that they found on his body? We heard it had something to do with a shepherd." He looked from Maureen to Caleb. "A clue, maybe?"

"Perhaps," Caleb offered, "but that's for us to determine." That was all Nathan Silk was going to get from him.

He gave them a winning smile and left.

Just then, Father Gabriel came around the corner. When he saw them, he walked over, his back slightly bent. "Good morning, detectives," he said warmly. "Are the boys being helpful?"

"They are," said Maureen as she and Caleb stood to greet the aging rector and introduce themselves. She had always judged every priest alongside her uncle, to whom no one could measure up to, and these young men were likely feeling the strain of a demanding class schedule and the death of their classmate.

The rector shook his head, exhaling a slow, heavy breath that Maureen noted carried a faint trace of whiskey. "This is a hard pill for me to swallow. Nothing like this has ever happened here at Saint Charles. You know, we're a historical treasure, never marred by anything as heinous as this." He looked at each of the detectives. "I hope you get to the bottom of this. I'm sure you'll find out that it was *not* one of my boys who did this." He shook his head again. "This is the work of someone who has sided with the devil and lost his way."

"Can you add anything, Father?" asked Maureen. "Anyone *you* suspect? And it doesn't have to be one of the students. Maybe a staff member or employee, or even someone from the outside, you think could be capable of murder?"

Father Gabriel creased his eyes in a scowl. "Young lady, these young men are of the highest quality and have been vetted, completed extensive psychological interviews, and come highly recommended by their bishops." He tugged at the clerical collar that was cloying around his neck. "Look, I don't mean to sound harsh, but you're barking up the wrong tree. My boys may be stressed, and I know how testosterone levels can rise when the living arrangements include all males, but I guarantee you, someone from the outside came in here and did this, not anyone from inside these hallowed walls—students *or* staff. We have visitors, delivery folks—all kinds of other people coming in at all hours of the day and night." He glowered at them. "Look to one of those people."

Maureen was stunned into silence.

Caleb intervened. "Father, I believe one of the deputies showed you that riddle and the note found under Joseph's body earlier. If you can shed any light on either, please tell us." He looked around, his eyes falling on the remaining seminarians they needed to question.

The rector twisted his lips. "I've never seen anything like that before. It's not Scripture, and it's from no poem I've ever read."

Caleb nodded. "Thanks, Father. We have a few more boys to interview, and I'm sure you have a full schedule. We'll keep you posted."

Maureen studied Caleb, knowing he was trying to fit the rector in as a potential suspect. And to her, that made more sense than for him to blame her cousin.

Father Gabriel gave an audible *hmph*, but then thanked them for being there, and after a curt nod, giving no indication he knew anything regarding the riddle, he turned and left.

"That man gives me flashbacks to Catholic school," quipped Maureen, taking her seat again.

"And makes *me* glad I'm a Presbyterian," said Caleb, winking at her. He gestured to the next seminarian.

Another young man proceeded over. Though neatly dressed in his cassock, a stray lock of ebony hair slipped across his forehead, nearly covering an eye. His skin held the golden warmth of the sun. Maureen tried to detect his nationality, one of her many inane hobbies.

The young man held his hand out, saying, *"Kumusta kayo."* A wide grin followed.

Maureen looked at him as she took his hand in hers.

He immediately gave a mischievous laugh. "That means 'hello to you both,' in Tagalog. I'm from the Philippines. Well, my parents are. I'm first generation."

"Ah," said Maureen, glad to have at least one mystery solved today. "Well, that sounded lovely. Won't you have a seat and tell us your name?"

"Manuel Bautista," he said with an air of pride.

They asked the young man the same questions that were asked of the others. Manuel had nothing of interest to say based on the same questions asked before.

"Did you ever think Joseph Lin might've been hiding something? We understand he spends a lot of his spare time in the library," said Caleb.

The seminarian hesitated. "None of us knew why Joseph spent so much time in the library. But there *was* a moment last week…but it seemed small." He twisted the lock of hair that had fallen across his face.

Maureen jumped in. "Describe that moment."

Manuel looked up at Maureen, then Caleb, and shrugged. "It really wasn't anything. He just had an uncharacteristic outburst. He shouted at Okeyo Masamba"—he pointed to one of the fellows still waiting to be interviewed—"during a theology debate, and the two of them got into it. I mean, their faces were so close I thought they were going to kiss. Spittle was coming out, and some of us in the front row got splattered." He grinned boyishly.

"So what happened?" asked Caleb, his pen moving furtively across his pad.

Manuel gave a small shrug. "Not much. The instructor broke it up, and they sat down."

Maureen waited for more, and when it didn't come, she continued. "So did they see each other later in the day, maybe duke it out somewhere?"

Manuel chuckled, a flicker of amusement breaking the tension. "If they did, I didn't hear about it."

Maureen felt her head beginning to ache. How many more of these boys did they have to question? "So you have no idea who could have killed your classmate, correct?"

Manuel shrugged again. "I guess if I had to choose, I'd say Matthew Mueller. He got under Joseph's skin and did all he could to aggravate him. He never said he didn't like Joseph, but anyone could tell he didn't." He picked at a piece of lint on his cassock. "Joseph *really* got on Matthew's last nerve." He looked up at the detectives. "Just saying."

Caleb laid his pen down and sank back into the chair. "One last question, son. Are you missing a rosary?"

Manuel looked at him in surprise. "A rosary? Sir, we all have *many* rosaries. We receive them as gifts at baptism, first holy Communion, confirmation—I could go on, but you get the picture." He gave Caleb a wide grin.

"All right, Manuel, I think we have enough."

Manuel began to stand, then asked, "So what was with that riddle that you guys found? Was it a clue, and do you think it'll lead to the murderer?"

Maureen sighed, wishing she had brought her bottle of ibuprofen in with her. "We can't divulge any information at this time. I'm not sure how you guys got your information so fast, unless it came directly from God." She'd ask Aiden later just how many of his friends he relayed this information to.

Manuel smiled and offered to send the next seminarian to them.

"And you are?" Caleb asked the boy who approached next, a tall young man with skin a rich, deep ebony, that spoke of sun-soaked heritage.

"I am Okeyo Masamba. I am from Kenya and am a first-year seminarian," he answered proudly, his accent thick.

"So, how well did you know Joseph Lin, and what was this argument you had with him last week?" Caleb rubbed his eyes and poised his pen over his notepad.

Okeyo's eyes closed for a few seconds. "I am a first-year seminarian. Joseph lived on my floor, and his room is close to mine. We had a disagreement on our religious viewpoints. I believe in a strong social justice-oriented theology, especially in places like Latin America, while Joseph argued that it was too political, and even felt it was Marxist-influenced."

Caleb turned to Maureen and, through tight lips, mumbled, "Way over my head."

"But I did not take offense," he continued, the pitch in his voice rising. "I assumed Joseph had been studying hard and felt the pressure to succeed, as we all did, especially over our first upcoming exam."

Maureen studied the young man. "Is that right? We heard it was literally a toe-to-toe argument, and you were nearly ready to go into fisticuffs if your teacher hadn't stopped you."

Okeyo spread his palms wide. "I can only tell you what happened last week. And I can also tell you that, after dinner, I returned to my room and took a shower, and after that, prepared my work for the following day."

Maureen noted the young man looked weary and was beginning to feel that none of these boys had information that would be of any use—or were they all sticking together, covering up for one of them? Or maybe for a teacher or staff member? And the forerunner, so far, was beginning to look like Matthew Mueller, who likely owned the rosary beads with the initials M.M. that just happened to be wrapped snugly around Joseph Lin's neck.

Maureen fiddled with the claddagh ring on her finger. "All right. Thanks for your time. If we need anything else, we'll be in touch." She motioned to Okeyo that he could leave, then signaled for the next seminarian.

The student who introduced himself as Daniel Caruso strolled over with an easy air of confidence. Tall and broad-shouldered, his hazel eyes caught the light, and the sharp line of his chiseled jaw gave him the look of a movie star who'd somehow wandered off the set and into a cassock. He took the proffered seat and folded his hands on his lap.

Caleb asked the same questions but, during the interview, noticed several scratches on the boy's neck and cheek. "How did you get those scratches, son?" He gestured to Daniel's neck.

Daniel touched the areas with a finger and smiled. "I got them shaving this morning. I was in a hurry, and my blade was dull."

Maureen's eyes narrowed as she watched his left leg jerk and pump, a staccato beat of nervous energy that gave away more than he intended.

Caleb continued. "Are you missing a rosary?"

Daniel laughed casually and shifted in his seat. "Seminarians have many rosaries. Why do you ask?"

Caleb ignored him. "You seem like a confident young man. Tell me, did Joseph Lin's piety ever get under your skin? Was your relationship with him a good one?" He pursed his lips and waited for an answer.

Daniel shrugged. "We all get along here. We're Catholic seminarians." He looked around at the other students milling about. "We'd never harm one of our own. You should look to an outsider." He gave Caleb a wide grin.

"Like who, for example?"

"Oh, I don't know," said Daniel, his leg pumping harder now. "I just know it wasn't anyone in here."

"You do, do you?" asked Caleb sarcastically.

Daniel leg stopped moving and he leaned in. "Look, if I knew anything, I'd tell you. I don't know who in here hated Joseph enough to murder him." He sat back. "I'm telling you, look outside this seminary." He folded his arms across his chest.

Maureen tried to summon some pity for Caleb, but if he insisted on blaming her cousin for Joseph Lin's death, she wasn't about to make things easier for him. They interviewed several more without getting any new information, leaving one more to be interviewed. Caleb dismissed Daniel Caruso and motioned for the last boy.

A tall young man approached, his strides wide and full of quiet confidence. With a glint of mischief in his eye and an air of self-assurance, he approached and seated himself with composed ease. Maureen studied his demeanor. He took his seat and waited for the questioning to begin.

"And your name, son?" asked Caleb, shaking his writing hand from obvious overexertion.

"Before we go any further, let me save you some time." He took a deep breath and placed his hands on his knees. "My name is Matthew Mueller, and I'm a second-year student here. After dinner last night, I went over to our gym, or what passes for a gym—we have a treadmill, some free weights, and an old elliptical that someone donated. And, unfortunately, I was the only one there, so no alibi. But I can tell you, I did *not* kill Joseph." He gave a slight shrug. "I know you can't just take my word for it, but when Joseph first came here, I was the one who guided him. He was so devout, you know? He would have made a wonderful priest, and it breaks my heart that someone here did this."

Maureen shot a look at Caleb as he continued questioning Matthew. "Thanks for that, but we still have additional questions." She watched the deputy's shoulders slump.

"So what was your relationship with him? Good? Bad?" she asked.

"It was good, of course. Joseph was a fine young man, very contemplative," began Matthew, easing back into the chair, spreading both legs forward in an extremely comfortable position. "You think his murder had anything to do with the riddle we heard was found on him?"

Maureen cast a glance in Caleb's direction, stunned at how fast news traveled in a place like this.

When Matthew received no answer from either detective, he continued. "Anyway, he was a first-year guy, and we all liked him." He looked over at Maureen.

Caleb glanced at the notes he had taken from Eugene Wingate. "We've heard otherwise, that you'd argue with him after he chastised you for your lack of reverence in class, in church, and just about everywhere the two of you were together."

Matthew laughed. "Oh, please, whoever told you that, and I know it was that fruitcake Wingate, it was all in fun. Lin was way too devout. I mean, at Mass, we all knelt on the kneelers, but him? He had to kneel on the floor like he was some kind of penitential saint. He found no humor in life. And wasn't it the Lord himself who gave us the gift of humor?" He settled back in his chair and once again, emitted a Cheshire cat grin.

"So did the two of you ever get into arguments over that? Did his treatment of you make you want to harm him?"

"Absolutely not," he shot back.

Maureen chewed on her bottom lip. His answer held no remorse for his fellow student's terrible demise.

"So what did you do after the gym?"

Matthew ran a hand through a perfectly coifed head of hair. "Let's see," he began, giving a sarcastic air of thinking. "After dinner, I went out back to throw some hoops. Then, of course, we all went to evening prayers."

"And afterward, or early this morning? Like when the victim was getting murdered?"

Again, Matthew gave a nonchalant shrug. "Back to my room to get ready for bed." His eyes darkened and he sat forward. "Look, I know my actions don't reflect well on me as a man who wants to become a priest, but we all have our strengths, and mine is in my sense of humor. Lin was a pain in my side, and the thought of more years with him in this place made me nuts, but kill him?" He leaned back again. "I'm a Catholic seminarian studying for the priesthood. It's all I ever wanted. After all our arguments, I found Lin and made my peace with him, Then, I knelt before my confessor and unburdened my soul." His eyes then went to Maureen and back to Caleb. "So you'll have to look elsewhere. I did *not* kill Joseph Lin."

"You own a black rosary, correct?" asked Maureen.

Matthew looked at her, his face revealing a smug look. "Of course. We all do. And we all probably have more than one. Why?"

"Do you all generally put your initials on them? Mark them in some way to denote ownership?"

Matthew sat up straighter, folding his hands. "Some of us do. There's a lot of them floating around, so yes, we do sometimes do that."

"Do you do that to yours?"

"What are you getting at, Detective?"

Maureen decided to keep that piece of information to herself until they had dug a little deeper. "Just asking questions here," she replied, ignoring his. "So you say you were in your room ready for bed? Your gym alibi only works for the hours after dinner."

Matthew let out a nervous laugh. "Why do you need to know that?" He looked over at the seminarians who had already been questioned and were now chatting in a group.

"Answer the question," urged Caleb.

Matthew scratched his head. "Like I told you, we're usually all back in our rooms by nine. We have exams coming up, and we all need to study." He frowned. "Why do you think I had something to do with Joseph's murder?"

Maureen leaned in closer to Matthew. "The rosary beads found around Joseph's neck had the initials M.M. on them." She retrieved her phone, pulled up the beads displaying the initials, and shoved the phone in his face. "Any other boy here with those initials?"

Matthew inhaled deeply. Maureen watched as the blood drained from his face. "I don't know how they got to be around his neck, but I never put my initials on my beads. We all know our own rosaries. We're Catholic seminarians."

Caleb narrowed his eyes but remained silent.

"Look," continued Matthew, "as much as I liked Joseph—and I *did* like him, regardless of what you've heard—he had a habit of coming into our rooms and taking what he wanted or needed. Not in any mean way. It's just, he sort of had a habit of losing his own stuff—class books, pens, sundries—it was all innocent, and no one minded it. It was an idiosyncrasy Joseph had, that's all." He picked at a nail. "He could have taken those beads from anyone. All I know is that they're not mine, and I don't put my initials on my rosaries."

Caleb chewed on his lip. "Anything to add that can explain why you *didn't* kill Joseph Lin?"

Matthew's lips were pressed so tightly they had turned white. "No, sir, only that I didn't do this. I couldn't have, and I'm sorry that someone here did."

Caleb tilted his head. "Why do you say 'someone here' did this? What do you know?"

His face seemed to darken as he looked around the room, and Maureen couldn't help but think he was checking to see who was watching.

"Look, I don't want to get into it here. Can we meet again? Maybe tomorrow? There's a lot I could tell you, but now's not the time nor the place." He glanced at his watch. "Besides, I have an appointment with my advisor in ten minutes." He looked at the detectives. "Can I give you a call later and let you know what works for me? And maybe I can meet you in your office, you know, so no one will suspect I'm giving you information that might hurt this place. Would that be okay?"

Caleb and Maureen looked at each other.

"That's fine, Mr. Mueller," said Caleb, tapping a finger on his notepad. "Please call us as soon as you can, and we'll set up an appointment." He handed the seminarian his card. "Just don't wait too long."

Matthew pursed his lips, gave a curt nod, and left.

"Maureen," began Caleb, "we need a lot more than what we just got."

Maureen nodded in agreement. "But maybe that Mueller boy has some good info. It might be the information you need to close this case."

Caleb nodded and motioned for the boys to come over one at a time. After they each sat, he got their names and all other pertinent information, and, as Maureen predicted, they didn't have much more to contribute. It was the same song the others had sung. No good alibi, no motive.

Caleb dismissed them, then leaned forward in the chair, rubbing his lower back.

Maureen watched as Caleb flipped the page on his notepad. They'd get no more from any of these boys right now.

The detective stood, still rubbing his back. "Well," he said to Maureen, "at least we have a starting point with that Mueller guy. Twenty-seven young men are living here, and minus the ones on retreat and the ones at their parishes, we're just scratching the surface. If Mueller didn't have a motive for killing him and the rest of them can't tell us anything more, then we're up the creek. None of these kids have a great motive. And if they all went to 'study' after dinner, then none have a decent alibi, either." He slipped his pad into his jacket pocket. "Is your uncle still here?"

"He should be." Maureen smiled, thinking of her uncle. "This is probably bringing back a lot of memories for him. Father Gabriel, the rector here, was a teacher when my uncle was attending. I'm sure he'll grill him, too. If you remember, my uncle was an intelligence officer when he was a young Marine during the first Gulf War and then got 'the calling' after several tours in Iraq, after getting hurt by an IED." She looked around the old building. "He was one of the older seminarians here, but I'm sure he has his stories."

Caleb nodded. "I'm sure he does." He was silent for a few seconds, and then said, "Hey, thanks for helping me out on this case. I'll take all the assistance I can get."

Maureen wasn't ready to forgive just yet. "No problem, just go easy on my cousin, will you? And you'll only have me for the next few days. Then you're on your own." But like her uncle, she couldn't resist a puzzle, so she told her fellow deputy she'd help where she could, while keeping to herself the unshakable belief that her cousin wasn't a murderer.

She didn't envy Caleb, knowing the difficult task that lay before him and the contempt their captain had for his underlings.

CHAPTER 4

Sunday Afternoon

B rendan walked the hallowed halls of Saint Charles. It was a small school, but each corridor flooded his mind with memories of the past—some good, some not so good. He rounded the corner, finding himself at a familiar office. Rapping lightly on an open door, he remained there until a wizened face looked up, squinting from behind glasses, and motioned for him to enter.

"Hello, Father Gabriel," began Brendan, waiting for the rector to recognize him.

The man removed his glasses and rubbed his eyes. Brendan felt a pang of sadness as he took in the rector's snow-white hair and the deep, sun-etched lines on his face, each wrinkle a testament to years of devotion and burdens carried.

"Do I know you?" he asked, his eyes narrowing with suspicion. "You look familiar." He motioned for Brendan to take a seat.

"It's me, Father—Brendan O'Clery. You taught the Eschatology class in Third Theology." He waited for the rector to speak.

"O'Clery, O'Clery...that glorious Irish accent...you were the boy who—"

"Who had been in the Gulf War and came back injured," Brendan finished the man's thoughts.

He glanced at Brendan's cane. "Ah, yes. I remember. Well, welcome back, Father, although I'm sorry it has to be under such disturbing circumstances."

He looked around. "Would you like some coffee? The boys got me one of those machines that use those little plastic things. A silly contraption, but convenient." He rose and headed toward a counter that held boxes of coffee pods, sugar, creamers, and stir sticks.

"Thanks, Father. That would be grand." Brendan watched Father Gabriel puttering with the coffee machine and decided to see what the old rector knew. "Father, what did you know about Joseph Lin? Why was he murdered in that particular way, strangled with rosary beads? And this ominous note, almost like a prophecy." He shuddered as he walked over to where the rector was, showing him the photo on his phone.

The older priest squinted as he read the words in the riddle-like lines. "As I told the detectives, I have no idea," he said curtly, returning to the coffee machine. He pushed a pod into the machine and turned to face Brendan as the dark liquid streamed into a mug. "Doesn't ring a bell or mean anything to me. There are many things we don't understand, Father. Why does one man get killed and another doesn't? Cream and sugar?" He turned back to the tray of coffee condiments.

Father Gabriel's cryptic answer baffled Brendan. He was unsure as how to answer the man, so he simply replied, "Cream, please."

Father Gabriel handed the steaming cup to Brendan and returned to his desk.

"O'Clery, O'Clery…would Aiden O'Clery be a family member, by chance?"

Brendan winced as the hot liquid burned his tongue. "He is. He's my nephew, my brother Finn's son."

"He's a fine boy, that one. He'll make an adequate priest." Father Gabriel leaned over his desk. "And how is the great archbishop doing these days?" He grinned at Brendan, and Brendan wasn't sure about Father Gabriel's feeling—or anyone's, for that matter—toward Archbishop Malachy O'Clery, the oldest of the seven O'Clery children.

"He's grand, Father. A true pain in my hind parts, but a hard worker for the archdiocese, so what can I say?"

The men chatted about seminary life, the state of the Church, and people they both knew, until Brendan realized he wouldn't be getting much from his former teacher about his students or the murder.

He studied the old priest as he sat hunched over in his chair. Father Gabriel had always seemed odd at best—enigmatic for sure. He remembered him as a relentless taskmaster, showing no patience for weakness, never coddling the seminarians. In fact, he barely seemed to care for them at all, let alone befriend any of them. Brendan needed to frame his next question correctly.

"Father, would you mind if I speak with some of the students here? And maybe have a quick look around the place? I'm a consultant now with the Porter Mills Sheriff's Department, and I might be able to help." He crossed his fingers, hiding them in the pocket of his jacket as he held his breath along with his lie.

The rector waved his arm over his head. "Go, do whatever you can to help solve this murder. Joseph Lin was a promising kid. He would have made a decent priest." He looked at his hands, examining them nervously.

Brendan couldn't help but smile at his old teacher's choice of the word "decent"—never anything more flattering, never excessive praise, just the bare minimum of approval. "Thanks, Father. I'll be discreet, and you won't even know I'm around."

After finishing his coffee, Brendan ended the meeting. He still needed to speak with his nephew, the adequate seminarian. Father Gabriel, he sensed, knew something, but either didn't want to share it with a former student or was hiding it. He was reminded of his days as a young seminarian, when the rector, then a teacher, hoarded knowledge as if sharing it would diminish his power.

"Thanks for the coffee, Father. And the chat." He leaned over the desk, his arm extended. "Maybe we can take in a lunch one of these days, you know, to catch up."

Father Gabriel took the proffered arm and shook it. "Perhaps we can. And now, I have work that needs attending to, and this place is now buzzing around with law enforcement all over. I won't have a minute's peace. You can see yourself out."

And with that, Brendan found himself looking at the top of a head of white hair. He grabbed his cane and left the office, looking back again, watching his old teacher as he immersed himself in paperwork.

He returned to the main hall, where the seminarians were still milling about. Spotting his nephew, they found a quiet spot where they could speak.

"Uncle Brendan." Aiden paused momentarily, then in a hushed tone continued. "I prayed hard on whether or not I should tell you this, and I don't want you to jump to conclusions," he said, wringing his hands, "but I overheard Matthew and Joseph arguing last night, before Joseph got killed. I only caught bits and pieces—something about betrayal and silence. Matthew kept inching his way closer like he was trying to intimidate Joseph. I honestly thought he was going to hit him." Aiden's pale skin appeared even more ghostly in the dim, cold light of the seminary, as though the weight of betrayal had drained the last trace of color from him.

Brendan let this information sink in before he gave his thoughts. "You did the right thing. And it could be nothing. You said exams were approaching, and everyone here is on edge. Trust me, I still remember those days." He gave his nephew a grim smile. "It might also mean Matthew's hiding something, something that could uncover who really killed Joseph, even if it wasn't him." He made a mental note to share this information with Maureen. "So what's on the agenda regarding the young man's body? Your cousin said they've expedited the autopsy so the family could get him sooner."

"They're having a Mass for him tomorrow since his body will have to be autopsied first," began Aiden. "Then after the autopsy, his body will be shipped back to New York, where his folks will have another funeral Mass for him in their parish. From what he's told me about their Masses, he'll have a good send-off."

Brendan placed a hand over Aiden's. "I know this is a lot for you to be taking in," he began, "especially since this is your first year." He rubbed his chin, his fingers brushing over the coarse wiriness of his short beard, each bristly strand a reminder of his perpetual battle with the razor. "Look, Aiden, I need to ask you a few questions. Do you mind?" When the boy nodded, Brendan continued. "What time did you go to the chapel and discover Joseph's body? And why were you there?"

Aiden looked around at his fellow students. "It was my week to sweep the chapel and dust around the altar." He hunched a shoulder, and Brendan could sense his nephew's discomfort.

"Go on," urged Brendan.

"I walked over there around seven. And that's when I…" He looked away.

Brendan put a hand on his shoulder. "I understand. Go on."

"The thing is, Uncle Brendan, Joseph owed me money. A lot."

Brendan removed his hand and narrowed his eyes. "Define a lot."

Aiden stared down at his hands, tracing the lines with his eyes. "One hundred dollars."

"What?" Brendan asked, having expected his nephew to give a much higher amount.

"I know I shouldn't have lent it to him, but his folks don't have a lot of money, and his grandmother back in China has been sick, and they needed the money for special medications." He looked at Brendan, his eyes pleading. "I couldn't say no. He's my—*was*—my friend. It was the money I had saved from my job this summer. And this gives me a good motive for murdering him, doesn't it?"

Brendan gave his nephew a wry smile and patted his knee. "One hundred dollars is a poor excuse for a motive. Look, you're a good lad, Aiden, and a credit to the O'Clery name, but as a seminarian, you need to keep any money for yourself. I realize that amount isn't much to us older folks, but to a kid, it's a lot. Father Gabriel could have found Joseph some help." He knew he'd have to divulge this new information to Maureen. He had a thought and pulled out his cell, scrolling to the photo of the prophecy. "Can you take a look at this again? Does it mean anything to you? Something from one of your classes maybe?" He held the phone out for Aiden to see.

Aiden squinted as he took the phone from his uncle, his lips twisted. Brendan could see the boy was trying to be helpful.

"Honestly, it doesn't look like anything I've seen or read. It's not scriptural, anyway." He looked at Brendan. "Maybe it's something that can be researched in our library. I can't say. Sorry."

Brendan looked into sad eyes. "No worries, kiddo. Anything else?"

Aiden gave a mournful sigh and shook his head. Brendan's heart ached for his nephew. He knew what it was like to lose a friend through senseless murder. The faces of his fallen comrades surged through his mind, ghostly echoes of the past that refused to fade.

He looked up, surveying the other seminarians. "Okay, then let me know if you think of anything else, no matter how insignificant. Just see if you can get a feel for the personalities of these guys and let me know if anyone seems suspect, okay?" He didn't want to push the boy any further. "Look, you've only been here a few months," he continued. "Your time here will test you again and again, but if you can survive it, you will be a wonderful priest to some lucky parish. I'm sorry this tragedy happened, but your life will be full of disappointments and sadness, and you'll have to learn to put your parishioners' needs above your own. Like my Irish banshee Ma used to say, 'Offer it up, boyo.'" He leaned over toward his nephew and tousled his red hair, which, for such a young person, was already thinning.

Brendan felt for his cane and stood. "Look, one of Mo's fellow deputies is handling the case, so if you need anything, don't hesitate to ask him. Or you can always call me or your cousin. Okay?" He looked at the boy and sketched a cross over his head, blessing him.

"Thanks, Uncle Brendan. I'll be okay." He stood and returned to his friends, blending into the sea of black shirts and trousers.

Maureen accompanied Caleb as he interviewed some of the staff but got the same answers from them as they did from the students. Joseph Lin was a saint, blah, blah, blah.

She finally rounded up her uncle and headed to the rectory to drop him off.

On the rough ride home in her Jeep, Brendan pulled his cell from his jacket and called his two comrades on speaker. Maureen listened intently as her uncle asked if they had time to meet with him. When he told them a little more about the murder and the personalities of the seminarians, he had a captive audience. The men agreed to meet for a late snack—Langdon's words—to see how they could inject themselves into the case.

Maureen started to argue with Brendan, but he gave her his most innocent smile.

When she dropped him off, she reminded him that Caleb still thought Aiden had something to do with the murder.

On the way back to her house to resume packing, she glanced in the rearview mirror, watching her uncle limping into the rectory's back door. She felt bad chiding him about getting involved in this case, but she also knew they were two peas in a pod—both problem-solvers, who stopped at nothing to fit all the pieces together in a puzzle. And how her uncle tore through pages and pages of crossword books! She realized he and his friends would be an asset, but they had to tread lightly—this was not her case.

CHAPTER 5

Monday Evening

Maureen, Brendan, and Caleb sat quietly in the nearly empty chapel for Joseph Lin's memorial Mass. They sat in the last pew and observed each seminarian, their teachers, and staff members. Events heavily attended were always a good place to see if the killer would return to observe the reactions to his deeds.

The seminarians sat in stiff rows, candles flickering against the stained-glass windows. After the funeral Mass, Father Gabriel delivered a somber eulogy, his voice strained.

"Joseph Lin was a young man whose faith was as steady as the sunrise and whose strength went far beyond the physical, rooted in kindness, conviction, and an unwavering sense of purpose. Let us remember that, in our trials, we must turn to God for strength. For even in our darkest moments, His light will guide us."

Maureen's eyes narrowed as she studied the various young men who had been tagged as being the closest to Joseph Lin. All eyes were on Father Gabriel, except for one. She observed Daniel Caruso staring intently at the casket, his lips moving in silent prayer. Nearby, she saw Okeyo Masamba whispering to Manuel Bautista. Aiden sat next to them, silent, facing the front. There were several empty spaces in the pew behind the young men, so she rose and, as silently as she could, inched her way toward the pew.

Squeezing past several seminarians, she took the space directly behind the young men.

"Joseph Lin was not exactly a saint," she heard Okeyo whisper. "Maybe someone finally called him on it."

Eugene leaned closer, frowning. "What are you talking about?"

Okeyo shrugged. "Nothing. Just saying he was not as holy as he wanted us to think."

Maureen watched as her cousin turned toward the two men.

"Don't speak ill of the dead. This is a funeral for our brother. Show some respect."

Maureen stifled a proud grin at her cousin's courage and turned her attention back to the eulogy.

After the Mass, Maureen and Caleb meandered the hallways, speaking with more of the seminarians and staff members and taking copious amounts of notes. Brendan followed along until he got bored.

"I'm going back to the chapel, Mo," he said to his niece. "I want to say a few prayers for Joseph Lin at the place where his soul left his body."

"Sure, Unc. I'll catch up with you later."

As Brendan made his way back to the chapel, he found Matthew Mueller kneeling and praying silently in front of the altar. He took a seat in a pew in the rear of the chapel and wondered what Matthew was praying for. Forgiveness? Absolution?

The air was still heavy with the smell of incense from the Mass, and the candles were casting long, flickering shadows in the evening darkness. Just then, his nephew entered the chapel, making his way toward the altar. Aiden silently acknowledged his uncle with a nod and continued toward the front.

"Hey, Matthew," whispered Aiden as he knelt beside the young man.

The acoustics in the old chapel allowed Brendan to catch most of the conversation his nephew was having. He saw Matthew glance at the boy, then bow his head again.

"I don't think anyone from here had anything to do with Joseph's…death. Do you think the police will figure out what happened to him?"

Matthew, his head still bent in prayer, as Brendan awaited his answer. "Maybe, or maybe they'll find something no one wants them to see."

Aiden glanced back at Brendan and then leaned in toward Matthew. "What do you mean?"

Brendan heard Matthew let out a loud sigh, then watched the boy stand, crossing himself. "This place isn't as holy as it pretends to be. Neither are the people in it." Saying no more, Matthew turned, and left the chapel.

Brendan watched as the seminarian left without looking toward him. Aiden, unsettled by the conversation, scurried over to Brendan to relay Matthew's strange words.

"I'm heading home," said Maureen to Caleb after they finished speaking to a few more people.

As she spoke, she saw her uncle turning a corner and walking toward them. "Come on, Unc, let's go. I'm beat." She grabbed his sleeve and left the building. On the way to the car, Maureen asked, "So, any thoughts?" She gave her uncle a sideways glance.

Brendan shrugged as he dragged his cane along the seminary's sidewalk. "From what you've said, that boy Mueller seems like the best suspect so far, although it's a bit early to pin it on him. But that rosary around that kid's neck with his initials… He's going to have to explain that one, even though he claimed they weren't his beads." He looked at his niece. "And when I was in the chapel Aiden came in and I overheard them talking. The Mueller boy made the comment that Saint Charles wasn't as holy as it seems. His words, not mine."

"Hmmm, wonder what he meant by that. He must know more than he's letting on. But, I agree, we've got to start somewhere. We have an appointment with him tomorrow." She let out an exaggerated sigh. "And that

Caruso kid had scratches on his face. Hopefully DNA will help with that, unless the killer wore gloves."

Brendan nodded, then added, "I told Ezra and Langdon about the murder yesterday, and of course, they wanted to help. I told them you were going on vacation and it was Deputy Martinez's case, but they insisted on helping anyway. You know I can't tell them anything."

Maureen pursed her lips. "Like I can't tell *you* anything."

"Well, I know it's your coworker's case, but don't forget, this is my old stomping grounds. I may not know *these* seminarians, but I still know the rector and some of the old teachers who are still around." His eyes twinkled. "And you *know* I know how to squeeze information out of people." He rubbed his hands together.

Maureen rolled her eyes. "I know I can't keep you from inserting yourself into this case, but remember, it's not mine. Anything you and the other two stoo—excuse me, *men*—find out will have to go through Caleb. Understood?"

Brendan gave her a mock salute. "Of course."

"Okay, then. Let's go."

Brendan and his friends had planned to meet at the rectory that evening. Mrs. Morrison had left a pan of lasagna warming in the oven, filling the air with its rich, savory aroma. As he was setting the table, both men appeared at the back door, letting themselves in.

"Hoo-ee," cried the big Baptist, removing a well-worn pork pie hat. "That November wind ain't like nothin' I ever seen down in Loosiana! Times like this, I be missin' Nawlins." He turned, looking around for his companion. "Where the little dude at? I swear he were right behin' me."

Seconds later, Ezra came through the door, a thick woolen scarf wrapped around his neck, hiding two reddened cheeks. He strode over to Langdon and gave his upper arm a firm, playful punch, the kind that carried both camaraderie and just a hint of challenge.

"Ouch," Langdon cried, rubbing his arm, pantomiming a hard blow, "the skeeters must be bitin'."

"The door to that old Caddy of yours is heavy. I had a hard time opening it up in this wind." He removed his scarf and coat and threw them over the back of a kitchen chair.

Langdon scowled at the little rabbi. "Don't be insultin' Aretha now."

Ezra rolled his eyes. "Aretha...who names their cars?"

"Boys, boys," said Brendan. "We're here for a late-night snack, and Mrs. M. left a doozy of one."

"Well, tell him to get hiself to a gym or somethin' an' put some muscle on them puny little twigs he got for arms, so he don't be insultin' Aretha no more."

The men sat down, said grace, and dug into the hot lasagna covered in freshly grated parmesan. For several minutes, the only sounds heard were grunts of pleasure and the smacking of lips. Just then, Brendan's cell rang. Wiping his hands, he reached for his phone.

"It's my nephew," he said to his friends. "Aiden, can I put this on speaker so my friends can hear you?"

"Sure, Uncle Brendan. Okay, you said to call you if I heard anything, and I did hear something tonight. Not sure if it's important or not, but I'm scared, and I want Joseph's killer to be caught before anybody else gets hurt."

"That's good, Aiden. So tell me what you've got." He moved the pan of lasagna out of the way and placed the phone down in the middle of the table, the volume pumped up.

"Well, tonight at dinner, Okeyo Masamba—that's the guy from Kenya— made a comment like, who's going to be next? Manuel Bautista, he's the Filipino guy, told him that his comment was not in good taste, and Okeyo told him that the truth was, that someone at the seminary was a killer. Then, Eugene—he's a weird guy and usually keeps to himself—he yells at Okeyo and tells him he doesn't know what he's talking about, that there's no killer here. Okeyo then goes on to say that it could have been anyone here, even Eugene, which made Eugene really angry. He was so mad, he pushed his plate off the table onto the floor, making a huge mess, and stormed out of the dining hall." He paused. "Eugene is a strange boy. He doesn't have a lot of friends, and he has nightmares all the time, and sometimes, he says he has visions. Don't ask me what kind. I've tried to be nice to him, but he keeps to himself. Uncle Brendan, do you think Okeyo could be the killer? Or Eugene?"

Brendan looked up at his friends and smiled. Aiden had always been a sensitive, shy boy, and here he was, thrust into the middle of a heinous murder in his school.

"Detective Martinez and his team will figure it out, Aiden, but I'll run it by Maureen just the same." He took the phone off speaker and put it up to his ear. "You have good instincts, Aiden. I'm proud of you. This *could* suggest that Okeyo knows more about Joseph Lin's final hours than he's admitting. Also," he added, "if he disliked Lin that much, maybe he decided to just be done with him. And Eugene may be strange, as you say, but he'd need to be more than that to be a killer. Good work. And if you have any questions or concerns about that seminary, just let me know." He lowered his voice, making it sound sinister. "I know where all the bodies are buried."

Aiden gave a nervous laugh, and Brendan was immediately sorry he had spoken those words. He ended the call and removed the cell from the table.

Langdon scooped out the last of the lasagna and deposited it on his plate. "So how we gonna get involved, Brendan? We just gonna sit here or what?"

Brendan rubbed his chin. "Not sure. Without Mo at the helm, we can't do much."

"We can eat some of that apple pie Mrs. Morrison has over there on that counter," said Ezra, rising to retrieve the dessert.

"That's sho' right, little man. I'll grab us some clean plates."

"This was just supposed to be a snack, not a six-course meal," said Brendan, laughing.

While he waited for a plate, he reached into his pocket and pulled out that morning's newspaper crossword.

"While we wait, help me with today's cross." He folded the paper until it showed only the puzzle. "Okay, what's a ten-letter word meaning the act of transferring ownership or legal title of something, typically property, from one person to another?"

Langdon came back with the plates, heard the question, and frowned. Brendan looked at his friends, who now appeared as if they'd been struck by lightning, completely stunned by a question they had no idea how to answer.

"You must be kidding," snorted Ezra, pushing his glasses up the bridge of his nose. "Those puzzles are your thing, not ours."

Brendan then looked to Langdon.

"Don' be lookin' at this high school dropout, boy. I know the Lord, but I ain't dealin' with them big words." Langdon passed out the plates while Ezra cut into the pie.

"Some friends," Brendan said, laughing. "All right, let's just concentrate on pie and murder." He folded the paper again and laid it aside. "I think the word is 'conveyance,' but I can write it in later."

The three friends then obliterated the housekeeper's apple pie in minutes.

As he quickly demolished the dessert, Brendan watched in irritation as Saint Peter, the stray-cat-turned-obnoxious-pet, unhinged himself from the kitchen curtain and leapt down on an unsuspecting Yorkie, who was begging for a bite of the pie.

Brendan enjoyed the rest of his evening with his friends as they discussed the murder of the young seminarian and how they could help. It pained him to think such a disturbing thing could happen at a seminary.

CHAPTER 6

Tuesday Morning

The following day, Maureen reluctantly called Caleb to ask if he needed help.

"Well," began the detective, "I was going to go through Joseph Lin's room. If you want, you can come with me. I don't need to involve another deputy."

Maureen agreed and met Caleb at the seminary.

Joseph Lin's room was sparse. His bed remained neatly made, and his nightstand had a lamp, a Bible, and a rosary on it. He had few items of clothing in his closet, and the desk was uncluttered.

"Let's go through his desk. There's nothing much here except his computer. We can go through it back at the office."

Caleb slipped on a pair of latex gloves and tossed another pair across the room to Maureen.

"You came prepared. That's a good start for your first homicide, Caleb," Maureen said as she put the computer in a large evidence bag. She pulled out a few drawers but found only writing tools, a box of tissues, and some photos that looked like family members, some of the older folks in traditional Chinese outfits.

"Hey, look at this," she said, pulling out a notebook filled with cryptic notes and drawings. "Check it out." She pointed to a sketch that looked identical to the confessional where his body had been found. The caption under the drawing read *Cleanse me.*

They exchanged looks.

"What do you make of that?" asked Caleb.

Maureen continued to peruse the notebook, when suddenly a note fell from between the pages. It read, *You can't hide forever. Judgment comes for us all.*

"It's unsigned," said Maureen, turning the note over. "But look, there's a smudged fingerprint on the edge." She handed the note over to Caleb, along with the notebook to be placed in evidence. "I wonder if this was sent to *him* or if *Lin* was going to send it to someone. This could hint at a larger conspiracy or maybe blackmail. It's worth looking into."

When nothing more was found, they left the building and walked the seminary grounds. Even in the stark month of November, they found the place oddly serene. The wind whipped at their faces, but they strolled to the edge of the property, and when they came to the black wrought-iron fence, Maureen heard a dog's ferocious barking. Looking up, she spotted a figure lurking on the other side.

"Come on, let's check him out," she urged Caleb. As she approached the man, her hand rested on her holstered Glock, her eyes focused on the large mixed-breed dog that kept circling the man.

Caleb flashed his badge. "We're with the Porter Mills Sheriff's Department. Mind if we ask your name?"

The man looked to be in his late forties. He wore an outdated tweed coat over worn jeans and had a woolen cap stretched over a ponytail. He yelled out a string of obscenities at the dog, flailing his arms in an attempt to drive him away.

"That your dog?" asked Maureen, nodding to the huge animal that was slathering saliva with each bark. "He, or she, needs to be put in the house."

The man watched the dog as it howled, its chest lowered to the ground as its hindlegs quivered in the air, as if it were ready to pounce.

"Nah. Not mine. It's been hanging around and, for some reason, follows me everywhere. Don't know why. I don't feed it or anything." He tried again to shoo the dog away. Eventually, it got bored and quieted down, its haunches lowered.

Maureen gave an inward sigh of relief as her hand left the butt of her Glock.

"So," continued Caleb, "again, can we ask you a few questions?"

"Sure," the man replied as he approached the fence. "My name is Marcus Dean. I attended this seminary years ago."

"So you're a priest?" asked Maureen.

The man gave a humorless laugh. "Heavens no. Oh, I got a great education, but before ordination rolled around, I—I decided that the priesthood wasn't the life for me."

"So, what are you doing here?"

"I'm a kind of handyman for this place." He swept his arm around. "I do odd jobs—electric, plumbing, landscaping, that sort of thing. I heard about the seminarian that got killed. Joseph Lin, correct?"

Maureen bristled. "Do you know something?"

Marcus shook his head and kicked at something on the ground. "I'm not here about Joseph Lin. I saw you two out here and wanted to warn you."

"Warn us about what?" asked Caleb.

Marcus waved his arm in front of him. "This place, it eats people alive. Joseph Lin wasn't the first, and he won't be the last."

The detectives looked at each other.

"What do you mean?" Maureen's eyes narrowed, and she felt the man had more to tell them. "Hey, talk to us. What do you know?"

But it was too late. Marcus had turned and strolled away and into a foggy mist, giving them a languid wave.

"Creepy guy," remarked Caleb.

"Yeah," said Maureen slowly. "He'd sure make a great suspect. Former seminarian turned killer." She elbowed Caleb. "Let's get out of here, but make a note to keep an eye on that guy."

TUESDAY NIGHT

That night, Eugene rolled around in his bed, tangling himself in the sheets as his dreams turned into frightful nightmares. He was in the chapel, surrounded by the other seminarians. One by one, they turned to him, their faces grotesquely distorted, pointing bony, withered fingers at him accusingly. One who didn't look like the rest of them—his face twisted with a quiet malevolence—stepped forward and said, "You're not innocent, Eugene. None of us are."

A scream woke Eugene, and he realized it was coming from him. He was in a cold sweat, shivering, but as his heart began to slow, he thought he heard faint footsteps outside his door.

He untangled himself from the knot of sweaty bed linens and made his way to the door. As he pulled it open, the hallway stretched before him, empty and still, yet the whispering lingered, curling through the air like a ghost that refused to leave.

CHAPTER 7

Wednesday Morning

Morning brought a cold chill to the seminary, inside and outside. The seminarians, filing out of the chapel after daily Mass, were beginning to eye each other. Everyone was a suspect—especially Matthew Mueller, who was conspicuously missing. The chatter began, and Father Gabriel sent two of the boys to locate Matthew. Perhaps he was sick, he suggested, but his thoughts went directly to Joseph Lin's murder. The rector had counseled Matthew on numerous occasions regarding his treatment of Joseph, but it had fallen on deaf ears.

When Matthew could not be found, the gossip ran wild. Matthew had murdered Joseph and was on the run! Father Gabriel tried to calm the boys down and maintain some semblance of order.

Early morning duties fell to first-year seminarians Manuel Bautista and Aiden O'Clery. They were to tend to the composting area, which lay adjacent to the old cemetery. To complement the enormous garden he had established a decade earlier, Father Sid Genario had promoted the composting area, ensuring a steady supply of fresh vegetables the following spring for the seminary's menus.

After Mass and breakfast, they grabbed their jackets and pails of discarded food scraps before heading out. The crisp morning air greeted them as they stepped outside. In the dim gray light of the morning, their breaths formed pale clouds in the crisp air. Their mood was solemn. Neither young man spoke. The silence was broken only by the crunch of frost beneath their boots.

"Let's shovel these scraps into the old stuff, Aiden," said Manuel, pointing to a heap of rotting vegetables. "My grandfather used to do that in his garden."

Aiden nodded and walked over to the pile with his shovel. As he perused the area, his eye caught sight of something in the cemetery, and he motioned to his friend. "Look over there, Manny, at that old grave marker." He pointed to the area, and Manuel squinted in the sunlight, trying to focus on what Aiden had seen.

"Come on," Aiden said, "let's check it out. Something doesn't seem right." He dropped his shovel and grabbed Manuel's coat sleeve.

When they arrived at the grave marker, they observed a mound of loose earth with what looked like a thin dowel sticking out. Aiden saw that Manuel had brought his shovel along, so he directed him to poke around the mound of dirt.

As Manuel began digging, his shovel hit something solid.

"I feel something," cried Manuel, looking at Aiden, his eyes bulging. He paused, his heart pounding, a cold dread settling in his chest. With trembling hands, he and Aiden scraped away more dirt, revealing something large, wrapped in a white sheet, and hastily buried.

The unease in Aiden's eyes mirrored Manuel's growing fear. Together, they slowly pulled the dirty sheet back, and what they saw turned their blood to ice.

Wrapped in the sheet lay fellow seminarian Matthew Mueller, his face pale and still, his chest pierced by a wooden dowel, revealed now as an arrow, and a clear plastic bag drawn tightly around his head, his face distorted in agony. The body appeared pale and lifeless.

Matthew's eyes were half-closed as if caught in some final, agonized prayer. His rigid hands clutched a tarnished crucifix to his chest, and his lips were stained crimson with dried blood.

Just then, a bitter wind swept through the cemetery, making the ancient trees groan as though mourning the discovery.

Manuel stumbled back, his breath catching in his throat. He stared at Aiden, who was frozen in a state of panic as the sinister realization set in—this was no ordinary death.

They ran back to the seminary, forgetting about their shovels. Father Gabriel was notified immediately, and the sheriff's department was called back in to another murder.

Detective Martinez arrived within fifteen minutes after receiving the call. He and two uniformed deputies met with Father Gabriel in his office. The rector had ordered tea from the cafeteria for the two shocked seminarians. Manuel and Aiden clutched steaming mugs, their fingers trembling against the ceramic. Their eyes, hollow and unfocused, stared past the room, locking onto something unseen yet inescapable. The weight of what they had witnessed clung to them, a silent, suffocating presence that time could not chase away.

Caleb felt a moment of empathy for the boys, but he had a job to do. "Boys," he began, hitching up his trousers, "I'm sorry, but you'll have to take me to the body."

Manuel and Aiden looked at each other, then, putting their mugs down, stood. They reluctantly escorted the detective, deputies, and rector to the horrific scene.

As they walked into the biting cold morning, they pulled their jackets tighter and shivered, but it was not from the cold. When they reached the body of Matthew Mueller, Father Gabriel clutched at his chest, gasping. After collecting himself, he muttered a quick prayer, making the sign of the cross over the boy's body.

"Not again…Lord, protect us."

Caleb donned latex gloves, knelt to examine the body, and addressed one of the deputies. "Call the medical examiner and tell them they'll be picking up a body, then tape this area up." He stood, wiping dirt from his trousers. Turning to the rector, he said, "Looks like someone shot him with an arrow, and he must not have died quickly enough, so they asphyxiated him with that plastic bag to finish him off. Somebody went to a lot of trouble to make a statement."

He held up a note that had been pinned to the seminarian's robe, missed by the boys in their shock. It read, *For pride—humility.* "Know what it means, Father?" He looked at Father Gabriel and the boys, who only shrugged.

"He wasn't at breakfast or Mass this morning," offered Aiden, as Manuel nodded vigorously.

Father Gabriel shook his head slowly, a stunned look on his face. "Must have happened last night." He turned to Caleb. "Detective, I'm at a loss for words. I had no idea Matthew was missing. We've had a lot of sickness going around here lately. You know how a change in Maryland weather can do that. Everyone just assumed Matthew was ill." He ran his hands nervously through his hair, his lower lip quivering. "This is most distressing." A tear formed in his eye, and Aiden and Manuel gently guided him back to the seminary.

Caleb pulled out his cell and called Maureen. "Your cousin's in a state at the moment. Another seminarian has been found murdered. Better get here quick. This is the second body he's found, Maureen. I don't have to tell you it's not looking good for him." He ended the call and began taking photos of the body and the surrounding area.

He knelt again, taking in the sight of another young person who would not get to experience any more of life. "What is going on here?" he asked himself.

CHAPTER 8

Wednesday Midday

Maureen had just taken out a frozen meal for her lunch when she got Caleb's call. Returning it to the freezer, she grabbed a candy bar instead and headed out to her car.

"I'm just canceling this vacation. Aiden needs my help," she muttered as she pulled the Jeep out of her driveway. She unwrapped the candy bar and devoured it. Her appetite sated, she called her uncle, relaying what had happened, once again.

"What in the world is going on over there?" he asked. "Poor Aiden. Another body. Do you want me to come over?"

"No, stay there for now. I don't want too many of us over there. You know my captain. If he gets the slightest whiff that I'm helping Caleb with the investigation when I'm supposed to be on leave, it'll be curtains for me, although I've decided to stay here. Caleb's hell-bent on Aiden being good for both murders."

Brendan let out a *"What?* What evidence does he have saying Aiden killed those boys?" He let out a sound of disgust. "Okay, but keep me posted."

The call ended, and Maureen broke all traffic regulations as she sped toward the seminary.

Arriving in record time, Maureen spotted Caleb just as the medical examiner's van was pulling out of the seminary.

"You know, Caleb, you're not making any points with me saying my cousin did these two murders."

Caleb gave her a defiant look as they headed into the building where the seminarians had gathered. "I'm just saying it's funny how he came across two bodies."

"There was another boy with Aiden this time, remember?"

He glazed over her question and showed her the photos he had taken of Matthew Mueller's corpse, quickly swiping each to show various views of yet another gruesome murder. Gathering some of the young men, he took them over to a corner, where several chairs had been placed, and began questioning them.

Maureen spotted several other seminarians and walked casually toward where they had gathered, stopping before reaching them, hoping to overhear what they were saying. She noticed Eugene Wingate was sitting alone. She felt a pang of sympathy for the young loner and wondered how he'd ever make it as a parish priest. She watched as Okeyo Masamba paced back and forth nervously.

"So, now we know it is not random," she heard Okeyo saying in a frantic tone, his thick accent punctuated with fear. "Someone is sending a message." He shook his head back and forth, his arms waving about.

Daniel laughed. "A message? Or maybe it was a punishment."

Manuel chimed in, his tone angry. "You're not helping, Daniel. This is serious business. Two of us have now been murdered—*murdered*." He wrung his hands. "I, for one, am petrified."

Okeyo nodded toward Eugene. "What about you, Eugene? You were the last person to see Joseph Lin alive. And last night, you and Matthew went to the chapel to say the rosary. What do you know about these two murders? Did you strangle Joseph? And then kill Matthew?"

Eugene stood slowly and turned toward Okeyo, his face flushed in anger. "What are you accusing me of, Okeyo?"

Okeyo shrugged and spread his arms, his lips curled in an accusing sneer. "I am just saying it is convenient. Two deaths, and you're always having visions of people getting killed."

Maureen could see Eugene's face turning the color of a beet, even from where she was standing.

"Aiden O'Clery's the one who found both bodies," challenged Eugene.

Manuel stepped forward. "Well, I was with Aiden, Eugene, so does that mean I helped him kill Matthew?"

Tension continued to escalate just as Father Gabriel walked over to intervene. "Enough! We are brothers in faith, not enemies. This division is exactly what the devil wants."

The group was silenced, and Maureen decided to take advantage of the situation. Walking over to the group, she interjected herself into the conversation.

"I couldn't help but overhear the discussion, Father." She looked at each of the young men. "This isn't just some random maniac, guys. Whoever's doing this knows your people, knows this place. And don't try to pin it on the staff. They've all been questioned by other deputies, and their alibis have been confirmed. What aren't you telling me?" Again, she looked at each face.

"I don't know what you want from us, Detective McNeely," spat the rector. "These young men came here to find salvation, just as your uncle did decades ago. Someone is punishing them for their flaws, and you need to find them fast."

"Something sinister is going on in this school, Father,"

Father Gabriel's face twisted in anger. "You think I don't lie awake every night worrying about these boys?"

Okeyo turned to Maureen. "Please, Father Gabriel is our revered rector and does not deserve these accusations. Please treat him with more respect."

Maureen turned to the young man, her eyes narrowing. "There have been two murders here, in the place you live. Law enforcement will do whatever it takes to find out who's behind these crimes, and we'll ask whatever questions need to be answered." Her eyes drilled into his as she took a step toward him. "Maybe we should take a look at you. Sounds like you didn't much care for either young man."

Okeyo's eyes widened as he took a step back.

Maureen didn't wait for a comment. The seminarians shuffled their feet and kept their eyes on the floor. Maureen knew she had hit a nerve.

"Detective Martinez and his deputies will be around to ask more questions, so no one leaves here. You'll all need to tell him where you were last night and early this morning." She started to walk away, but turned. "I suggest you answer them honestly. All of you." Again, her eyes narrowed as she regarded each of them with quiet menace.

WEDNESDAY NIGHT

Later that night, unable to sleep, Eugene ventured into the cemetery, a cold wind whipping at his face. The fog hung low, and the air felt heavy. He knelt at the place Matthew's body had lain, whispering a prayer. "Lord, if this is a test, I don't know if I can pass."

Eugene heard the sound of frozen ground crunching beneath a boot. He turned to see Nathan Silk coming up behind him, startling him.

"You shouldn't be out here alone, Eugene, old boy."

Eugene stared up at him. "Neither should you."

Nathan knelt beside Eugene, placing an unwanted arm on his back. Eugene flinched at his touch. "Do you think God hears us when we pray for answers? Or does He already know what we're going to do?"

Eugene sensed something dark in Nathan's words. "What do you mean?" he asked.

Nathan stood, looking down at him. "Only that, sometimes, silence speaks louder than words." He walked away, back into the fog, leaving Eugene even more unsettled.

THURSDAY MORNING

After morning Mass, Brendan's day was clear. He called Ezra and Langdon and asked if they were ready for some sleuthing, which they eagerly agreed to.

Ezra and Langdon pulled into the rectory's driveway, Langdon in his baby-blue Caddy, Aretha, and Ezra in his yellow Mini Cooper with black racing stripes.

Langdon heaved his body out of the Caddy and watched as the little rabbi exited his Mini, a grin forming under an impeccably trimmed beard, giving him an effortlessly sharp look.

"Little man," Langdon began raucously, "that vee-hicle looks like a big ol' bumblebee just flew in and landed here." He slapped his thigh and turned to Brendan, who had walked out to meet them.

Ezra lifted a shoulder. "Well, you could *live* in that thing you drive, it's so long. I'm sure when folks see you coming around the corner, they're wondering when the other half is going to follow." He nudged his glasses up and adjusted the yarmulke that the wind had blown askew.

Langdon walked over to his friend and swiped at the yarmulke, but the rabbi ducked and evaded the large man's hand.

Brendan ushered the men into the rectory's kitchen. "Hey, if you two are done and haven't had breakfast yet, let's go to that new place in town and check it out."

"Which one is that, Bren?" Ezra grabbed a chair and sat.

"I know 'bout that place," said Langdon. "Some of my church crew rolled through, jus' the other day. Said it was decent and you got lots o' food."

Ezra hit Langdon with an elbow. "Is that all you ever think about is stuffing your ugly face with food?" He looked at Brendan. "So what's the name of this new place?"

"Are you ready for it?" asked Brendan. "Hamlet and Eggs. No kidding! A nod to Willy Shakespeare. But I'm for trying something new. And then we can go to the seminary on full stomachs."

Ezra's face lit up. "Hey, is that the new place where the servers are dressed in Tudor and Elizabethan costumes?" He looked at each man, grinning.

"Maybe I can find the next Mrs. Lieberman there, you know, all decked out looking medieval and stuff, with those low-cut gowns."

"That all *you* think 'bout? The next Miz Lieberman?" Langdon clucked. "Well, let's get goin'. All this talk 'bout food is makin' *this* Loosiana boy hungry." He pushed his chair back and stood, grabbing Ezra by the collar, lifting him out of his chair, and walking the rabbi out to the Caddy.

Hamlet and Eggs was everything the men had heard. The food was good, the costumes outrageous, and although Ezra was unable to replace his beloved late wife, Mindy, who had died from cancer, the food made up for his disappointment. The friends had found another place to meet and eat.

"All righty then," said Brendan, patting his stomach, "let's get out to the seminary."

With full bellies, the three friends walked out to the old Caddy. Ezra got in the back while Brendan rode shotgun.

When they arrived at the seminary, Brendan watched his friends' faces as they gawked at the castle-like building.

"This place is gargantuan, Bren," said Ezra as he perused the grounds.

Langdon studied the rabbi. "Little dude, you'd get lost in there. If we go in, you hol' my hand." He held out a huge paw, and Ezra slapped it away.

"Come on," encouraged Brendan, grabbing his cane. "Let's check out the cemetery. I told Mo we'd look around and see if we could uncover anything interesting."

They meandered to the back of the cemetery first, where mossy grave markers were leaning adjacent to newer ones.

"This place goes back over a hundred years," said Brendan wistfully, "and I have friends and acquaintances out here, too." He wound his way around to where Matthew's body had been found. He ducked under the crime scene tape and, after crossing himself, he knelt, scooping up a handful of cold dirt and letting it sift through his fingers. His eyes searched the area, but he could see nothing out of the ordinary. The crime scene investigators had been thorough.

He looked back at the seminary where he had spent so many years and felt saddened for the young men who had to deal with death, as he had to during his time in Iraq, and years later in Afghanistan, when he returned to the Middle East as a chaplain. He had walked away with his life when so many had not. Even with a bum leg, his life had continued.

"Hey, lookie there," said Langdon, pointing to a gray stone mausoleum. "Looks like how we bury our loved ones back home in Nawlins." He turned to Brendan. "Who's in there?"

Brendan scratched his head. "I don't know *everyone* who's in here, Langdon." He walked over to the crypt, his friends tagging behind. When he read the family name chiseled in stone, he gave a wry smile. "Dean," he said slowly.

"Know them?" asked Ezra.

Brendan turned to his friend. "I know—*knew*—Marcus Dean. His grandparents donated the land and helped fund the building of this seminary. They supposedly were swimming in money." He turned back to the decaying burial chamber. "Marcus was a seminarian here, two years ahead of me, but he got expelled right before ordination." He shook his head slowly. "It was a shame. He went through all that training, then met up with—actually, that's *his* story to tell, not mine."

"So what happened to him?" asked Ezra.

Brendan tugged at his chin. "From what I understand, he does odd jobs and has been here ever since, as a sort of handyman." He added, "Mo said she and Caleb met him yesterday."

"Can we get into that mausoleum?" asked Ezra, changing the subject. "Looks scary. And kind of fun." He rubbed his hands together for warmth. He grinned and awaited an answer.

"I'm sure it's locked," said Brendan, but as he spoke, Langdon had already ambled ahead and found the entryway open. Brendan walked toward the stone edifice, glancing down at the frigid grasses. "Look," he said, "footprints. They look fresh."

Brendan saw his friends exchange a look.

"What?" he asked, palms out. "I'm overly observant, okay?"

The men stepped cautiously into the mausoleum.

Ezra gave a timid laugh. *"Really* spooky, huh?"

Langdon frowned, waving away spider webs. "Ain't nobody made you come. This here's all you."

The only light was coming from the open vault door. Standing at the stairwell, Brendan switched on his phone's flashlight and took his first step into the waiting dark of the crypt. Motioning for his friends to follow, the group began their descent down the cold concrete steps.

As they reached the bottom, Brendan spotted something in a darkened corner. As he walked over, he shined the light on several empty wine bottles scattered about, yet not a single glass in sight, as though the wine had been drained in secrecy or haste. "Either someone's been hiding in here, or doing something they're not supposed to be doing," he muttered.

"Brendan," came a weak voice. It was Ezra's. "Brendan," he said louder, but shakier.

Brendan turned in time to see Marcus Dean standing at the top of the steps, a huge dog lingering several feet away, growling.

"Visiting my family, O'Clery?"

Brendan's mouth went as dry as the Mojave Desert. "M—Marcus," he stammered. "What are you doing here? I haven't seen you since—"

"I know, I know." The man smirked. "Since I got booted out of here." He picked up a stone and threw it at the dog.

Brendan strengthened his resolve. "You've been here awhile. Care to comment on these murders?"

Marcus pulled a pack of cigarettes from his jacket and lit one. "I don't know anything. But maybe I know some of the skeletons in the seminary closets."

"Like what?"

Marcus gave Brendan a sardonic grin. "That seminary isn't as pure as they want you to think. People disappear, and secrets stay buried. You think *two* bodies are bad? Try looking deeper."

"Did you kill those boys, Marcus? I'm sure you're still harboring anger over…the incident."

Marcus flung the half-smoked cigarette into a corner. His eyes narrowed, and he stepped deeper into the musty space. "I had no beef with them, or any of those kids." He inhaled deeply and exhaled, his breath rising in ghostly white puffs.

For several beats, no one spoke. A bug, immune to the cold, scuttled across the dusty floor.

Marcus turned to go, zipping his jacket. He smiled at Brendan. "Good to see you, O'Clery." He glanced at Ezra and Langdon as if seeing them for the first time, then walked out into the cold.

The men watched Marcus walk away, the dog, now wagging its tail, following close behind, as Marcus kept waving his arms and stomping his feet, in an attempt to rid himself of the mutt, who appeared to be a stray.

"Now *that* was terrifying!" Ezra exclaimed, stepping out from behind Langdon's towering frame, his wide eyes still reflecting the shock of the moment. "Don't know what was scarier, the man or that dog."

Brendan continued to stare at the steps going up and out of the mausoleum. Seeing Marcus Dean after all these years had rattled him. He shook his head, collecting his thoughts. He remembered how shocked everyone had been when Marcus was expelled from the seminary.

He slapped a hand to his forehead. "His untimely appearance threw me, and I never got to ask him if all this stuff was his." He waved his hand at the items they had discovered. "Who left this stuff here?"

The appearance of Marcus Dean certainly added another layer of suspicion to this investigation. Using the phone's camera, he took several photos of the wine, shoving the latter into his trouser pocket.

A chill ran down his back, and it wasn't from the cold. "Let's get out of here now."

CHAPTER 9

Thursday Midday

Caleb Martinez sat in the seminary's ancient library and played with a pair of handcuffs as he ticked off the qualities that had made him a highly decorated patrol deputy. He was outspoken, yes, but held his tongue when necessary. He was certainly not afraid to push boundaries, and when it came to reading people, he was usually spot on. But now, being assigned his first homicide meant he'd likely be facing a lot of internal pressure to prove himself.

He glanced at his watch and was glad he had asked—begged—Maureen to help interview seminarians. As far as anyone, like Captain Pollard, was concerned, he'd say her cousin was a first-year seminarian here, and she wanted to remain close to him. And then a pang of guilt swept over him. Here he was, asking her for help, when he felt he couldn't rule out her cousin as a suspect…but he did have to remain neutral.

Just then, Maureen walked through the heavy mahogany doors that led to the shadowy, musty-smelling library.

"Hope I'm not late," said Maureen, throwing her canvas tote bag on the table and dropping down onto a chair.

"You're fine. I've asked that Wingate kid to meet us here. There's something about him. I think he'd be the best candidate to let us know what's going on here."

Maureen emitted a laugh. "You mean you want him to spy on his class-mates? Well, if it takes some of the heat off my cousin, then okay." She absently ran a hand through her hair, and the smile left her face. "You know, Matthew Mueller had your card and was supposed to get with us to tell us about all the 'secrets' in this place, and maybe even tell us who murdered Joseph. But then he got murdered." Her lips pressed into a thin line as the thought kindled her anger.

Caleb nodded and looked up just as Eugene Wingate walked in, his eyes taking in the table filled with folders and crime scene photos. He quickly shoved the photos under a manila folder. He nodded to the young man. "Sit. We need to talk about the dynamics in this place."

Eugene squirmed in his chair uneasily. "Dynamics? What do you mean?"

Caleb leaned forward, narrowing his eyes. "You're all supposed to be training to be priests, but let's be honest. Everyone has skeletons in their closets. I need to know who's hiding what."

Eugene gave a nervous laugh. "I don't know what you mean. We're all just trying to survive this."

Maureen spoke up. "Survive? That's an interesting word choice for a place meant to foster faith."

Eugene looked away, clearly uncomfortable.

Caleb let the moment pass and then added in a more gentle tone, "Look, I get the feeling you want to help us, and you're closer to this place than I'll ever be. If you've noticed anything—anyone acting off—I need to know."

The seminarian's shoulders sagged. Maureen could see he was weighing his next words. "There's been tension. Manuel's now started pushing people, questioning their faith. Daniel Caruso is quiet, but something about him feels...heavy, like he's carrying something he can't share. And those scratches on his face...come on, *you* know. And Okeyo is—well, he's from Kenya, and he's still getting used to how things are done here in the States."

"Anyone else?" asked Caleb.

Eugene shrugged. "Nathan Silk is a first-year guy, and he's kind of standoffish, but he's okay, I guess." He looked at Maureen. "And Aiden's okay, too. He's kind. Very devout."

Maureen had been scribbling notes. She looked up. "And how about Father Gabriel and other staff?"

Eugene screwed his face into an uncomfortable mask. "Father Gabriel's trying to keep things together, but I've caught him locking doors and hiding files." He fidgeted with a button on his shirt. "I guess you've figured out he drinks occasionally." He added quickly, "But he never drinks during the day, or at least not that much." He looked nervously around. "I shouldn't have said anything. It's never caused any problems, so I should have kept my mouth shut."

Maureen leaned in. "It's fine, Eugene. We all have our secrets."

Eugene lifted his head, and his eyes drilled into hers. "Well, there's something else. It's Okeyo." He snorted. "He treats our rector like he's the pope. If anyone criticizes the man, Okeyo is ready to fight them. I truly believe that, if Father Gabriel did anything wrong, Okeyo would lie to protect him." He picked at his fingernails for a time. "Anyway, the rest of the staff here seems okay."

Caleb continued in his most compassionate voice. "Interesting...thanks, Eugene." He glanced at his watch. "It's lunch time, so go on. But please let us know if you hear or see anything. You could be a huge help."

The young man nodded but said no more. Caleb laid his pen down and smiled, dismissing him. They watched as he slunk out of the library.

"He knows something," observed Maureen. "And you're right to use him as your eyes and ears."

"Yeah," sighed Caleb heavily, "but I have a feeling that, whatever's going on, these young kids are going to stick together." He looked at Maureen. "We'll have to figure it out all by ourselves." He began laughing.

"Go ahead and laugh, Caleb, but know this...I've canceled my vacation to help get this resolved."

Caleb immediately ceased laughing.

CHAPTER 10

Thursday Midday

Aiden was late getting to lunch after his last class, but after he had grabbed a plate of fried chicken and a small bowl of steamed broccoli, he set his tray down at the table that Manuel, Daniel, Okeyo, and Nathan occupied. At the end sat Eugene, reading from one of his textbooks. Aiden's eyes lingered on Eugene for a moment, studying him carefully, before he finally took his seat at the table.

"Don't bother him," said Daniel sarcastically. "You know he prefers his own company." The others didn't laugh at Daniel's mean comment.

Manuel turned and greeted Aiden, welcoming him enthusiastically. "So what's new on the murders? Since you have an in, I imagine you get all the juicy details."

Aiden gave a pert *hmph*. "They tell me nothing. I leave all that gore to my cousin and uncle. They actually *thrive* on it." He crossed himself, said a brief grace, then bit into a piece of chicken. "You guys hear anything?"

"Nah," said Nathan. "Looks like the cops are stumped. Must be someone from the outside."

"Why do you say that?" asked Aiden.

"Take a look around," Nathan said, sweeping his arms wide to encompass the room of seminarians.

Aiden took a cursory look, his eyes resting once again on Eugene. He felt sorry for the boy. Eugene was nice enough and a smart student, but socially awkward, for sure. Aiden wondered how he'd be able to manage an entire parish with his lack of social skills.

And then his gaze rested on the gold chain around his neck. Along with the Miraculous Medal most of the seminarians wore, there was another one with a woman's image stamped on it.

Aiden felt his skin prickle. Should he say something? Keep his mouth shut? The latter sounded like the best solution, but then he thought about Maureen and what she'd do, and he decided to make his cousin proud.

"Hey, Eugene," he began, his voice quavering, "what's that behind your Miraculous Medal? Is it your patron saint?" Aiden held his breath.

Eugene peeked up from his book and stared at the faces now gawking at him. Fingering the two medals, he held up the one that interested Aiden. "This one?" he asked. "Joseph gave it to me. Said it was some Chinese saint." He began removing it from around his neck. "Want to see it?"

"Sure," said Aiden. He saw the others staring at him in confusion.

He took the chain from Eugene and examined it. Sure enough, it was good old Saint Anna Wang, Joseph Lin's favorite saint. Aiden felt a lump in his throat.

Handing it back to Eugene, he thanked him and returned to his fried chicken, which now tasted like dust, as his mouth was as dry as a desert.

He decided to hold on to this new discovery and tell his cousin about the medal the next time he saw her. Poking around at his broccoli, he finally excused himself, using his philosophy class as justification.

THURSDAY EVENING

After dinner that evening, Eugene returned to the dormitory, where he found Manuel and Nathan arguing in the common room. He stood in the doorway, feeling the tension, and thought about going to his room instead.

Manuel was standing and pointing at Nathan, speaking in a heated tone. "How do we know you're not behind this? You're always sneaking off, praying at weird hours."

Nathan shrugged, his face lacking emotion. "Praying is part of why we're here. Maybe you should try it instead of throwing accusations."

Daniel and Okeyo, who'd been sitting off to the side, stood and walked over to the two. Daniel placed himself between them, a palm on each chest. "Enough! This isn't helping anyone."

Eugene took that moment to enter the room. "What's going on?"

Manuel grew agitated, waving his arms around. "Nathan's hiding something, I can *feel* it."

Eugene looked at Nathan, not knowing what to do or say.

Nathan, still unperturbed at the assault, turned to Eugene. "And Manuel's paranoia is going to get someone else killed."

Eugene pursed his lips and did his best to calm the group. "Look, we're all scared, but fighting each other won't solve anything. Detective Martinez and his team will do their job. Let's let the police figure this out."

Manuel, crimson darkening his caramel skin, stormed out, muttering under his breath. Okeyo stood silent. The remaining seminarians looked at each other, seemingly upset with the argument, and left in uneasy silence.

Later that evening Brendan's phone rang. Seeing it was his nephew, he quickly picked up his cell.

"Uncle Brendan, I know it's late, but I can't sleep. Can you come over and talk with me for a while? My nerves are shot. I'm not used to dead bodies, and I don't want to speak with anyone here."

Brendan's heart broke. His nephew was lucky, never having to deal with dead bodies until now. He closed his eyes, told his nephew he'd be over shortly, and went upstairs to his medicine cabinet.

For several painful minutes, Brendan studied the face in the mirror. He didn't see Maureen's constant reference to Ewan McGregor when he looked at himself. He saw a young Marine fighting in Iraq during the Gulf War. An ugly face. A killer's face.

He clenched his jaw and opened the cabinet, perusing his pharmaco-poeia of drugs. He went for the Xanax first, but the thought of two young seminarians brutally murdered made him bypass the Xanax and go for the oxycodone. That one would not only relieve the pain in his leg but also allow him to speak with his nephew about the murder of innocents—something he knew a great deal about.

He arrived at the seminary around nine o'clock and found his nephew fast asleep. Not wanting to wake the boy, he silently closed the door and left the dormitory.

On a whim, Brendan decided to walk around the building. He wandered down the hallowed halls, memories stirring with each step, their echoes whispering from the walls like old friends. As he was passing the seminary archives, he thought he saw a flash of light coming from inside. Stopping, he entered the room, his hackles raised. Who'd be in here this time of night, and better yet, for what reason?

His hand found the light switch, and when he flipped it on, a startled Father Gabriel looked up in horror. When he saw it was Brendan, he relaxed for a moment but then tightened his lips and scowled.

"Late-night reading, Father? Or hiding something?" Brendan asked sarcastically, glancing at the flashlight the old priest had in his hand.

"These archives are restricted. Sensitive Church documents."

Brendan crossed his arms and glared at the old rector. "Sensitive? Or incriminating?" He waited for an explanation from Father Gabriel.

The old priest let out an agitated sigh. "My patience with you is growing thin, Father O'Clery. You're not here to investigate murders nor to dig into the Church's past. Let the police do their job." His eyes flashed. "I've heard about you and your ragtag group of clergy that ingratiate their way into police investigations. Well, you'll not do it here."

Brendan was undaunted. "Well, Father, the past has a funny way of catching up, and from where I'm standing, it's looking pretty messy. The police will find out if you're hiding anything. It's only a matter of time."

He watched Father Gabriel's face twist in anger. He shoved past Brendan and left the archives.

Brendan turned the lights off in the room and left. There had been secrets when he was here, and there were still secrets, he opined. What was it with this seminary, anyway?

FRIDAY MORNING

Sometime after midnight, Aiden awoke from a restless sleep. He glanced around the room, remembering he had called his uncle, but then must have fallen asleep. Did his uncle come to the seminary and find him asleep, not wanting to wake him? It was too late to call him now, but determination in discovering who murdered his fellow seminarians overrode his fears and anxieties. He eased his feet into a pair of slippers and headed to the library. He thought he might be able to find answers to the cryptic messages located on the seminarians' corpses in theological texts, although the thought of walking around the spooky seminary creeped him out.

While searching the various volumes, his hand hit a loose panel in the back of one of the bookshelves. Feeling behind the panel, he found a small metal box.

Intrigued, he gently lifted the box from its place and set it down on a table. It wasn't locked, but the latch stuck, and as he pried it open, he saw several old photographs. One caught his attention. Aiden's brows furled as he studied the photo, recognizing Father Gabriel as a younger man, with several seminarians standing around him, one standing apart from the group, looking almost forlorn and distant. He pocketed the photo and replaced the box behind the panel. He'd take it to Detective Martinez in the morning, after he called Maureen.

He returned to his room and, upon entering, stepped on a piece of paper, which appeared to be a note slipped under his door while he was gone. Picking it up, he didn't recognize the handwriting.

He went over to his bed and sat down. His lips moved as he read the note: "Stay out of this. You're not as innocent as you think."

Shaken, he folded the paper and stuck it in his jacket. Something else to take to the detective, he thought, as he slipped in between the sheets, knowing sleep would not come to him tonight.

CHAPTER 11

Friday Morning

The following morning, Maureen, Caleb, and Brendan returned to the seminary. Caleb gathered the same group of students into a classroom to glean more information, while Maureen and Brendan headed down the hallway to see if they could find Father Gabriel.

They hadn't gotten far when Maureen heard footsteps walking swiftly behind her. She turned to see Aiden, giving him a warm smile.

"Hey, Cuz." She halted, as did Brendan.

Aiden's face was as pale as a corpse's. He kept looking around nervously. "I found this hidden in a box in the library." He shoved the photo into Brendan's hands, looking nervously over his shoulder.

Brendan studied the photo, then passed it over to her. He pointed to one of the men. "This is Father Gabriel, but I don't know the others. This one looks vaguely familiar. Maybe a seminarian back in the day?" He gave it another glance then shrugged.

Maureen saw Aiden trembling and felt bad that these murders had come to such a holy place.

He looked up at her. "What if Father Gabriel's connected to the murders or is covering for the murderer? Or maybe he killed these guys himself."

"Then we just found our next lead," said Maureen.

Aiden fumbled around in his slacks and pulled out a crumpled paper. He handed it to Maureen. "This was under my door. Someone knows we're related and that I've probably been talking to you."

Brendan peered over his shoulder. "What's it say?"

Maureen read the note out loud. "'Not as innocent as you think.' What's that supposed to mean?"

Aiden looked like he was in a state of near panic. "I don't know. Does someone think *I'm* not innocent, or do they mean Joseph and Matthew?" He shook his hands, and Maureen saw his eyes well with tears. The boy was scared to death, she thought. She should get him out of this place and maybe even have the seminary closed down until the killer was apprehended.

She reached for his hand, grabbing one in hers and squeezing it tightly. "It's meant to scare you," she said, her voice calm and soothing. "Don't let it. But it does mean one thing: whoever's doing this must think we're getting closer to uncovering the murderer, even though we have no motives and no suspects."

Brendan glanced between Maureen and his nephew. "Look, this place will have deputies all over for the next week or so. Try to stay calm, and don't go anywhere alone, especially at night. Stay close to a group."

Aiden nodded numbly, thanked them, then turned and walked slowly down the hall.

Maureen's mouth twisted grimly. "That poor boy. I'm thinking we should evacuate this place to keep everyone safe."

"Not a bad idea, Mo," agreed Brendan.

She twisted the claddagh ring on her finger. "Well, let's go see if Caleb uncovered anything new." She looked over at her uncle, her head slightly tilted. "I guess nothing like this ever happened while *you* were here, huh?"

"It's a different time, Mo. Strange things going on everywhere, so why should a seminary be any different?" Pounding his cane into the floor as they walked, he continued. "I'm just baffled by Father Gabriel's evasive behavior. I know he's anxious to get these murders solved, but I really feel like he's hiding something, or covering up something, or covering *for* someone."

Maureen could only shrug as they continued their way down the hall. She turned and peered down the dark corridor, half expecting her cousin to come running back with a knife protruding from his back or something just as gruesome.

As they turned a corner, they ran into Caleb.

"Get anything more from the staff?" Maureen asked the deputy.

"Nope. They're all either lying, holding something back, or doing whatever their rector is telling them. And that group of students had nothing new to add. So we still have no motives, no good alibis."

Brendan frowned. "Well, I know they're only human, but I can't believe an entire group of seminarians and staff are lying or hindering a murder investigation. It's got to be someone outside."

The deputy's face flushed crimson, as a burst of curses flew from his mouth. "Sorry," he apologized. "I guess I'm just frustrated, this being my first homicide and all."

Maureen put a hand on Caleb's shoulder. "Don't worry about it. The forensics team has sent everything down to the lab, and while I don't know everyone in that department, I know the ME for Porter Mills, and *she* knows everyone in forensics, like her husband." Her face warmed with a grin. "She'll let us know what they find on the bodies and on that parchment."

Caleb's face returned to warmer tones. "Thanks, Maureen. I won't forget this."

"You bet your sweet—"

"Maureen! Stop!" cried Brendan, halting her in mid-obscenity.

CHAPTER 12

Friday Midday

The trio chatted for several minutes outside until Caleb got in his unmarked police car and left.

Brendan turned to Maureen. "How about lunch? I'll call the guys, and we can discuss what we've found so far."

Maureen turned, an exasperated look on her face. "I've already canceled my vacation plans, and while I'd love to go, why don't you go with the guys, and I'll go home and call my friend, Victoria, at the ME's office. Call me after lunch, and I can let you know what she's found out—that is, if she *has* found anything out yet."

"Nice to have friends in high places," he said, kissing her cheek.

"Please," she said drolly, "with *your* connections, you should be able to part traffic like the Red Sea."

They both laughed and walked toward the parking lot. Before they reached Maureen's car, they heard their names being called. Turning, they saw Aiden running toward them. Maureen turned to her uncle, her brows knit together.

Panting, Aiden bent over when he reached them, his hands over his abdomen. "Glad I caught you both." He stood, his breathing more measured. "Look, there's something I forgot to ask you." He turned to Maureen. "Can you tell me if your crime scene techs found a medal of Saint Anna Wang when they picked up Joseph?" He crossed himself, making Maureen stifle a smile. Her cousin had learned that from her uncle.

"Saint *who?*" asked Brendan.

Aiden emitted an abrupt laugh. "Saint Anna Wang, the patron saint of Chinese youth, among other things. Joseph revered her for her martyrdom during the Boxer Rebellion." He looked at their uncle. "I've been so upset thinking about Joseph's murder, I forgot all about the medal, but I know he always had it on his chain." His eyes went to a squirrel running across the seminary's lawn. "I've been trying to recall anything I could about that night, and I'm positive I didn't see it on his neck chain when I came across his...his body. He *always* had that chain on." He looked down. "I didn't see the medal around his neck that night...only that...rosary, but I'd know it anywhere. This medal was unlike the others we usually see. It wasn't just metal, but vividly colored, like maybe it was enamel or something like that."

Maureen looked at Brendan. "So the killer may have taken it with him as a souvenir."

Her uncle nodded.

"Find the medal, find the killer?"

Aiden cleared his throat. "I saw Eugene Wingate with the same medal around his neck, so if your forensic folks haven't found it, maybe that's why. Eugene says Joseph gave it to him, but I'm telling you, Joseph was very attached to that medal and would never give it away."

Maureen narrowed her eyes at her cousin. "You don't think there could be two medals of that saint?"

Aiden's shoulders lifted. "Hey, this is a pretty obscure Chinese saint. You'd either have to be Chinese to know about her or a hagiographic prodigy."

Maureen jotted the information in her notebook. "Guess we'll be sitting down with this young man again." She closed her notebook and turned her attention back to Aiden. "Thanks for that info, Cuz. Hey, keep an eye out for stuff like that, but be careful." She gave him a warm, familial smile and changed the subject. "They're going to test the rosary Lin was strangled with for DNA. The other boys agree it was probably Matthew Mueller's because a lot of them put their initials on their rosaries since this place must have thousands of them floating around. But even if his DNA is on it, that won't prove he murdered Joseph. Between the data on the cell phones Caleb's been checking out, the rosary, those strange footprints with that tacky substance, and that prophetic saying on the parchment, along with those threatening notes, forensics should be able to get DNA off *something*." She gave her cousin's shoulder a warm pat.

Aiden looked down at the driveway, kicking at an acorn that had fallen from a tree. "There's something else, Mo."

"Oh?"

"Joseph owed me some money—a hundred dollars." He looked at her, his face racked with guilt. "Will the cops haul me in for questioning? Does that make me a suspect?"

Maureen squeezed her eyes shut. "Aiden, why didn't you tell me this earlier?"

"I told Uncle Brendan." He looked at their uncle, who immediately looked away.

Maureen huffed but was in no mood to get into it with Brendan.

"That's not a big thing. Anything else I should know?" She looked at Brendan, giving him a chastising stare.

"A few days before Matthew was murdered, he and Okeyo had a big blowup. Okeyo said Matthew must have cheated on a theology exam because he got a perfect score, and Okeyo passed, but with a lower score." He looked around and dropped his voice. "They almost got into a fistfight. One of the deacons came by and broke them up. Okeyo said if they were in his country, he'd be taken out and hung for cheating."

Maureen and Brendan exchanged looks.

"This is now the second time that boy has been heard arguing with another seminarian, and now two of them are dead." Maureen inhaled deeply, her chest rising with the chill of the air. As she exhaled, a cloud of white breath escaped her lips, disappearing into the air.

"Do *you* think he was cheating?" asked Brendan.

"I doubt it. Matthew is—*was*—super smart. Okeyo has a temper. He's always on edge. He's usually quiet, but he's over here in a strange country, and he feels he *has* to make it through this seminary and return to Kenya as a successful priest, or face disgrace from his family."

Maureen gave Aiden a wan smile and tousled his curly red locks. "That's a big help, Aiden, but from now on, tell me *everything*. Don't feel you need to keep your friends' secrets. Remember, two young men have been murdered."

"How can I forget?" Just then, Aiden turned as he heard his name being called. "Got to run. Bye, Uncle Brendan. Bye, Maureen." He ran off before they could say their goodbyes.

"What do you think?" Brendan asked.

"I'll have to see what Victoria has found out, but this Okeyo Masamba is certainly a good start for these murders." She chewed her bottom lip. "Let's go. I'll drop you off and call you later."

"Sounds like a plan."

Brendan got in the front seat and threw his cane in the back. "Aiden's a fine young man, isn't he?"

Maureen turned the ignition and exited the seminary's grounds. She looked over at Brendan. "He's always looked up to you. You know you're the reason he wants to be a priest."

Brendan grinned. "Yeah, I'm a model of piety and devotion, and if you look up the word 'holy' in the dictionary, you'll find a picture of me with my halo." He formed a circle with his thumbs and forefingers, lifting it above his head like a makeshift halo.

Maureen reached over and gave his upper arm a solid punch.

CHAPTER 13

Friday Midday

"I don't care if God Himself came down and told me, I'll not do it. No way!" Brendan felt his face heating up as he paced the rectory's living room, punctuating each step with his cane. Mary Magdalene thought he was playing a game and nipped relentlessly at his heels.

"This is not a request, *Father*, this is an order, and you'll obey." A rich, thick Irish accent bellowed over Brendan's cell.

Brendan pressed his lips together so tightly that one of his teeth accidentally found its way into his lower lip. He pulled a handkerchief from his pocket and wiped the blood from his mouth. "You know I hate driving in Baltimore, and besides, I've got too much on my plate to entertain one of your harebrained ideas."

"*Harebrained?* How dare you speak to your archbishop like that! I gave you an order, and by God Almighty Himself, you'll carry it out."

Brendan felt like reaching through the cell phone and grabbing a handful of neck. "Right now, Malachy, you're acting like my brother, not the high and mighty archbishop. I don't have the time to help out at Saint Ann's, let alone set up an outreach program there." Brendan felt his heart beating wildly.

The archbishop brought his volume down. "Look, Brendan, Father Timothy Mahoney is in his eighties and needs help. He can only—"

"So get him a deacon, Mal. Or a layperson from his church."

"Have you seen his parish? His parishioners are just as old, if not older. His church is in the worst section of Baltimore and probably won't survive much longer. They need some kind of program to help the poor families that live there." Brendan heard his brother's frustrated sigh. "Look, can you at least take a drive down there soon and get him started? We have to help our brother priests out, so."

Brendan continued pacing. "Don't try to lay that Irish Catholic guilt on me, brother. It won't work." He paused for a moment, feeling trapped by his vow of obedience. "Okay, Mal, you win. But I won't be able to do it this week. I'm still trying to help out with Aiden. He's upset about the two seminarians who got murdered. As soon as I think he's ready to handle things on his own, I'll head down to the city and give Father Tim a hand." He couldn't let it go. "But that's the last favor you ask of me for a while."

Before his brother could respond, Brendan ended the call, hurling his cell phone onto the sofa. Throwing himself into a chair, he fumed for a few minutes, but then his thoughts turned to Aiden and his murdered friends.

Putting Father Tim on the back burner—along with his brother—he checked his watch. Friday…an impromptu poker night with the guys would be just the thing. That might take his mind off the murders for a while.

He grabbed his cane and stood, and he and Mary Magdalene went into the kitchen to see what snacks and goodies Mrs. Morrison had left.

That night, five off-the-clock clergymen entered the rectory's tiny utility room, the only room Mrs. Morrison would allow them their "sinful pleasures." A wobbly card table had been set up, and Brendan took out a box of bootlegged Cuban cigars from a devoted parishioner and set it next to a bottle of Jameson.

By seven o'clock, the room had become thick with swirling cigar smoke as serious faces hovered over their hands, eyes flicking between cards and opponents in silent calculation.

Langdon was the first to call. Throwing his cards down, he reached past Ezra and grabbed a handful of chips.

"Hey," cried the little rabbi, "watch it! You're pushing my cards around, and Milo's going to be able to see my hand." He brought his cards to his chest, giving the hulking Baptist a menacing look.

Milo Hendricks, pastor of Porter Mill's Grace Lutheran Church, snorted. "Ezra, you could show me every hand you're dealt, and I'd still lose." He placed his cards down. "I call." He looked at Ezra. "See what I mean? All the years we've been playing poker with you losers, I can count on one hand how many times I've won." He waved three fingers around in demonstration.

Langdon, now holding a buffalo wing in each hand, chimed in. "An' you ain't that lucky in love, either, dude."

Ezra elbowed his friend. "That's not nice." He turned to Milo and gave him a toothy grin. "Milo and I are holding out for the perfect woman, right, Milo?" He reached for a wing, but Langdon slapped his hand, snatching it for himself.

"Little man, you be lookin' at every woman you see, on the prowl for the next Miz Lieberman."

"Well, I miss my Mindy," snipped Ezra. "So kill me."

Langdon grabbed the yarmulke from Ezra's head and waved it around, teasing the rabbi.

"Speaking of killing," interrupted Ritchie Kim, the youth minister at the Korean Praise to Jesus Our Eternal King of Heaven Church, "clue us in to what's going on at that seminary." He shuffled the cards and then dealt each man a new hand.

"It's a nightmare," said Brendan, grimacing at the hand he had been dealt. "And my poor nephew has been traumatized by the entire thing. I mean, one murder is bad enough, but *two*?" He took a sip of Jameson.

"Any suspects?" asked Milo, running a hand over his balding pate.

"No real ones. And it's too early for forensics to have found anything."

Ezra piped in. "We'll have to solve these murders all on our own, the three of us."

"Really?" asked Ritchie.

"Of *course* not," Brendan said, rolling his eyes. "Caleb Martinez has the case—his first homicide. Know him?"

Some of the men said they knew Caleb from town.

"Anyway, one boy was strangled, and one was shot by an arrow and finished off by placing a plastic bag over his head. As of now, no one knows if it was done by a seminarian, a staff member, or someone outside." Brendan turned when he heard scratching at the door, realizing it was Saint Peter, smelling the sandwiches. "But, for now, can we just play cards?"

The men groused for several minutes and then went back to their game, putting the murders quietly behind them.

CHAPTER 14

Saturday Morning

Maureen was rubbing a bronzing lotion on her arms and legs, hoping it would help her look tanned, since she wouldn't be getting any sun from Bermuda, when the phone rang.

"Mo, have you heard anything back from your friend, Victoria?" Brendan asked.

"Not yet, but she's working today, even though it's Saturday, so I'm going over there as soon as I can get myself together." She added playfully, "And if I tell her it's *you* that's asking, I'm sure she'll fall all over herself getting that information. She has the biggest crush on you."

Brendan expelled an exaggerated sigh. "Mo, you know she's playing with you. She's got a husband."

"I know, but I like to imagine you with a halo on your head, that's all tarnished and hanging on by a thread."

Brendan rewarded her with a soft laugh. "You two have your fun. I just wanted to tell you I'm going over later to check on Aiden. His folks can't leave North Carolina for another couple of days, so I want to make sure he's okay until they can get back."

"You're a good uncle. At least to Aiden."

"You're funny, kiddo."

Each rang off and Maureen squirted a heavy line of bronzer down her legs, muttering under her breath. If she couldn't go on vacation because of work, then she'd at least *look* like she had.

After three cups of coffee and a microwaved sausage biscuit, Maureen steered her Jeep to the medical examiner's office. The parking lot was nearly empty on a Saturday, so she slipped into a spot right by the door.

She buzzed the intercom, and Victoria Chen appeared almost immediately, smiling as she let her in. "Good timing," she said, ushering Maureen inside the empty building.

They exchanged quick hugs before Victoria headed for the coffeemaker. Within minutes, the aroma of fresh brew filled the room, and they sat down together, cups in hand.

"My uncle asked me if you've found anything out from the autopsies," she said.

"Then tell him to come over here and find out for himself. I'd *love* a visit from him." Victoria giggled girlishly.

Maureen laughed at her friend's audacious but harmless banter. "Remember...that pesky little vow of celibacy," she said, studying her petite friend with her glossy black hair tucked neatly in a paper cap.

"Oh, stop it," retorted the ME. "You know I'm kidding! I'm happily married to my own hunk. But getting back to why I called you, when it's something *you're* working on, I try to rush it through, especially when the victims are young seminarians."

Maureen's face warmed at the gentle lilt of the medical examiner's Asian accent. The pleasantries faded quickly, though. There was now too much at stake.

"So whatcha got?"

"Joseph Lin was strangled, that's a fact, but not by those rosary beads. There are bruises around his throat, and he suffered from contusions. It looks like someone attacked him, got control of him, and laid him out on the floor, where they began choking him. Dark red marks encircled the neck, consistent with manual or corded strangulation. There's petechial hemorrhaging in the eyes and face from vascular compression. The perpetrator was facing the boy as he strangled him." With a wicked grin, Victoria looped her hands around Maureen's neck in a pantomime of strangulation, squeezing just enough to make her point. "I detected thumb marks on the neck, and the hyoid bone was fractured. That's commonly found in strangulation, especially manual strangulation, where force is applied directly to the neck. The rosary was simply added on for effect, not the murder weapon. And no fingerprints from either that piece of parchment or the note, or anything, for that matter. And nothing under the boy's fingernails. I'm trying to sweet-talk my hubby into getting the DNA testing pushed to the front of the line, but don't be surprised if nothing shows up. You know criminals these days. Everyone watches cop shows and knows how to cover their tracks."

"Any defensive wounds?"

Victoria nodded and again pointed to various sections of Joseph's body. "There's defensive wounds, like deep abrasions and bruising, on the forearms and backs of the hands, likely from blocking or grabbing at the assailant's hands or weapon. There're also crescent-shaped nail marks on the victim's neck, suggesting he clawed at whatever was constricting his airway."

Maureen tilted her head slightly, eyes narrowing as a low, almost absentminded *hmmm* slipped from her lips. "So how about that sticky substance that was on the floor?"

"That's for the forensic folks. I'm the dead body person."

Maureen laughed, then let this information digest. "And the other boy? Mueller?" Behind her, she heard the clicking of Victoria's signature stiletto heels, worn by the diminutive ME "for height," and then the shuffling of papers.

"Matthew Mueller. Just my opinion, but from the depth of the arrow that went into him, it looks like someone shot him from a fairly close range, then finished him off by wrapping a plastic bag over his head and suffocating him. We're still working on the arrow. Hopefully, I'll be able to glean some more info from it. Also, there weren't any defensive wounds on him, so his attack must have been really quick and a total surprise to him, and maybe even by someone he knew."

"So I guess nothing on any of those notes or that parchment, either, huh?"

"Not yet. And both tox screens came back negative. Nothing unusual there."

Maureen was silent for several moments, racking her brain, seeing if she had left anything out. "By any chance, did you find a medal? Like one of those holy medals? It was of a Chinese saint…Anna somebody."

The ME's voice brightened. "Saint Anna Wang, patron of Chinese youth!"

Maureen smiled to herself. "You've heard of her?"

"Gracious, yes. I'm not Catholic, but I am Chinese and have a ton of family who married into that religion. Anna's really popular with the young people."

"Who knew? You're like an onion—layers hiding more layers. And I'm starting to wonder what's buried at the center."

Victoria let out a soft, melodic laugh. "You're hilarious, but no medal of Anna on his body or in his clothing."

"Hmm…well," Maureen said, changing the subject, "I canceled the Bahamas, since my cousin's a seminarian there, so I'm trying to help Caleb Martinez. He caught the case. Do you know him?"

"Maureen, I know all the deputies and most of the state police. I'll help you both in any way I can." She paused for a moment, then in a syrupy voice added, "So will your hunky uncle be helping you out?"

Maureen rolled her eyes. "I keep telling you…celibacy…" She laughed at her friend, and after several more quips, the visit ended and Maureen turned to leave. "Oh, I almost forgot," she said, reaching into her pocket and handing Victoria a small evidence bag containing the note that had been slipped under her cousins door. "Probably win't have much on it, but we can hope." The ME took it, and Maureen exited the room.

Maureen promised herself she'd tell her uncle what she had just been told. But not right now. She started the Jeep's engine and began humming along to a Beach Boys tune playing on the radio. And suddenly, the happiness drained out of her soul as she remembered the familial chore she had to face later that day.

Aiden tried to study later that afternoon, but his mind was filled with visions of dead bodies. Slamming his book shut, he walked down the hallway to Okeyo's room to see if he wanted a study mate.

When he reached the room, Okeyo's door stood ajar. Aiden gave a light knock on the frame before stepping inside, only to find the seminarian gone.

Wanting to leave a note asking about studying together later, Aiden went to the desk to grab a pen and a piece of scrap paper. After locating one, he shuffled through a stack of books for some paper.

As he moved the books aside, his hand froze. He had just uncovered something that made his heart skip a beat.

Joseph's Saint Anna Wang medal! Just like the one Eugene had!

He reached for the medal, then paused, remembering all the stories Maureen had told at O'Clery's family meals—*no touching the evidence*. He quickly shuffled some papers over the medal, making a mental note to call Maureen as soon as he left Okeyo's room.

Suddenly, he felt the urgent need to get out of there. As he turned to leave, his eyes flicked to Okeyo's bed and then froze. Something was there.

His pulse quickened. He didn't have time for this. But after finding the medal, he couldn't ignore it. A Bible lay on the bed, and the cover on it was not the cover he had seen on the Bible Okeyo always carried. Scanning the room, Aiden found Okeyo's Bible on a shelf over the desk and wondered why his friend would have two.

Heart pounding, he pulled his sleeve down over his hand and carefully lifted the cover. His breath caught. The name inscribed on the inside was Matthew Mueller! The words stared back at him. First Joseph's medal, now Matthew's Bible. Both belong to the murdered boys. And now Okeyo appeared to be connected to them.

He closed the Bible and turned to leave. Before he left the room, however, something in the corner caught his eye, barely visible in the dim light, but just out of place enough to make him stop.

Walking slowly over to the object, he stooped down to examine it further. It was a bloody handkerchief, poking out of a jacket. Was Okeyo hiding something? Had he used his handkerchief to wipe blood from his hands after murdering Matthew Mueller?

He stood slowly, his body trembling from the weight of the discovery. His pulse pounded in his ears, and for a moment, he just stared at it, unable to believe what he was seeing. Whatever it was, it didn't belong here. He had to call Maureen.

Footsteps echoed in the hallway. His stomach clenched. He had to get out—now.

Amused by Victoria Chen's innocent crush on her uncle, Maureen sang along to songs on the radio, but her good mood was soon thwarted as she remembered where she was headed—her grandmother's.

She loved her grandmother, Eabha O'Clery, *"of the County Mayo O'Clery's,"* as her Gran always insisted on adding, but any time spent with that little banshee left Maureen, and anyone else, drained of all energy. Still, it had been a while since she had last visited her grandmother. After stopping and picking up a bouquet of colorful flowers at the local florist, she aimed the Jeep toward Our Lady of Grace, the retirement home where her grandmother now lived.

She arrived at the facility and found a parking space close to the front entrance. Taking a deep, steadying breath, Maureen squared her shoulders and entered the building. She greeted a few of the sisters who tended the elderly residents, then made her way down the hall to her grandmother's apartment, knocking softly, already bracing for the storm—or silence—she might find.

Upon entering the small suite, her nose picked up on something cinnamon-y. From the doorway, she spotted her tiny grandmother pouring tea from an old, chipped Belleek teapot. Maureen's eyes narrowed as she watched her, like a suspect in an interrogation room.

Eabha always had tea and something sweet to lure Maureen into a false sense of security, where she could then pounce on her and pummel her with questions about her marital status.

"*Duit dhuit, a stor.* You look tired," began Eabha. "And pale. Have you been eating at all, or are you surviving on coffee and spite?"

Maureen sighed, shrugging off her coat as she watched her grandmother pour tea into two chipped floral cups. "Nice to see you, too, Gran."

"I call it as I see it, so. And what I see is a woman who should be minding her own business instead of chasing criminals around like a mad thing. You know, your cousin Fiona married a lovely accountant. Steady job. Home every night. Have you ever considered a real career, *cailin?*"

Maureen took a slow sip of tea, her patience already wearing thin. "You mean a real career like Fiona's husband, who just got caught embezzling from his company?"

Eabha didn't even blink. "Well, at least he was clever about it. Unlike you, running into danger with nothing but a badge and bad judgment."

Maureen sighed. It was going to be a long visit.

They sat in silence for several minutes, Maureen glancing at her watch way too often.

Eabha stopped stirring her tea and laid her spoon down. "Malachy called me the other day." Her grandmother's face glowed at the mention of the archbishop. "He says you haven't been to confession in months."

Maureen rolled her eyes. "Years is more like it," she muttered, taking a sip of the hot tea and reaching for a cinnamon bun. "Maybe because I don't have anything to confess?"

Eabha snorted. "Oh, please, *mo chroi.* You have a mouth like a sailor, a temper like your father, and I'd bet my social security check you've thought about murder at least twice this week."

Maureen lifted the teacup to her lips, glared at Eabha, and, under her breath, muttered, "Three times, actually. Once just now."

Eabha waved her off. "And speaking of sins, why are you still unmarried? Remember my friend, Brigid McNamara? Her Tommy came over the other day for a visit—handsome lad, owns his own pub, so. You could do worse."

"Gran, I'm not interested in Tommy," she moaned. "He's his own best customer."

Eabha scoffed. "Of course you're not interested. He's got a job, hair, and a decent smile. Not brooding enough for you, is he?"

Maureen shook her head, already regretting her visit. "Gran, if you must know, I've been seeing a handsome Maryland State Police detective for several months now. His name is Simon Archer, and he's very nice, and I think even you'd like him."

Eabha set her cup down and stared at her. "Are you, so? Is he Irish? Or better yet, is he Catholic?"

Maureen could only raise her eyes heavenward.

Suddenly, Eabha leaned forward, pushing Maureen's cinnamon bun aside. "Girl, you're not letting him have his way with you, are you? You keep your legs crossed and your rosary close, or I swear I'll be lighting candles for your soul every Sunday until the day I die!"

"Okay," Maureen said, getting up from the table. "Gran, I love you, but I'm a big girl. Old and divorced, that's me." She took her dirty cup and plate to the sink and returned to the table. Leaning over, she kissed Eabha on the cheek. "I haven't been here in a while, and I wanted to see how you were doing. Uncle Brendan will be over as soon as he can. And maybe he'll even take you to lunch."

"And maybe he can bring Malachy with him, do you think?"

Maureen loved her Uncle Malachy, but she always tired of hearing her grandmother tout the virtues of the grand archbishop, who only saw her a few times a year. She had a perfectly lovely son who lived minutes away.

"Yeah, whatever, Gran. Hey, get me a list of stuff you want me to bring over on my next visit, and I'll start working on it." As she walked to the door, she blew Eabha a kiss.

"*Slan agat, mo chisle*," said Eabha, lapsing into her native tongue, blowing a kiss back to Maureen. "And don't go letting that fellow charm the sense right out of you, so. Kisses won't pay the rent, lass!"

When Maureen got back to her car, she rummaged through her purse for Tylenol and reached for her water bottle, gulping two pills down all at once. That's what it took her to live through a visit with her grandmother, she thought. But as she pulled out of the parking lot, a grin began to spread over her face. Her grandmother knew what buttons to push, but the two of them loved the sparring. It had been their love language since Maureen could walk.

Just as Maureen was losing herself reminiscing, her cell phone rang. It was Caleb.

"We've got us a situation."

CHAPTER 15

Saturday Afternoon

Brendan, along with Ezra and Langdon, had scarcely sat down at the Bean Barn when the debate ignited. He struggled to keep hold of Mary Magdalene, the little Yorkie wriggling furiously beneath his arm.

"I'm jus' sayin'," Langdon argued, stirring his coffee, "if Jesus were here today, I think He be a black coffee kind o' man. Strong, bold, no-nonsense, like me."

Ezra snorted. "Please. He was Jewish. You think He wouldn't appreciate a little honey and cinnamon in His coffee? Maybe a nice bagel on the side?"

Brendan shook his head and turned to see why his order was being delayed. "You're both wrong. He'd drink wine. Probably wouldn't even *bother* with coffee."

There was a beat of silence before Langdon pointed his spoon at him. "Okay, that's fair."

At that moment, the barista walked over and set down a monstrous caramel Frappuccino, a monstrous blended caramel cappuccino, in front of Mary Magdalene. Ezra and Langdon looked at each other, stunned.

Ezra raised an eyebrow. "Tell me that's not for that dog."

Brendan casually slid the cup toward himself. "Of course not," he said, lifting the straw. "It's mine. But the Magdalene, here, does enjoy a little whipped cream." He scooped some onto his finger, and the tiny dog eagerly licked it off.

Langdon chuckled. "A priest, a rabbi, and a Baptist minister walked into a coffee shop...and the priest orders dessert."

Before Brendan could get a word in, a loud tapping sound came from Ezra. They turned just in time to catch Ezra jabbing furiously at his mocha milkshake lid, the straw bending but refusing to go in.

With a resigned sigh, he lifted the lid and shook his head. "Well, would you look at that? They forgot to poke a hole in the lid—again. It's like they're trying to wean me off caffeine."

Langdon shook his head. "Little dude, I think it be time to cut you off." He lunged his massive body across the table in a playful scuffle, swiping at the cup with exaggerated determination.

The three shared the moment until their peaceful morning was interrupted by the ringtone of a cell phone.

Brendan looked at his phone. "It's Mo," he said, answering the call.

"Looks like they arrested that Kenyan boy," Maureen told Brendan as she drove to the seminary. "If you want to hear the details and be there for Aiden, you'll have to drive yourself. I just left Gran's."

She heard a faint chuckle. "One step closer to heaven, Mo! Look, I'm at the Bean Barn with the guys." He paused, then asked meekly, "Could they tag along? Might be helpful."

Maureen made a sharp turn, nearly losing her grip on the cell phone. "Sure, why not? At this point, Caleb would probably take help from a psychic...or a parrot."

"I wonder what evidence Caleb has on this kid to lock him up."

"Guess we'll find out. Okay, look, I'm almost there. Grab your crew and get over here. And it might be a good idea for tomorrow, or sometime soon, to call his parish priest and see what kind of person he is, and if he's capable of doing something so heinous."

"See?" asked Brendan. "Always thinking, always planning. That's a wonderful idea. I'll make that call." Changing the topic, he added, "So how was the little banshee? How many times did she mention Malachy?"

Maureen's scowl melted into a laugh. "Plenty of times, but thankfully, her lecture on why I'm still single lasted far longer than her rant about the grand archbishop."

Pulling into the seminary's driveway, Maureen ended the call. "Meet you when you get here."

The men left the Bean Barn and headed for Brendan's car. Brendan yanked open the passenger door of his Honda for the hulking Baptist, but Ezra, with his short stature, slipped past him with surprising agility.

"Shotgun!" the rabbi crowed, adjusting his yarmulke as he hopped into the seat beside the driver.

"That ain't right," boomed Langdon, eyeing the cramped back seat. At six feet seven, with a build like a linebacker, he looked at the tiny car like it had personally insulted him.

Brendan sighed. "Fine, Ezra, you can ride in front, but if I end up with Langdon's knee in my back, I'm blaming you."

"Blame God for making him so huge," the rabbi quipped, already buckling in.

The three clerics wedged themselves into the Civic with much groaning, squeezing, and a final shove. It tilted slightly to one side.

Langdon huffed. "Next time, I'm driving."

Brendan muttered, "Next time, we're taking separate cars—and staying friends." He turned the ignition, and the car lurched forward as they headed toward the seminary.

"So what do *you* think, Bren?" asked Ezra. "Think the Kenyan kid did it?" He turned around to slap at Langdon's knee that was poking into the seat.

"It's too soon to tell. It's hard to believe a first-year seminarian wouldn't even be able to make it a few months into the school year before killing two of his fellow students. I mean, maybe it's a cultural revenge thing. And maybe he didn't even do it."

"You still thinkin' 'bout that dude we seen walkin' 'round the grounds?"

"I am, Langdon." Brendan nodded, thinking about Marcus Dean. "He was a bitter man back in the day."

"Why won't you tell us what happened?" asked Ezra.

Brendan's voice softened as he slowed the car down for a stop sign. "That's his sin to tell, but I kind of feel sorry for him. Like Adam, he didn't have to take the apple offered to him. He could have slung it out of the Garden of Eden and been done with it."

"Huh?" Langdon's wiry brows furled.

Ezra piped up, ignoring the Baptist. "You think *any* of those boys could have done it?"

Brendan shrugged, turning into the seminary. "Anyone's capable of murder under the right conditions, but seminarians? Men of God?" He shook his head slowly as he pulled into a parking space. "It's unimaginable."

Maureen approached a uniformed deputy and asked where Caleb was, just as Brendan's Honda was pulling in. The deputy immediately pointed her in the right direction. She took the stairs to the seminary's second-floor dorm two at a time, spotting Caleb and another uniform leading a serene Okeyo Masamba from his room, hands cuffed behind him.

"Is that really necessary, Caleb?" asked Maureen in a hushed voice, glancing around. "He's a seminarian, for heaven's sake."

Caleb shot her a look. "He's a murder suspect, and he doesn't deny it." He gave a nod to the gloved deputy holding several evidence bags. "We found Mueller's Bible, that medal that was missing, and several sheets of that paper—parchment, is it? Also, a bloodied handkerchief was stuffed in a jacket pocket. Anyway, it's enough to tie him to at least one of the murders. All we need now is to find out why he did it."

He turned and began walking downstairs with Okeyo wedged in between himself and the deputy.

He stopped walking, nodded to the deputy to continue walking Okeyo down the stairs. He cupped his hand and leaned in, his mouth close to her ear. "It was your cousin who called me and told me what he saw in that kid's room."

Maureen smiled sadly. "He was brave to turn his friend in. It *was* the right thing to do."

The deputy's shoulders rose. "And now we've got us our first good suspect."

Maureen, still stunned at this revelation, followed them down the stairs, scanning the first floor for her cousin. Instead, she found her uncle and his friends chatting with some of the bewildered students.

"Mo, what's going on?"

Maureen shook her head. "I hate to think that young man killed his friends, but Caleb said he didn't refute the charge." She added, "And he said it was Aiden who called him and turned him in."

Brendan's lips twisted, and his hands went up in the air. "I don't know. Remember what I said earlier? We're all capable of homicide, it just takes the right ingredients. But, from what I've been hearing, the boy did have a temper." He gave her shoulder a gentle pat, a silent gesture of reassurance. "And Aiden did the right thing. If this boy did these murders, then he should pay, seminarian or not. But let's give him the benefit of the doubt for now. You know, innocent until proven guilty, and all that."

Ezra piped in. "Brendan's right, Maureen. And coming from a different culture, he may have struggled with either teasing or outright bullying from these guys." He looked over at Langdon, frowning. "As a Jew, I can identify with that with all the violence aimed at *my* people."

Maureen tapped her foot impatiently. "Yeah, you're right on all counts, guys." She balled her fists. "Grrrrr…" She growled, then looked at each of the men. "You know I'm going to have to follow Caleb to the station and sit in on the questioning." She shot her uncle a look. "And you should come, since you understand the workings of the seminary and may be able to support the boy as a priest."

"And the guys?" He gestured toward his friends, a playful, pleading look tugging at his lips.

Maureen rewarded him with her usual eye rolling but nodded her assent.

Brendan thanked her and turned to Ezra and Langdon. He glanced at his watch. "I have Mass later this evening, but we won't stay too long at the station. Don't want to get Mo in trouble with that captain of hers."

With that, Brendan and friends piled into the Honda and followed Maureen to the sheriff's department.

Captain Lamar Pollard stood at a table in the roll call room, sipping a cup of hours-old coffee. He frowned as his lips met the thick, tepid liquid.

Grumbling to himself, he slammed the cup on the table and exited the room. "Don't know why these female station clerks can't make coffee around here like they used to. It ain't the same department it used to be."

As he turned a corner, heading to his office, he heard a commotion coming through the front door. Seconds later, Pollard watched as a parade emerged: deputies, a young man in handcuffs, that pesky priest, a little guy with a tiny cap perched on his head, and a towering Black man bringing up the rear.

Pollard narrowed his eyes, locking in on Maureen. She gave him a weak smile and kept walking, head down.

"McNeely!" hollered Pollard as he watched the parade halt. "I thought you were on vacation." He gave her no time to respond as he looked at Brendan, his upper lip curling into a snarl. "And once again, you've brought civilians in on a police matter." His gaze fell on the young man, whom he assessed. "So what do we have here?" He directed his question to Caleb, ignoring Maureen completely.

"Murder suspect, Captain," said Caleb. "Okeyo Masamba. He's a seminarian over at Saint Charles." He looked at Brendan. "Father O'Clery's nephew attends there, and he's friends with this boy." He nodded at Okeyo.

Pollard hitched his pants and took a step toward Maureen, glaring at her. "So why are *you* here, and especially *him*?" He jabbed a finger toward

Brendan. "And who are these others?" He grimaced as he waved an arm toward the other men.

Maureen stood her ground. "I canceled my leave so I can help Martinez on this case. We thought this young man would be more comfortable speaking with a priest and may be more open to questioning." Pollard just stared at her, so she continued. "He's Kenyan and not familiar with our police procedures."

Finally, Pollard looked at the seminarian again. "Then do what you have to do. Just hurry up and get out of my hair." He turned and, as he walked away, muttered a string of colorful curses under his breath.

Brendan and Maureen followed Caleb and the uniformed deputy as they led Okeyo downstairs to the interrogation room. After they had entered the room, Caleb unlocked the handcuffs and motioned for the seminarian to sit. The deputy took his place at the door as Maureen, Brendan, and his friends, sat at the far end of the table. All eyes were on Okeyo.

Taking a notepad from his jacket, Caleb began speaking in a calming tone. "Okeyo—did I pronounce that correctly?"

The young man nodded, remaining stoic, his hands folded neatly on the table, indicating the seminarian understood.

"Okay," he began, "I read you your rights back at the school, so you know why you're here. We found items belonging to both of the dead boys in your room. Why did you keep these items after you killed them, and what was the reason for killing them?" His pen was poised over his notepad.

Okeyo looked at Caleb and then over at Brendan. "Yes, I suppose I am at fault."

"What do you mean by that?" asked Caleb, his eyebrows coming together.

The young man shrugged. "I am to blame. I have a temper that I sometimes cannot control." He inhaled deeply and rearranged himself in the chair. "I am learning to control it so I can become a good priest."

Langdon leaned over toward Brendan and whispered, "A priest with a temper? I done thought holy water an' all was s'pposed to wash that stuff right out."

"*Shhh*," hissed Ezra, shooting a sharp glare at the big guy.

Caleb shot a glance at Maureen. "So, are you saying you did or did not kill either of those boys?"

"I am saying their deaths are my responsibility."

The deputy chewed his lower lip. Brendan knew he needed a confession.

Caleb leaned in toward Okeyo. "Look, I'm trying to help you here, son, but I can't do that unless you talk to me. What you're saying is too cryptic. I don't understand what you mean. Are you confessing to these two murders or not? It's a simple yes or no."

This time Ezra leaned over. "Gee, Bren, if guilt could solve murders, we Jews would have the killer in handcuffs already!" He sat back quickly when Maureen glared at him.

Okeyo's eyes drilled into Caleb's. "I am saying, I am at fault. It is my doing that they are dead. The punishment is mine and mine alone."

Caleb looked over at Maureen again, frustrated.

Brendan asked, "Mind if I speak?"

Caleb shrugged. "Go ahead. If you can elicit *anything* from him, I'd appreciate it."

Brendan stood, leaving his cane with Maureen, and went to where Okeyo was sitting. He pulled out a chair next to the seminarian, placing a hand on his shoulder. "Okeyo, we're all here to help you and get to the truth of what happened. These boys' families need to know how their sons died and why." Gently, he continued his urging. "Please, talk to us. I don't think you did this, but you may have information regarding the person who did."

An uneasy hush settled over the place, as if the room was holding its breath.

"Are you covering for someone?"

Okeyo's head jerked up, his eyes drilling into Brendan's. Still, he offered nothing, but Brendan suspected he knew more and would remain silent.

Caleb cleared his throat. "Father, if he won't talk, I have no choice but to put him in a cell and hold him. He can contact an attorney if he wants to, but for now, my hands arc tied. Sorry."

Brendan patted Okeyo's back, a brief but solid reminder that he wasn't alone. "Do you want me to find you an attorney, Okeyo?"

Okeyo gave Brendan a weak smile. "I am good, Father. You have been most kind. Thank you."

Caleb stood, nodding to the deputy. "The deputy here will take you to a cell after he gets your fingerprints, and we'll find you something to eat." He gazed at the young man, and Brendan saw a sharp pang of sorrow twisting on the detective's face. "And I'm sorry, but we'll have to confiscate your passport."

Caleb watched as the deputy handcuffed Okeyo and walked him out of the room, his hand clenching the boy's upper arm.

When they were gone, Caleb turned to Maureen. "I appreciate the help." He looked at Brendan, who reached for his cane. "And, Father, thanks for trying to get the boy to talk. He'll be held here while we review the evidence." He stood, shuffling some papers and returning his notepad to his jacket. "I don't get the kid. Did he do it or not, or is he covering up for the person who did it? Or is he afraid of the person who did it?" His breath left him in a quiet sigh, heavy with unspoken words.

"You did your best, Caleb," said Brendan. "I'll go back to the seminary later, after evening Mass, and see what I can discover."

Caleb's grabbed Maureen's wrist. "I'm sorry about your vacation. I can handle it from here. I'll see if I can arrange for someone to pick up the kid after he sees the magistrate."

Maureen shook her head. "Nope, as long as there's a murder that needs solving, I'll help you in any way I can." She gave him a weak smile. "Besides, now that my cousin's off the hook in your eyes, we can be friends again." She winked at him.

Caleb gave her a weak nod as the group left the room.

Maureen said goodbye to Brendan and friends and threw open her car door, climbed in, and let it slam shut with a satisfying thud. The interview they had just endured had clearly left her frustrated.

Brendan slid into the Honda's front seat, throwing his cane in the back. "Wow, that poor kid. Not sure what his game is, but if he's going for martyrdom, then I'd say he's got a good chance." He turned the ignition and pushed the accelerator down hard. "And Mo won't leave Porter Mills knowing two murders—of seminarians, no less—have been committed. And my poor nephew is a wreck, because it's likely one of his friends did this horrible thing, and he was the one who ratted him out."

As he was pulling out of the seminary's parking lot, something caught his eye.

"Hey, I see something." He rolled the window down, a blast of cold wind hitting his cheeks. "Over there!" He pointed to a figure standing under a tree, a mangy-looking dog next to him, watching them as dusk fell around them. "Guys, I think it's Marcus Dean."

He turned the car around and drove slowly to where the man was standing. When he reached him, he shut off the engine. Grabbing his cane he looked at Ezra and Langdon. "Stay here, guys. This will only take a minute." He made his way over to the man, wary of the menacing dog hovering nearby, barking incessantly.

"Father," said Marcus blandly. "Looks like the cops got their man."

The dog stopped barking and began growling at Brendan.

Brendan zipped up his jacket. "Not necessarily. They took one of the boys in, but he didn't confess." He glared at the dog. "Can't you get him to shut up?"

"He's not mine. He's a stray that I can't seem to get rid of." He waved his arm around and stomped his feet. The dog eventually backed away but kept his eyes on them.

"So no confession?"

"This boy's different," began Brendan. "It's only my opinion, but either he knows who did it or is protecting someone."

Marcus laughed. "Now, isn't that nice. He's protecting someone. I wonder who it could be. Someone in authority, perhaps?"

Brendan watched the man's face as it darkened.

"No one protected me when I got kicked out. I committed *one* sin—and who hasn't been tempted—and no one gave *me* a second chance."

"Marcus, if you know anything, you need to tell the police."

Marcus shrugged. "What's it to me? This new breed of seminarians is different from when we went through. They're more entitled and more self-absorbed. They're driven by ego, always chasing what benefits them most. Their flock will always come second."

"That's not true. You're bitter, and I understand that, but if you can help that boy who just got arrested, then it's your Christian duty to do so."

Marcus laughed again. "Christian duty! That's a good one. Hey, you think this kid is innocent, but you have no idea what goes on in there nowadays."

"He may not be innocent at all, but he still deserves someone's help if that person knows something." Brendan tapped his cane onto the cold ground just as he heard a bellowing voice coming from the Honda.

"Dude, let's roll." Langdon's tone left no room for argument.

Marcus glanced toward the Honda then turned to go. He waved his hand casually at Brendan. "Sure, Padre. If I hear anything, I'll let you know." He shook his head and laughed louder this time.

Brendan watched him walk away, the shaggy dog following him, then returned to his car.

"What a piece of work that man is. Good thing he *isn't* a priest."

"What did you expect to get out of him?" asked Ezra, as Brendan backed onto the street.

A slow sigh escaped him, laced with frustration he didn't bother to hide. "I'm sure he knows more than what he'd ever tell me, but he's so bitter, I guess he'd rather see this seminary fall than help save it. And after his family spent so much money building it." He let out an exasperated grunt, shaking his head. "I've got to get back for Mass. Hang on tight, guys," he said, and with a sudden, wild turn, he sent Ezra slamming his shoulder into the door.

"*Oy vey!* I'm too short for this kind of holy violence!" He reached for his yarmulke that had slipped down as he grabbed the arm rest.

CHAPTER 16

Sunday Morning

Sunday rolled in with a bite, the frigid November air nipping at everyone who stepped into Saint Margaret Mary's for the first Mass of the morning, souring moods before the first hymn was sung.

Brendan's mind was on Okeyo and how he must be feeling sitting in an eight-by-eight holding cell. Maureen had told him Father Gabriel had gone to pick the boy up, and Brendan thought how those two were as thick as thieves—or had what they used to say when he was younger, a "mutual admiration society." Maybe Okeyo was covering up for the rector. Was Father Gabriel capable of murdering two young men? Was it because he didn't approve of their personalities, or was it something deeper, something unspoken? The man was in his dotage—maybe his mind had convinced him they needed to be eliminated for whatever reason.

After Mass, Brendan walked Mary Magdalene along their familiar wooded path, where the trees stood bare, their skeletal branches swaying like silent sentinels in the crisp autumn air. When they returned to the rectory, he unsnapped the Yorkie's pink coat and gave her a treat. Saint Peter strutted into the kitchen, tail held high, letting out a demanding meow.

"I know, I know," said Brendan, hands on hips, lecturing the cat. "Mrs. M. feeds you *before* the first Mass, but it's Sunday and she's not here, so you have me to deal with." He stared down at the persistent feline, who continued meowing and nuzzling his head against Brendan's trousers as if claiming ownership of his attention.

Sighing, Brendan gave in to the recalcitrant cat and filled his bowl. Observing his two non-human companions for a few precious moments, he decided to go into the living room and work on an especially difficult crossword puzzle he had been trying desperately to finish.

Setting his cane next to an end table, he sank into his favorite chair, pulled out the thick puzzle book, and opened his current project. Already feeling defeated as he looked at the cryptic hints, he wished Langdon didn't have to spend his entire day in church and that Ezra hadn't agreed to dinner with two rabbis from synagogues in Baltimore. Maureen might be with Simon, and he certainly wasn't going to interrupt whatever shenanigans were going on over there. Even Mrs. Morrison had the day off. Time to dig in and get on this crossword.

He read the first clue: one across, a twelve-letter word for "an instrument for measuring the amount which a ship heels at sea."

"How does anyone even know these words?" He threw his hands up in the air and decided to take a peek at the answers in the back of the book. Skimming the pages, he finally came to the puzzle he had been attempting. "Nauropometer," he said, sarcastically. "Never heard of it and will likely *never* use it in a sentence."

The chiming of his cell phone interrupted the frustrating crossword. Squinting at the image coming through, he saw it was Aiden.

"Uncle Brendan, I feel horrible about turning Okeyo in. Deputy Martinez said Okeyo didn't have to know it was me who did it, but I can't shake the feeling that I'm a despicable rat."

"Look, Aiden, you did the right thing. I know it must have been hard for you, but if Okeyo did this to one or both boys, then he needs to answer for his sins. And if he didn't? Then all is well." He decided to change the subject. "You want me to come over?" Brendan had the second Mass yet, but felt his nephew needed him.

"No, I'm good. Unfortunately, and I don't mean that in a bad way, we've got a bus load going to the basilica in Baltimore for an afternoon Mass. We're going to sing some Gregorian Chants, so I'm excited. One guess as to who orchestrated this field trip!"

"I'd only need one guess, Aiden," said Brendan. "You go on and make the archbishop happy."

Aiden grinned. "Hey, how do you think Okeyo did with the questioning? Father Gabriel brought him back but I haven't spoken with him yet."

"He was very enigmatic," said Brendan, his voice tinged with sadness. "I just don't understand why he isn't talking. I think he knows more than he wants to say."

"Yeah, he's always been quiet, unless he's arguing with someone. I've seen his temper in action."

Brendan couldn't think of anything else to add. "Enjoy yourself, kiddo. And remember to stay in a group."

"No need to worry about that, Uncle Brendan," said Aiden. "I'm always with the guys, and at night, I lock my door and push my dresser in front of it."

Brendan grimaced at the thought of his nephew being so fearful of his fellow seminarians. "Good lad. Now go chant your heart out."

He ended the call and, after celebrating Sunday's second Mass, spent the rest of the day reading, doing anagrams or puzzles, and watching old movies. When evening fell, he walked Mary Magdalene, then went upstairs to his room, where he grabbed his pajamas and went into the bathroom to shower.

As the water heated up, the steam began to swirl around the room, curling in the air like a soft, warm mist that seemed to wrap everything in a quiet embrace.

Brendan stood in his underwear, staring at the medicine cabinet like it held the secrets of the universe—his personal pharmacopoeia of happiness, the little pills that turned "meh" into "right, I can survive this night."

Slowly, he opened the door, a tingle running down his spine, as the warm mist surrounded him. His eyes viewed the amber bottles, all neatly standing in a row like little soldiers. The thought of soldiers immediately took him back to Iraq in 1991.

His heart began to race, and his mouth tasted like gunmetal. His breathing increased, and he was starting to become lightheaded. The bodies, the blood, the screaming—and now the bodies were morphing into seminarians, lying on the floor in sticky pools of blood.

He squeezed his eyes shut so tightly that he began to black out. Opening them, he found himself calmer, once again staring at the pills. Not a Xanax night, he thought, his eyes resting on the oxycodone. Yes, that was the one.

Reaching for the bottle, he shook several pills into his palm with the precision of a man who had turned this ritual into an art form. After taking them, he stripped down and entered the shower, the scorching hot water searing his skin—a perfect penance for his sins.

CHAPTER 17

Monday Morning

Maureen awoke to the familiar ringtone she had assigned to Simon Archer. Smiling, she answered groggily.

"Good morning. What's so important that you felt you had to wake me up at"—she held the phone away from her face as she checked the time—"six thirty?" She sat up in bed, easing her feet into a pair of slippers.

"I have to drive to headquarters today and thought maybe I could stop in for a quick lunch or dinner, or maybe just a kiss?"

Maureen laughed as she stumbled her way to the kitchen in search of a clean coffee mug.

"I'll have to let you know." She proceeded to update him on Caleb's murder investigation. "I want to run over to the medical examiner's on my way to pick up some dry cleaning. We haven't heard anything about that arrow that killed the second boy, and I want to see if Victoria's husband, who runs the forensics lab for the state, was able to track down where it came from."

"That's fine," he said. "I'll keep you posted on my twenty when I get close."

Maureen laughed. "I love it when you talk in police codes." She heard Simon laugh, and the call ended.

While she and Simon had met during her last homicide investigation, after purloining the case from the state police, they had only known each other for a few months. Just as they had started to really vibe, he got transferred out to western Maryland, a three-hour drive from Porter Mills. This had put a real kibosh on the budding relationship.

Even so, she took it as a good sign. The wounds from her divorce to a psychologically abusive ex-husband hadn't healed completely, and her trust level was at an all-time low.

Finding a coffee pod, she stuck it in the machine and walked sluggishly to the bathroom to prepare for her day that did *not* include a balmy island with an adult beverage in hand.

A short time later, with a travel mug full of coffee, Maureen made her way down the familiar stairwell to the medical examiner's office.

"I'll let Dr. Chen know you're here, Detective." A painfully thin young woman, with a Latin phrase inked on her forearm, stood and left the room. Moments later, she returned, motioning for Maureen to follow her.

"Maureen!" came the soft accented voice. "I treasure these cases because I get to see you often." The tiny Asian woman, barely five feet tall and teetering on her trademark spiked heels, threw her head back and laughed. Her sleek black hair was coiled into a tight, flawless bun atop her head today, not a single strand daring to stray from its place. The cloying scent of a floral perfume hit Maureen like a tidal wave as the ME gripped her tightly.

"Likewise, Victoria." They parted, and Maureen followed Victoria over to a well-lit table. "And if you can give me something that will make me happy, you'll get a dinner at your choice of very expensive restaurants."

Victoria's bright red lips parted into a mischievous grin. "Then you'd better get a part-time job to pay for where I want to go. Check this out. The hubby sent this over from the lab just for you, along with his findings." She put on a latex glove and picked up the arrow and a magnifying glass. "See these numbers etched on the shaft?" She handed Maureen the round glass. "Newer, more expensive arrows now have numbers that identify their manufacturer. This is an expensive carbon fiber arrow with a really fancy, broad head. It's specifically designed for hunting. The blades are super sharp and made to cut through vital organs. Whoever bought this would probably be considered a very valuable customer."

Maureen nodded slowly. "So, a higher-end sporting goods store might have that person in their computers?"

"Very likely. And that person might very well be somewhere on video, if the store has surveillance cameras. It's worth a shot."

"Anything else?" asked Maureen, as she watched Victoria place the arrow back in the evidence bag.

The ME slipped off the glove and threw it on a nearby table. "Well, if you're asking about DNA or that fingerprint we found on that piece of parchment, the print was too degraded, and the lab couldn't get anything from it. And as for any DNA"—she gave Maureen a mocking pat on the back—"you'll have to keep your big girl panties on. Forensics hasn't finished testing yet."

Maureen nodded slowly and hunched her shoulders. "Well, at least that arrow's given me a place to go." She scratched at her cheek and then grinned at her friend. "Guess I'll start looking for that part-time job to pay for dinner." She pulled out her phone. "Let me get a few shots of that arrow. Maybe I can get my uncle and his friends to visit some of the local sporting goods stores and see what they can dig up on it."

Victoria shot her a look. "Well, if your hunky uncle needs any help, tell him I'm available."

Maureen rolled her eyes. "I keep telling you, Victoria—Catholic priests are celibate! And you're married!"

"But like *you* always say, he looks so much like Ewan McGregor." She sighed, worthy of an Oscar for drama.

Maureen's eyes went upward again as she gave a hearty laugh. "You're too much—but you *are* one amazing medical examiner."

Victoria feigned a modest shrug. "I am, yes, very amazing."

The two hugged again, and Maureen left a happy woman, armed with new information.

CHAPTER 18

After daily Mass and the usual chatting with his faithful daily attendees, Brendan took Mary Magdalene for a walk around the church grounds. The wind was dry and brisk, a sharp reminder that fall was fading fast and winter was approaching. Before entering the rectory, he stooped to unhook the dog's leash and clenched his teeth when, through a window, he saw Saint Peter scaling a kitchen curtain. He walked over to the window and, with his cane, tapped on the glass, inches from the animal, yelling for the cat to get down. Saint Peter simply looked at him, gave an angry meow, and continued climbing the fabric.

Giving up on the demon cat, he entered the rectory, setting his cane down, his mood improving when his eyes took in the breakfast Mrs. Morrison had prepared for him—sausage links, poached eggs, homemade biscuits, and gravy.

"Mrs. M.," he crooned, "you are a real treasure." He said a blessing over the breakfast and dug in.

"The butcher had these beautiful links that just called out to me. I knew you'd enjoy them." The housekeeper's face beamed with pride. She walked over and filled his coffee cup.

"I've got a visit with my mother lined up later," Brendan told her, "so I'm savoring this breakfast while I still have my sanity."

"Oh, Father, stop it," chuckled Mrs. Morrison. "You'll be fine."

Brendan's cell rang, and when he saw it was his niece, he answered the call, but not before shoving a huge piece of sausage in his mouth.

"Hey, can you do me a favor?"

"Sure, Mo. Name it." He spooned gravy over the biscuits and lifted a portion to his lips.

"Victoria found a serial number on the arrow that killed Matthew Mueller. If I send a few pics over to you, can you and your Musketeers visit a few sporting goods stores and see if you can dig up who purchased this?" Her voice became sarcastic. "You're so adept at lying, I'm sure you can come up with a story or two."

Brendan set his fork down. "Maureen McNeely," he said, feigning shock, "the only people I lie to are my archbishop and the banshee who birthed him." He waited for her laughter to die down, then told her he'd be glad to help out. "So, did Okeyo get bail?"

"Believe it or not, Father Gabriel sprung him."

"He's always been a bit odd, but a decent man, even when he was my teacher." Brendan brushed several crumbs from the table. "Hey, speaking of the banshee, I need to go see Ma soon. Maybe I should call her and tell her Malachy wants me to attend some stupid meeting or something, so she'll excuse me from the visit."

"Good try, Unc," she replied, "but Gran would only call Uncle Malachy to ask him to dismiss you from that meeting."

He exhaled sharply, the sound carrying more than a hint of resignation. "So send the photos and I'll call the guys."

"Thanks. I owe you."

"You sure—" But the call had already ended.

"You need to get a lawyer, Okeyo," Father Gabriel said as he pulled into the staff parking lot, having retrieved the boy from the sheriff's department.

"Thank you, Father, but I do not need one. God is watching over me, and I have placed my trust in Him."

Father Gabriel led the young man into his office, motioning for him to sit. "Why aren't you defending yourself?" His gaze swept over the thin seminarian, his deep, dark eyes unreadable against his equally dark skin. He walked over and placed a hand on his shoulder. "You know you can tell me anything—under the seal of the confessional if you'd like."

Okeyo looked up at the rector. "Father, you are most kind. And you are like a real father to me. I have not been here that long, and it has been difficult for me to—how do you say—fit in with the others here." He brought his folded hands to his mouth. "I would do anything for you, Father, protect you in any way I could." His eyes remained cast down.

The rector stared at the young man with pity. Realizing the boy was probably tired and hungry, he returned to his desk and sat. "Go to the dining hall and see what they have left over from lunch. Then, take the rest of the day off and clear your mind. Pray, study, or do both. I want you to know that I and the entire staff are behind you."

Okeyo stood, pressing his black clerical slacks with the palms of his hands. "Thank you, Father. You have been a blessing to me today. I know your time is precious, and I am beholden to you for your generosity." He bowed obsequiously and turned to go.

Father Gabriel waved a dismissive hand. "Nonsense, my boy. Now go, get some food in you."

He watched him leave and wondered what Okeyo could have meant by *protecting him*. From what? Did he mean from—no, he thought, don't go there.

His head began to throb, and he rubbed it with the desperation of a man trying to massage the pain, and the regret, right out of his skull. He shrugged, forcing indifference onto his face.

Before going through the pile of forms demanding his signature, he reached into his bottom drawer, pulling out the bottle of whiskey, burying his emotions beneath the cold, familiar weight of paperwork.

Okeyo walked slowly back to his room. He wasn't afraid. Not for himself. He was afraid for the rector. He knew the priest had never cared for either Joseph Lin or Matthew Mueller and had made no bones about it. Joseph and Matthew had shown promise, and Okeyo would see Father Gabriel bristle every time he asked a theological question during one of his impromptu debates. He sensed the jealousy simmering beneath the surface, sharp and unmistakable, as both boys walked away, victorious from their arguments with their rector.

Entering his room, he threw himself on the bed. Father Gabriel had been so helpful in securing a place for him at Saint Charles that the very mention of the man's name sent his mother back in Kenya into tears of gratitude. *Whatever* the rector, his mentor, had done, Okeyo would protect him, even lie for him. He owed him that much.

He closed his eyes and was soon fast asleep.

Brendan pulled his battered Honda into the Beit Ahava Synagogue's parking lot next to Langdon's Caddy. Walking up to Ezra's front door, he could hear his two friends bantering back and forth. Smiling to himself, he rapped on the door.

"Hey, Bren. Come on in. Want something to drink?" Ezra laughed as he swatted at Langdon's hand, which kept trying to snatch his yarmulke.

"Nope. Let's just go. I'm supposed to be visiting my mother later, but I told her some blarney about the parish secretary needing help with something."

"You sho' lie a lot, bro. That cain't be good for your soul."

"Don't make me feel any worse than I do, Langdon. So whose car are we going in?"

"Like there's a choice? Aretha, of course."

Ezra shook his head as he put his jacket on. "I get lost in that monstrosity. But I guess as long as you're paying for the gas."

"That's right, little dude, so you put your tiny self in the back, and I get you out when we get there."

Ezra emitted a groan, making Brendan laugh as the trio walked down the driveway to the baby-blue Cadillac. He threw the cane in the back seat and slid into the passenger side.

They arrived at the first store—Iron Trail Outfitters—and got out after parking the Caddy and walked toward the entranceway.

Langdon's massive legs made it to the door first, and he grinned as he held the door open for his friends. "You sure you wanna go in here, little man? They might be cardin' you at the entrance. You know, for height requirements."

Ezra pursed his lips and adjusted his yarmulke. "Oh, very funny. I'll have you know, David was small, too, and he took down Goliath."

This made Langdon chuckle. "Uh-huh. But David had hisself a big ol' slingshot. You plannin' on pickin' one up today?"

Ezra stroked his beard. "Now that you mention it, I might. You, on the other hand, could use a stepladder for that high horse you're always riding."

"Hoo-ee! Good one, little man," said Langdon, laughing as they walked inside. "But let's jes' hope they got kid-sized golf clubs for you."

Ezra gave the big man a deadpan stare. "And an oversized lawn dart for that ego of yours."

Brendan shook his head, laughing, as he went through the door.

Once in, they made their way to the archery section.

"Can I help you, gentlemen?" asked an older man with a craggy, sun-wrinkled face, his snow-white beard bobbing up and down on his chest as he spoke. When he smiled, it looked like his teeth had packed up and left town, one by one. He took a baseball cap off and wiped his forehead with the back of his hand.

Brendan took a step toward the clerk. "Yes, we'd like to know if you sell this brand of arrow." He turned his cell phone to the man, flashing the photo of the arrow that had killed Matthew Mueller.

The man shot a whistle through the few teeth he had. "You boys have expensive taste, that's for sure." He looked at Brendan. "That there's an Easton Axis 5mm carbon arrow. Depending on the size and shaft weight, that baby can run you almost a hundred dollars."

"That's a lot of money for an arrow. Can you tell us a bit more about it?" asked Ezra, edging his body in front of Brendan's.

"Sure. This here's a small-diameter hunting arrow, and it's built so it can fly faster and penetrate deeper." He grinned. "It can deliver a mighty fast kill, for sure. It's made of carbon composite fibers. That's better than any standard carbon arrow, as far as speed and accuracy. Perfect for big game hunting."

The three clerics exchanged looks after hearing the words "big game hunting." After he recovered, Brendan asked the man, in his most sincere and pious voice, if they had records of anyone who had purchased an arrow like this in the past year.

The man narrowed his eyes. "We don't give out that information. I'm afraid you boys are out of luck."

Brendan's tongue pushed into his cheek as he considered his next move. He reached for his wallet and pulled out his clerical credentials, urging Ezra and Langdon to do the same. "Here," he said to the man. "We're clergy. My friends and I found this arrow the other day, and it looked expensive. We thought we'd do the right thing and see if we could return it to the person who lost it." He then gave the man the most beguiling look he could muster—the one his brother, the great archbishop, detested. "Maybe like the purchases for the past year?"

The man pulled at his beard, the hairs giving off an odor of onions and cigarettes. "Okay, I'll tell you what I'll do." He turned and reached under the counter and pulled out a tattered notebook. Shuffling through the pages, he said, "Let me see that photo again, Vicar."

Brendan ignored the incorrect title and pulled out his phone again, showing it to the man.

Several minutes later, the man jabbed at a spot on the page. "A-*ha*. Here it is." He leaned toward the trio and whispered conspiratorially, "Now I'll let you look at this list, but if you boys see the person's name, you'll have to find them on your own. I can't give you an address." His eyes met each man's gaze.

They nodded, agreeing to the man's rule.

"All righty, then," he said as he turned the notebook around for the men to see. "Whoever lost that arrow will be mighty happy to get it back." He winked at them. "I'll even bet you get a reward. They're expensive toys."

Brendan's eyes bugged. There were at least a hundred names over several pages. Not wanting to complain, Brendan set his attention to the book, scanning the names until he came to one that he recognized.

His breath caught. It couldn't be, he thought, but turned the book back to the clerk.

"Thank you, sir. Thank you so much. God bless you." He gave a nod to Ezra and Langdon, and they headed out to the car.

Once inside the Caddy, Brendan looked at his friends, grinning so hard his lips seemed to crack.

Regaining his wits, Brendan mumbled, "I've got to tell Mo. *Now!*"

"I can only stay about an hour," said Detective Simon Archer, as he brushed past Maureen, shedding his jacket and throwing it on the sofa. Turning, he grabbed Maureen and crushed her to himself, kissing her softly at first, then embracing her so tightly she laughed as she fought to free herself from his lock.

"I missed you, too," she said, dragging him over to the couch. "Here, sit." She patted the space beside her.

"I have to tell you, Maureen, this separation has been hard. I can't believe how much I've missed you." She noted the sincerity in his eyes, and it warmed her heart.

"I've missed you, too, Simon, but I'm happy to see you, if even for a few minutes."

His eyes fell on the open suitcases. "So…how come you haven't left yet? Shouldn't you be lying somewhere on a beach of white sands, slathered in suntan lotion?"

Maureen twisted her lips and rolled her eyes. "Yes, I *should* be. But these two murders forced me to cancel my vacation." Hearing her own words, she quickly rebounded. "I mean, the murders of these two boys are tragic, but what I meant was that Caleb, another deputy…well, this is his first homicide, and my cousin is a seminarian there, and I'm concerned for his safety. I think that place should be closed down until these murders are solved, but that would be up to that old rector."

She inhaled softly and looked away. "Anyway, I remember my first homicide and how I got no help from anyone. So, I feel compelled to assist him on his first case. My cousin has not taken these incidents well at all." She traced what appeared to be an old scar on Simon's wrist.

"You're a good soul, Maureen McNeely. I understand." He patted her hand, then inched closer to her. "So maybe we should make the most of the precious time I do have."

Maureen followed suit, and just as their lips met, her cell rang, to the tune of "Ave Maria," her uncle's untimely ringtone.

She looked at Simon, her eyes full of regret. "Sorry," she said, shrugging apologetically. She stood and went over to the table where her phone sat, chirping out the hymn.

After ending the call a few minutes later, Maureen read the disappointment in Simon's eyes. She sat down beside him, placing a hand on his knee. "We have a suspect—well, a second one—and this one looks promising." She stood, shaking her head. "I'll explain it all later, but I really should get over there and help Caleb. These murders are personal for me and my uncle, since we have family there." She combed her fingers through his hair, the strands thick and heavy beneath her touch, then watched him stand, unfurling his lean frame in front of her.

Simon gave her a knowing smile. "Hey, it's the nature of our vocation. Of course, I understand. And look, maybe if you're available tomorrow, I can swing by in the morning on my way home." He winked at her as he reached for his jacket.

"Sounds good."

Maureen walked Simon to the door and opened it, a pang of regret hitting her hard. She liked this guy, a feeling she hadn't experienced in years.

Simon kissed her chastely on the cheek. "Until then," he said, giving her a mock salute as he ambled off to his car.

She watched him with a tender smile, savoring every small gesture. This one, she thought, just might make it to meet the family. Other "romantic crash-and-burns" never made it past a week, let alone up to the family-introduction level.

Simon hit the horn, jarring Maureen from her reverie. He waved, and she waved back.

Closing the door, she picked up her Glock, holstered it, threw on her coat, and dialed Caleb's number. Her voice was steady as she instructed him to grab a uniformed deputy and meet her at the seminary. Without skipping a beat, she dialed her uncle next, her tone leaving no room for argument. She needed *him* there, too.

There were now just as many suspects as there were murdered bodies. And all this at a seminary. What next?

CHAPTER 19

Monday Afternoon

When Maureen pulled up to Marcus Dean's house that afternoon, she was glad Caleb had brought two uniformed deputies with him and was equally happy to see her uncle and his friends had arrived before her and were just exiting Langdon's Caddy. After parking, she met with the group in the parking lot.

"Were you able to find a judge to issue a warrant quickly?" she asked. Caleb gave it a quick wave in front of her.

"I begged Judge Ryder, and she issued it on the spot after I explained the situation." He gave her a boyish grin. "You know she has a crush on me."

Maureen chuckled. "Glad your ego is so big."

"That info that your uncle and his friends passed on to you was golden," he told her.

Maureen turned to her uncle. "Uncle Brendan, you guys can come with us, but you stay outside, understood?" She made eye contact with each of the men, ensuring they got the picture.

Pounding on the door, Maureen waited for it to be answered. Caleb perused the grounds, and she suspected he was looking for that stray dog.

The door opened, and a smiling Marcus Dean greeted them. "What can I do for you, detectives?" he asked cordially. His smile faded when he caught sight of Brendan and the squad cars.

Caleb stepped forward, thrusting the document into the man's hands. "We have a warrant to search your house." He gave a sharp nod to the other deputies, his hand slicing through the air as he motioned for them to move in, the tension palpable as they pushed roughly past the man.

Marcus looked back at them, then at Maureen. "What's the meaning of this?" he spat. He glanced back again at the deputies who were moving things aside roughly, opening drawers and cabinets.

"Mr. Dean, do you own archery equipment?" Maureen studied the man's craggy face. He looked tired and beaten.

"I do," he answered slowly, "but what does that have to do with anything?"

Maureen held up the photo of the arrow that was on her phone. Marcus's eyes widened, letting Maureen know he recognized it.

"That looks like…but it can't be." His voice cracked.

Inside, Maureen instructed Marcus to sit. She sat across from him at a rickety old dining room table, years of scratches etched on the surface. She placed the phone on the table, ensuring Marcus could see the arrow, and took in the small abode. The place held little in the way of furniture or any personal effects.

"Where…where did you get that photo?" Marcus stammered, his face pinched, eyes wide with suspicion.

"Is it yours?" asked Maureen.

Marcus shrugged. "It could be. Looks like one of mine." He stretched his neck to study the photo.

"This arrow"—she nodded to the cell phone—"came out of the body of Matthew Mueller." She narrowed her eyes and moved closer to Marcus. "I'm curious to know how your arrow got into that boy's body." She sat back and waited, pulling out a pen and notepad.

Marcus fixed her with a seething glare, his eyes narrowed and burning with frustration. He kneaded his hands together, then placed them on the table before Maureen.

"Look at my hands, Detective. I've had rheumatoid arthritis for the past twenty years. Yes, I was a champion archer back in the day. I won all kinds of awards. Taught archery in colleges, even. And some of those seminarians asked me if I'd teach some archery techniques. That's why I bought those arrows. For *them* to use. They should learn on the best equipment." He inched his gnarled hands closer to Maureen. "Look, I have a hard enough time doing the chores around the seminary with these. Do you really think I'd waste my time pulling a recurve bow back to kill someone?" He waggled them in front of Maureen, and she pulled her face away.

"Then how did your arrow—and incidentally, your name was on a list of purchasers at Iron Trail Outfitters, so it *could* be yours—find its way onto the chest of a seminarian? And if *you* didn't kill the boy, are you going to tell me that someone got inside your house and stole your arrows?"

Marcus placed his hands on his lap, remaining silent—maybe preparing a false alibi? "That's exactly what I'm going to tell you. On the night of that boy's death, I was in my shed, sorting through the tools I was going to use to trim the bushes over at the school. The killer must have been watching me to see when I left the house to go up to the seminary." He examined his hands. "I do what I can with these. And if you come with me, I can show you how someone could have gotten anything from inside here while I was out." He pushed back in his chair and motioned for Maureen to follow him.

They walked back to a claustrophobically small bedroom, where one of the deputies was ransacking the bureau.

"Hey!" cried Marcus. "Those are all folded. Stop it!" He made his way over to the deputy, who blocked him.

Holding up a cylindrical tin container full of arrows, the deputy addressed Maureen. "We found these. Looks like the one in the photo. I can check the numbers if you want."

"Thanks, Deputy. Can you give us a minute?"

The deputy nodded and left the room.

When they were alone, Marcus stepped over the clothes the deputies had dumped onto the floor. He pulled the curtains away from a small window and pointed to a large piece of cardboard taped up to cover broken glass.

"Someone broke in here?" asked Maureen, making her way over the obstacle course of yellowed underwear.

Marcus nodded. "I don't have much to take, but some of my arrows were gone, as was the bow I used to win most of my competitions. Some change was missing, but like I said, I don't know what they were looking for." He looked at the clothes on the floor and began picking several items up and putting them back in the drawers.

Maureen took her cell out and began photographing the window, then jotted something down in her notepad. "Did anyone at the seminary know you had these arrows?"

Marcus shrugged. "Sure. Sometimes the boys would come over, and I'd let them have a go at it. I couldn't do much more than give them verbal instructions. Not like I could show them." Again, he held up his disfigured hands.

"Which boys?"

Marcus shrugged. "The Mueller kid. And Daniel something, and the Black guy. Can't pronounce his name, but he was *really* good. Almost as good as I was at that age."

Maureen froze. Okeyo Masamba. She stepped across more piles of clothing and made her way out of the room and back to the kitchen table. Taking a seat, she motioned for Marcus to do the same.

Her eyes searched the man sitting in front of her, his face so forlorn and beaten down. She wondered what had brought him so low. According to her uncle, he had been a promising seminarian, close to being ordained, then suddenly he was gone, and years later, discovered to have returned to Saint Charles as a mere handyman, working for not much more than lodging.

So Father Gabriel had let him back into the fold, thought Maureen. Interesting.

She paused, scrutinizing his hands. "Look," she began, her tone softer. "I admit, it does seem as though it would be difficult for you to pull a bow string back, and also, it's obvious your house did get broken into." She shook her head. "But why didn't you call the police when you discovered the window?"

Marcus inhaled loudly, looked away, then exhaled. "And what would they have done? Taken a report, then filed it somewhere?" He rubbed his gnarled hands roughly. "I've learned it's better just to keep your mouth shut. No one wants to help someone like me anyway, so why would the cops?"

Maureen sensed the meeting was over. Maybe someone did break into the house, or maybe Marcus broke the window himself, staging a break-in, while he gave the arrow to someone. She clicked her pen and put it and her notepad away. And if Marcus wasn't able to shoot an arrow, then he likely could not have mustered the strength to strangle Joseph Lin, either.

"You know not to leave the area. We may have more questions for you later." She stood, waiting for Marcus to say something, but when he didn't, she turned to leave.

Caleb came out from another room and brushed past her, exiting the house with several evidence bags. Maureen glanced at them, then followed him out. Brendan and his friends were waiting outside.

Marcus poked his head out of the door, his head swiveling at all the activity. Maureen stopped when she saw Marcus glaring at Brendan. She waited to see if there would be any trouble.

"I guess this makes you happy, huh, O'Clery? Marcus Dean finally gets his comeuppance?"

Maureen turned to her uncle.

Brendan took a tentative step forward. Ezra and Langdon took a step back.

"That's not true, Marcus. I've never wished anything but peace for you." He took another step forward, his cane crunching into the frozen grass. "And I'm sorry you're having to go through all this. If you ever want to… talk…please know I will make time for you. I'm a phone call away." He stood there, rooted to the spot, as the deputies climbed into their vehicles and drove off, the sound of their engines fading into the distance.

Maureen watched Marcus's face soften. He looked down at his feet. His work boots were caked with mud.

"Thanks, O'Clery," he said, then closed the door.

Brendan looked over at Maureen. "Well, that's something, I guess." He turned and went to stand with his friends.

"You a good man, bro," said Langdon, giving Brendan's back a hard slap.

"Yeah," added Ezra. "That guy's scary, for sure. And if he's the one that killed that boy—"

"I don't think he did it," interrupted Maureen as she made her way over to the trio. "But evidently, Mueller, Caruso, and Okeyo all came here for some so-called archery lessons from Dean. He had plenty of arrows, but says he bought them for the boys to use." She paused, then added, "And it looks like someone broke into his house, unless he did it himself, so Dean *could* be off the hook." She looked back toward Marcus Dean's house. "But with Okeyo using the archery equipment, along with the evidence we have against him so far, he could be the one we're looking for, unless those scratches on Daniel Caruso's face came from one or more of the dead boys." She checked her watch. "Too much to get into. It's late. You guys go home. We'll talk tomorrow." She kissed her uncle on the chin. Rubbing her hand over his beard, she said, "If you want to keep looking like Ewan McGregor, then you'd better get to a barber. You're starting to look more like Rip Van Winkle." She laughed as Brendan playfully swatted her hand away.

As Maureen ambled toward her Jeep, Brendan looked at each of his friends. "Well, I guess that's a wrap. I was hoping to check in on my nephew again, but I've interrupted enough of his classes, so let's just head on home. Sound good?"

Langdon scratched at his neatly trimmed Van Dyke. "Well, ain't nothin' like a good *po*-lice search to end up the afternoon, I always say."

"Yeah, just another quiet day for three clergymen," laughed Ezra, pushing his glasses up the bridge of his nose.

As they walked back to the Caddy, Langdon put his arms around each man. "I don't know 'bout y'all, but I'm stoppin' for a snack. All that second-hand stress made me hungry."

Ezra frowned, shrugging the big man's arm off. "You're *always* hungry."

"And yet, somehow, he still moves faster than us when it's time to eat," said Brendan.

Langdon gave an impolite grunt. "That's the spirit o' the Lord, gents. And also the spirit o' fried chicken callin' my name." He dashed ahead of them, twirling in the cold evening, each breath appearing as a tiny puff of swirling white. "I'm stoppin' at Poultry in Motion if y'all wanna come."

Brendan glanced at his watch, then at Ezra. He shrugged. "I'm game. Ezra?"

Ezra gave his friends a glib look. "I could eat."

Piling into the Cadillac, they headed off to Porter Mill's most popular chicken shack, Marcus Dean and the murders in their rearview mirror.

Fifteen minutes later found the three clerics in a booth at Poultry in Motion, the scent of fried food and sizzling wings thick in the air, each of them nursing a half-eaten meal.

Brendan twirled his napkin around his finger, eyes narrowed as he stared across the table. "Those two seminarians weren't random targets," he said, his voice low but certain. "Someone wanted to send a message. But the question is, what *kind* of message? The cryptic notes, the ones left on each body, make no sense."

He rubbed the stubble on his chin, then pulled out a piece of folded paper from his slacks pocket where he'd copied the messages. *"When the shepherd is blind, the flock shall bleed...* That's what was found under Joseph's body, and *For pride—humility* was under Matthew's." He looked up at his friends then folded the paper and shoved it back in his pocket. "We don't know these boys well enough to know how it might relate to their demise. And trust me," he added, dipping a wing into a thick sauce, "I've pulled out all my analytical skills on this one. I can't crack these riddles."

Ezra chewed thoughtfully on a wing, wiping his mouth with the back of his hand. "I still think it's someone inside the seminary," he offered, glancing at Brendan. "A rivalry? A grudge? Or maybe someone's trying to bury something darker."

Langdon shook his head, reaching for a biscuit and staring at it lovingly. "It ain't one o' them boys. You know how it is. Kids these days get worked up 'bout things like social media an' stuff, but murder? That's a whole diff'rent ballgame. You talkin' 'bout some pretty serious darkness there. Someone done come in there and kilt them." He slathered butter on the biscuit. "It be Satan and his minions." He shoved half the biscuit in his mouth.

Brendan cocked an eyebrow. "And you don't think there's *anyone* there that could possibly have a few screws loose? You've met that group of young men, right?" He picked at a wing, then placed it on the paper plate. "I know some of those boys simply want to be good parish priests, but others, I fear, may have other ideas."

Ezra laughed. "I believe you're describing you and your brother, Bren."

Brendan gave the little rabbi a knowing grin.

"But getting back to the topic," continued Ezra, trying to push his glasses up on his nose with a greasy finger, "it's hard to ignore the coincidence. *Two* murders? Same place? That seminary may have more secrets than they want to admit."

Langdon shrugged, taking a bite of his chicken. "Could be some sort o' religious zealot gone too far. I mean, we talkin' 'bout people who dedicate their entire lives to somethin' they can't always prove. It messes with your head."

Brendan paused, then dropped the napkin onto his plate. "Okay, but here's the kicker—what about the staff? Maybe one of them could have had something to do with it. Maybe someone had a little too much sway over the students. You know how some of these guys get if they think the students may be smarter than they are."

Langdon leaned back in his chair, eyes scanning the ceiling. "Professors, seminarians, zealots… you two be makin' my chicken look like the *leas'* complicated thing in this here room."

Ezra snorted, wiping his mouth again. "You're telling me. What do you think, Bren? We've been talking in circles for over an hour, and you still haven't said anything definitive."

Brendan raised his eyebrows, a sly grin tugging at his lips. "Well, there's a difference between solving crimes and keeping my cholesterol in check. But I'm starting to believe it's an inside job. You know, someone who's been hiding in plain sight. Someone who's either convinced they're doing the right thing, or someone with an axe to grind." He paused. "Though I do find it hard to believe anyone could be *that* devoted to a cause. I can barely get through my own sermon half the time."

Ezra chuckled. "It's true. You'd think if we were all that smart, we'd at least be able to keep track of our socks, let alone two murders."

Langdon sat up in his chair and looked over at Ezra. "Let's go back to the little dude's place and check out his famous murder board again. We got us more clues now, so somethin' might jump out at us. And maybe he can crack that Zodiac case, too, while we be there."

"Are you making fun of my board?" Ezra slapped Langdon's arm. "If you remember—though I doubt your little brain can remember that far back—that board was a tremendous help in the past."

"Okay, okay," interrupted Brendan. "I, for one, think that's a good idea." He looked at Ezra. "Let's do it, Rabbi. It's worth another look."

Ezra stuck a tongue out at Langdon. "See? Someone thinks my board is a good idea. Anyway," he continued, wiping his lips and placing the napkin on the table, "on a serious note, we've got to get our hands dirty on this one. We need to start pulling some threads before someone else gets hurt."

Langdon sighed, shaking his head with a slight smile. "Well, at leas' we're not pullin' chicken bones outta our teeth while we be at it."

The three exchanged glances, their banter lightening the mood for a moment before the reality of the situation settled back in. They had a case to crack, and the clock was ticking before the murderer struck again.

CHAPTER 20

Tuesday Morning

After morning Mass, Brendan sat down to one of Mrs. Morrison's hearty breakfasts—two eggs, over easy, sausage and gravy, home fries, and a cup of fresh fruit.

"Mrs. M," cried Brendan, patting his stomach, "you spoil me. And if you ever feel the need to murder me, please do it by using foods high in fat, calories, and cholesterol." He rubbed his stomach again. "That's the way I want to go."

The housekeeper waved a hand at him. "I only make you a big breakfast occasionally, Father, and you know that." She took his plate away, placing the dirty dishes in the sink.

Brendan's cell rang, and the angelic picture of his nephew appeared on the screen. Smiling, he answered. "Good morning, Aiden. What's up?"

"Uncle Brendan, can you come over sometime today? I don't have any classes after lunch." He paused, and Brendan waited. "I just can't stop thinking about these murders. I know I should place my trust in God, and I do, but that doesn't mean everything that's happened here isn't disconcerting. Can you come?"

Brendan smiled, the love for his nephew tugging at his heart. "Of course I can come." He glanced at his watch. "See you after lunch then, okay?"

Brendan heard the anxiety in his nephew's voice. "Sure, and thanks."

The call ended. Brendan watched Mrs. Morrison washing and rinsing the morning's dishes. He couldn't help but notice the way she hummed under her breath, her back to him, her thoughts lost in the suds. It was almost as if she were in a world of her own, untouched by the weight of whatever was going on outside the rectory's walls.

"Is he all right?" asked the housekeeper, placing each dish on a drying rack.

Brendan pushed away from the table, reaching down and picking Mary Magdalene up. "Short answer? No. And I'm not happy with him being there with some maniac running around murdering seminarians. Father Gabriel should really close the place down for a bit." He grabbed the Yorkie's leash from a hook and walked toward the back door. "I'm going to walk this one and do some paperwork, then head over to the seminary and see if I can calm him down…and maybe pick up another clue or two."

Mrs. Morrison laughed. "You're becoming a regular Father Brown." She stopped washing and turned to him. "So, does that make me Mrs. McCarthy?" She shook her head, a wide smile breaking across her face.

"Well, you both sure know how to cook, so absolutely, you can be the Mrs. McCarthy to my Father Brown any time," he said, referring to the popular British television series.

Mary Magdalene tugged on the leash as Brendan grabbed his cane and exited the backyard just in time for the little dog to find relief.

Later, Brendan stood before the old seminary, its stone walls worn and weathered by years of secrets. The wind rustled the bare branches of the trees, sending a shiver through the air. In his arms, Mary Magdalene sat calmly, her small body nestled against his chest. Brendan's eyes scanned the familiar building. The quietness around him seemed almost too peaceful for what was to come, a place where memories always had a way of catching up to him.

He walked in and found his nephew sitting in a winged-back chair in the foyer, reading. When Aiden saw him, he closed the book and began to rise, but Brendan gently patted his raised hands in the air, signaling him to stay seated.

"Let's talk here for a while," he began, setting his cane across his lap as he sat. "Tell me what's on your mind?"

Aiden shifted in his chair, his body tense before his hand reached out to give Mary Magdalene a gentle pat. "Joseph and Matthew were friends of mine. Oh, I know we had all just met in August when we arrived for orientation, but we bonded, even though Joseph was a first-year student and Matthew was second-year." He gazed at two seminarians who had just walked in the front door. "We all got along great, Uncle Brendan. I know you and Maureen heard that Okeyo had a temper, and this one or that one spoke harshly to another, but you were here once, and you know how stressful it can be. Egos and personalities clash sometimes."

Brendan gave a knowing nod, recognizing that his nephew was only at the beginning of a journey that would test, not just his faith, but his body and mind as well.

"I don't know," said Aiden, emitting a frustrating sigh. "I don't know what to do or who to trust anymore. Did one of the guys I'm living with do this? Did a staff member do it or some serial killer stalking seminaries?" His shoulders rose as he spread his hands, a wordless gesture of uncertainty. "And who's next?" He stared at Brendan, his cheeks a bright pink on a background of pale skin. "Me? Uncle Brendan, you've helped Maureen solve a couple of murders in the past. Can you do it again?"

Brendan sat up and leaned in toward Aiden, putting a hand on the young man's knee. "Maureen's doing the best she can. She's helping out that deputy who's in charge."

Aiden nodded. "I know, but I trust you and Maureen. Can't *you* do more?" His urgent plea tugged at Brendan's heart.

Brendan's hand drifted to his chin, rubbing the beard his niece always nagged him about as he considered his next words. "Aiden, I don't have any pull here anymore. Actually, I never did, but I'll do what I can." He looked around, his eyes narrowing. "How about we go back to the scene of the crime? Maybe there's something more we can discover."

Aiden's face brightened. "That's a great idea, Uncle Brendan. At least we'd be doing *something.*" He set the book on the table in front of him and rose.

Brendan carefully picked up Mary Magdalene from his lap and was glad to see a subtle change in Aiden's demeanor that hadn't been there before—a spark of something more hopeful, more resilient.

Okeyo sat in his room, trying to study his notes from the catechism class the previous day, but found he was unable to concentrate. His parents would be so ashamed if they ever found out he had been questioned by the police and was still considered a suspect in two murders.

With a heavy sigh, he dropped his face into his hands, overwhelmed by a tangle of fear and uncertainty. He couldn't study. He hadn't even been able to eat since the police let him go. Father Gabriel had wanted him to get a lawyer, but did he really need one? He had no alibi, not a good one, anyway. But no one there had a good alibi. All of the students said they had been in their rooms. Anyone could have killed his two classmates. And maybe he'd be the next one to die. He began to tremble.

His thoughts went to Father Gabriel. The rector *had* to be protected from all of this. This seminary *was* Father Gabriel. He, Okeyo, would do anything to protect his mentor, his friend. No one would touch him, no matter what the rector had done, he'd see to that.

He shoved his chair back and sprinted to the bathroom, barely making it before a surge of green bile came up, its bitter taste lingering in his mouth, a harsh reminder of the life he now faced.

He wiped his mouth and stared in the mirror. A young Kenyan boy, full of promise and his parents' pride, stared back at him. How proud his folks were to have been able to send him to America to become a priest! But now, he was a suspect in two murders.

He exited the bathroom and grabbed his jacket. He needed to leave this dorm and find somewhere to think and pray. Closing his door behind him, he headed for the library to find peace.

CHAPTER 21

The chapel was empty. The only sound was the mournful whistling of the wind, slipping through the cracks of a drafty window and finding its way into the cold, empty building.

"Let's start here," Brendan suggested as he walked toward the old mahogany confessional, ducking under the tape that still surrounded the crime scene.

He studied the ornate structure, remembering being on the penitent's side many, many times. But now, as a priest...he swung open the door to the confessor's side and glanced around, taking in the dimly lit space with a quiet, thoughtful gaze. The seat was plushly padded, albeit worn from the years of use.

"Get in," he instructed Aiden, pointing to the penitent's side. He slipped into the middle stall where the priest would sit and, after placing the Yorkie on his lap, immediately slid the screen open, seeing the slightly obscured face of his nephew.

"Are you getting anything?" asked Aiden.

Brendan chuckled. "I'm not a clairvoyant, Aiden."

He studied the inside of the compartment, feeling around, although he had no idea what he was looking for. He fingered the rich fabric lining inside the space. The solid mahogany, so old and strong, sounded solid under the rapping of his knuckles. Tucking Mary Magdelene under his arm, he stood in the cramped space and lifted the padded seat. To his amazement, he found it opened easily. Peering inside, he found a box of tissues, a rosary, some old holy cards, and a few dated Catholic prayer books.

Putting the seat back down, he sat on it again and continued his survey of the space. He moved his hand deftly across the sides of the compartment until his hand ran over of metal knob barely protruding from the wood. Opening the confessional's door for more light, he toggled the knob until a soft click sounded.

His heart began pounding as he gingerly pushed the wood inward. A draft of cool air hit his face, and the faint smell of something musty assailed him.

"Aiden," he whispered, "come here, quick."

Aiden opened the confessional's door wide enough for him to peer into, and when he saw what Brendan had discovered, his eyes nearly popped out of his head.

"Uncle Brendan," he gasped, "what's that?"

"I don't know, but we're going to find out."

He pushed the panel open further. Placing Mary Magdalene on the floor, he stepped into a narrow passageway. Cool plastered walls, yellowed with age, created a cramped corridor. He held the panel door open for Aiden.

Brendan fumbled around and grabbed a Saint Margaret's bulletin from his jacket, folded it in half, and closed the secret door over it. "So we don't get locked in," he explained to Aiden when the boy gave him a questioning look. "Turn on the flashlight on your phone."

Slowly, they inched their way down the hallway, each step deliberate, the weight of the moment pressing on them both. At the end of the corridor, they reached a closed door. Brendan's heart began to race. He could feel the tension in the air, thick and suffocating.

He picked up the Yorkie, turned the doorknob, and as they stepped into a small room, he found himself frozen, unable to find his voice. The space was well-lit, the soft glow of several wall sconces casting flickering shadows against the walls. Despite its cramped size, the room exuded a quiet reverence, like a place meant for contemplation—or maybe secrecy. Shelves lined the walls, jammed with books and old manuscripts, some so worn they seemed to whisper their secrets. It felt like an archive of forgotten knowledge, the kind of room that held more than just history. It held mysteries waiting to be unearthed.

"So what is this place, Uncle Brendan? Was this here when you went through?"

Brendan could only shake his head. "I've never seen it before."

Brendan put Mary Magdalene back on the floor and began perusing some of the books. They were old—some hundreds of years old. An old shoe box sat next to a pile of books, and Aiden uncovered it, finding it chock-full of old photographs.

"Look at this," he said to Brendan, who was thumbing through the pages of an old book on the men and women considered the doctors of the Catholic faith.

Brendan took a place next to his nephew, and the two began flipping through the old photos. The photos captured the seminary and its grounds, showing young saplings that had since grown into the recognizable towering trees that now graced the seminary's landscape.

"Here's the only one with people in it. Hey, check it out! It's the same one I found in that library book. The one with Father Gabriel and those guys." He let out a quick, surprised chuckle. "Father Gabriel looked like a hippie back then!"

Brendan's heart melted at the sound of his nephew's joy.

Brendan took the photo from Aiden. "This is how I remember him. No gray hairs, no wrinkles. He was a secretive man, even back then, and he was always a little odd." He picked up several more, but they were only shots of the seminary and the surrounding area. No more photos of people.

Aiden stared at the photo and then took it from Brendan's hands, examining it more closely. He handed it back to Brendan. "Take another look, Uncle Brendan. Does this guy look familiar to you?" He pointed to a stocky young man.

Brendan studied the photo. Scratching his head, he replied, "A little, but the guy in this picture is older now. Or dead." He pointed to faded initials over the familiar-looking young man's head. "M.M.," he said to himself. "Same as Matthew Mueller." He continued rifling through items until he came across something that had been placed between the pages of an old book. "Look at the note in this manuscript," he said to Aiden, "It's the same prophecy the killer seems to be following."

Aiden's lips moved silently as he read the note. He looked incredulously at Brendan. "What *is* this place, Uncle Brendan?" asked Aiden, his head swiveling around to take in the shelves of books.

"I don't know, but someone's been using it recently, that's for sure. It smells musty, but the books and boxes don't have any dust on them, and the lights are on. It beats me." He looked at the photo again and put it in his pocket. "Come on, let's get out of here. We don't want to be caught snooping." He searched for Mary Magdalene and found her pawing at a mouse hole.

Aiden nodded as they made their way out of the small room, back through the narrow corridor, and back into the confessional.

Before leaving the structure, Brendan stuck his head out, ensuring they were alone. Satisfied, he ushered his nephew out, grabbed the church bulletin from the latch, and headed toward the front of the chapel.

"Now don't discuss what we found with *anyone*," warned Brendan, "especially about that photo. We need to find out who M.M. is. It may lead to some vital information. I'll tell Mo about it and this room, and we'll figure it out. Meanwhile, next time you're in the chapel, try to see who goes in and out and how long they're in there, but don't be obvious about it." He clapped the boy on his shoulder. "I'll walk you back to your dorm, but then I want to tell Maureen what we found."

As they walked down the path that led back to the seminary, Mary Magdalene barked madly at falling leaves.

"See you soon?" Brendan wrapped his arms around his nephew's fragile frame, catching the faint, clean scent of shampoo as he held him close.

"Yeah, sure, but tell Maureen"—he glanced around for eavesdroppers—"as soon as you leave here, okay?"

Brendan released the boy from his embrace and gave a mock salute. He waited for Aiden to enter the building before he left, waving one more time.

And then he was off to relay to his niece what they had discovered.

A formless shadow had been kneeling in the back of the empty, dimly lit chapel, his whispered prayers blending with the occasional groan of aging pews and the distant caw of birds outside. The stillness was sacred—until he heard it. A soft scuffling sound. His head lifted sharply. It was coming from the confessional.

The stranger's pulse quickened. Was someone inside? A penitent murmuring sins to a priest? He strained to listen, but the hush swallowed the words. Then, to his shock, the entire confessional seemed to shift—just a fraction, but enough. A shadow flickered against the carved wood.

The figure barely had time to register what was happening before the door creaked open, and a leg poked out into the aisle. His breath caught. Instinct sent him ducking low behind the pew, heart hammering.

Peering through the narrow space between the seat and the kneeler, he watched as two figures emerged, not from the penitent's side, but from the center, where the priest would sit. Aiden O'Clery stepped out first, followed by his uncle, the priest.

The figure swallowed hard. They had found the room!

He remained still, his mouth as dry as a cotton ball, his nerves tingling, watching the two as they passed what looked like a photograph between them. He picked up on several phrases: "looks familiar," "wrinkles," "Father Gabriel," and other words that made his heart race—especially when he heard "M. M.".

As they descended the aisle toward the exit, he ducked back behind the pew, praying he wouldn't be discovered.

Finally, he heard the chapel door slowly closing, and he sat upright again, his mind whirring. What had those two been up to, and how had they discovered that room? And what did they mean by speaking of Father Gabriel? Did they suspect him of committing these murders?

With shaky hands, he hastily shrugged on his jacket and slipped out of the chapel. His shoes kept sticking to the floor. He hadn't cleaned his shoes thoroughly from the duct tape! The odd sound echoed against the stone floor as he quickened his pace, his mind racing as fast as his legs carried him.

CHAPTER 22

Tuesday Midafternoon

"**S**aint Monica, patron saint of the impatient, *please* make that woman pick up her phone." Brendan drummed his fingers agitatedly on the worn steering wheel of his battered Honda, his irritation growing with each passing second.

Not wanting to relay what he and Aiden had discovered over the phone, he told Maureen to meet him at the Rusty Rooster, a popular diner in Porter Mills. After dropping Mary Magdalene off at the rectory, he texted Ezra and Langdon, asking if they had time for a midafternoon snack. He got a quick reply in the affirmative and planned to meet in an hour.

When they arrived at the restaurant, the place was jammed, even though lunch had been long over.

Brendan surveyed the room. "Why do we always pick the busiest place in town?"

Ezra gestured to the only available booth—an extremely small one. "I'll sit on this side. Last time, I was sandwiched between you two, and I spent the whole meal wedged like a knish in a too-tight box."

Langdon gave the little rabbi a wicked grin. "Little dude, you so small. You fit anywheres."

"I'm also over fifty," replied Ezra. "I creak. Give me some space."

Brendan broke in. "Fine. Langdon, you and I can sit opposite the whiner."

Langdon shrugged. "Okay, but if I get sick o' lookin' over at him, I expect me some divine intervention."

An attractive woman in the diner's uniform made her way through the crowd. She was a petite brunette with a tumble of curls that refused to stay pinned back, freckles dusting her nose. Her lips were painted a daring crimson, and her dark-lined eyes carried a hint of mischief. The pad and pencil in her hand looked almost out of place, as though she should have been striding down a runway instead of scribbling notes.

"What can I get you, gentlemen?"

Brendan jumped in. "Just an iced tea for me, thanks."

"I'll have the small spinach salad," said Ezra, eyeing the captivating woman. "Dressing on the side and water with lemon."

Langdon, grinning, said, "And I'll take me the double bacon cheeseburger with a double side o' fries an' a choc'late milk shake, an' a piece o' that bee-*yoo*-tiful apple pie I seen comin' in."

"Did you order that just to torment me?" asked Ezra. "And didn't you already eat lunch?" He glanced at the waitress, giving her the most flirtatious smile a rabbi was allowed to give.

Langdon let out a hoot. "I'm hungry again. So what? An' don' be checkin' out that woman for your next wife." He elbowed Brendan. "Like the little dude got a chance with *her*."

Ezra's face burned, and he looked away, embarrassed by his friend's statement.

Brendan squeezed his eyes shut and rubbed them, as if that alone could erase the tension of what he and Aiden had just been through. As soon as the waitress left, he leaned in, relaying what he had uncovered.

Just then, Maureen walked in. Seeing six arms flagging her over, she rolled her eyes and came to their table.

"Scoot over, Rabbi," she said, sitting beside Ezra.

"Thanks for not being big and bulky, Maureen," he said, throwing Langdon a spiteful look.

"Huh?"

"It's nothing, Mo. Let me just tell you what I told the guys. You are *not* going to believe it." Brendan relayed the story of the secret room to Maureen, who sat dumbstruck.

"Wow," was all she could say. "That's a lot to unpack. Wait until I tell Caleb."

Ezra looked at her, his eyes narrowed. "Hey, I heard you canceled your trip."

Brendan blanched, waiting for the fireworks, but none came.

Maureen smiled sweetly. "I postponed it. I have two weeks' leave, so I'll still be able to enjoy some downtime, as well as help solve these murders."

"I'm shocked," said Brendan, puzzled. "I thought you'd be chomping at the bit and madder than a hornet stuck in a soda can."

"You know how I like to solve things, Unc. Caleb can use the help. Pollard gave *me* no help when I had to solve those murders at Windy Meadows, remember? So, if I can help out, I'm willing."

Ezra piped in. "I remember those murders. They sure were scary."

The waitress returned and set down the food and drinks, turning to Maureen. "Anything for you?"

Maureen shook her head. "No, thanks."

With a nod, the waitress spun on her heel and walked away. Brendan watched Ezra ogling the woman.

"She's not on the menu, Rabbi," Brendan quipped before blessing their food and digging in.

During the meal, the discussion turned serious.

"So what's our next move, Mo?" asked Brendan.

"I'll get with Caleb later and fill him in on what you discovered. We're definitely going to want to see that place. Meanwhile"—she gave her uncle a glib look—"you can make a few copies of that photo so Caleb and I can see if we can find out if anyone knows who that boy is, or *was*, and the significance of that photo. And finding that secret room is unbelievable. I wonder who else knows about it and what it's used for."

"Trust me," said Brendan, "we'll find out. I just need some more snooping time." Changing the subject, he said, "So what else is on your agenda for today?"

With a scowl, Maureen chewed her lip and leveled a malevolent glare at Brendan. "Uncle Malachy called earlier. He told me Gran's in crisis and that you were supposed to have gone and checked in on her. She called *him* just to tell him she's out of Rheb's chocolates. You remember her getting hooked on them when we first came to Baltimore, don't you?" She waited patiently for the laughter to die down. "Well, apparently, that's *my* problem now."

Once Brendan calmed himself, he said, "It's so nice to hear the grand archbishop doling out meaningless tasks for others. It's not just me for once."

"What's he got *you* doing?" asked Maureen.

Brendan grunted. "What *doesn't* he have me doing? Now, he wants me to start some kind of outreach program at Saint Ann's in the city. Where am I going to get the time to do that?" He hunched his shoulders. "And I hate driving into Baltimore."

Again, Maureen scowled at him. "Like maybe, instead of having breakfast, lunch, or dinner almost every day with your friends?"

"You're a real comedian, Mo," said Brendan.

Maureen checked her watch and groaned. "Gotta bounce. Gran's tolerance for delays ranks just below airport security's."

She kissed her uncle's cheek, said her goodbyes to Ezra and Langdon, and left the restaurant.

Brendan watched her go, then turned to his friends. "Well, gentlemen, I hope you're free later." He rubbed his hands together like a scheming villain, his eyes twinkling. "How about a little game of poker this evening? I'll call Milo and Ritchie and see if they're ready to lose some money."

Ezra looked at Langdon and bumped the big man's outstretched fist. "And maybe figure out a way to help Maureen and Caleb solve these murders."

Brendan nodded, frowning. "Yes, and make sure my nephew isn't on the killer's menu."

Aiden had skipped lunch and stayed in his room. With each passing day, the tension within the seminary grew, and so did his fear. Being around his fellow seminarians was making him anxious, always looking at each one and thinking, *are you the murderer?* Today felt like a day he needed to keep to himself.

He reached into the mini-fridge his parents had given him and retrieved a water, then grabbed a bag of chips from a care package and threw himself on his bed. These would more than suffice as a decent meal.

Ripping open the bag, he grabbed a few chips and chewed them slowly, his thoughts spinning like a pinwheel. How much more stress could he take?

A faint bonfire scent drifted to his nose as he reached for more chips. The crunch echoed in his head as he sniffed the air again. The smoky smell was stronger now.

His gaze flicked to the closed window. If it wasn't coming from outside, then where was it coming from? The seminary, he knew, was heated with oil, and what he was smelling was not oil-based. He sniffed again.

Setting the bag of chips down, he eased himself off the bed and walked out to the hallway. He inhaled, looking up and down the hallways for the origin of the smoke, but all he caught was the stale blend of gym socks and the faint, buttery trace of old popcorn.

Closing the door, he then walked over to the window. Peeking through the venetian blinds, he was surprised to see Daniel Caruso standing at the fire pit in the garden, feeding papers into the flames with unsettling urgency. Smoke curled upward, snaking its way toward Aiden's window. Most of the seminarians were at lunch, so was Daniel trying to hide something? If so, he wasn't doing a good job of it, thought Aiden, as the fire pit was out in the open where anyone could see him destroying—what?—evidence?

Grabbing the handles on the window, he prepared to open it but then decided at the last moment to just observe what was going on. What was so secretive about what Daniel was burning that he couldn't have just thrown it in the trash? Was it something that would connect him to the riddle found on Joseph's body or the other notes? Perhaps it was the parchment paper he used to write the notes.

He continued watching, keeping his body hidden from view, peeking out only occasionally at the strange action. Something else to tell Maureen, and perhaps another suspect with something to hide.

After watching Daniel throw the last of the papers in the fire pit, Aiden waited for his friend to leave, then grabbed his phone to tell his cousin.

Maureen pushed open the door to Our Lady of Grace Residence, the scent of lavender air freshener and disinfectant hitting her nose. She knocked on her grandmother's apartment door and had barely stepped inside when she heard Eabha's sharp voice.

"There she is, finally! I thought maybe you'd forgotten your poor old Gran, so, left here to rot among people who think salt is a spice."

Maureen sighed and walked toward the sitting area, where her grandmother was perched in a floral armchair, her cane propped against the side like a scepter. Another older woman sat in a separate chair, her head tilted to one side, lost in a deep, peaceful sleep. Maureen assumed the woman was a friend of her grandmother's.

"Gran, I was here last week."

Eabha scoffed. "A week? Might as well be a year at my age. And look at you. Still too skinny. Are you eating properly or just living off coffee and whatever nonsense Americans call food?"

"I eat just fine, thank you very much, Gran," Maureen said, dropping a box of Rheb's chocolates, a Baltimore staple, onto the table. "Here's your fix of candy for the week."

Maureen saw Eabha's eyes light up as she inspected the box, but she knew her grandmother wasn't about to admit gratitude that easily.

"Hmm...did you buy them today or did one of your practice boyfriends buy them for you last Christmas? Because if it's the latter, I'll need to have Malachy give me last rites read before I take a bite."

Maureen rolled her eyes and decided not to take the bait.

Eabha nodded approvingly and took one. "Well, at least you did one thing right today." She took a bite, chewing thoughtfully. "So, my son—the priest, not the archbishop one—was *supposed* to come see me, but he could only spare me a phone call." She gave a dramatic sigh. "He tells me you're off on another murder case and my grandson is a target?" She picked up another piece of candy and shoved it in her mouth.

"Gran—"

"Don't 'Gran' me. I'm just saying, you need to find a more suitable job, so I don't have to worry. I'd like to meet my great-grans before I'm stuck in this place permanently, listening to Gertrude drone on about her 'good old days.'" She nodded toward the sleeping woman and leaned in, lowering her voice. "The woman was a school librarian. Sure, and what kind of 'good old days' are those?"

Maureen stifled a laugh. "You do realize Gertie's sitting right over there?"

Eabha glanced over Maureen's shoulder again, completely unfazed. "She can barely hear a thing, so. Poor woman's ears gave up on her out of sheer boredom. Ah, sure, she's fast asleep, isn't she? And wouldn't you know it, peace at last from all her blathering!"

Maureen shook her head. "You're impossible."

"And you love me for it," Eabha said, popping a third piece of chocolate into her mouth. "Now, tell me something interesting. And don't you dare bore me, or I'll pretend to fall asleep right in the middle of it."

Maureen lasted about forty-five minutes, and in her mind, that made her practically a saint. She finally kissed Eabha on the top of her head, then quietly slipped five twenty-dollar bills onto the counter and left.

Once inside her Jeep, she checked her phone for messages and returned Aiden's call regarding the unsettling detail that Daniel had been burning papers in the fire pit, rather than throwing them in the nearest trash can.

"I figure he thought they were too secret to dump in the trash." He added in a hushed tone, "Maybe it has something to do with the murders."

Maureen thought for a moment, wondering if this was an important clue or just some strange behavior of a seminarian.

"Okay, I'll swing by later and check it out." She added, almost in a scolding voice, "Don't go near that pit."

After Aiden promised, Maureen reached into her tote, her head pounding from the visit with her grandmother.

CHAPTER 23

Tuesday Afternoon

After surviving her grandmother's visit, Maureen shook a Tylenol into her hand, swallowed it with a can of flat soda, and proceeded to the seminary.

Parking by the seminary's gardens, she exited the car and walked over to where the fire pit was located. The odor of smoke still haunted the air, faint but unmistakable, causing Maureen to sneeze twice.

The fire pit loomed at the center of the stone patio like a forgotten altar, its rim chipped and blackened by old heat. She sensed, by the number of outdoor chairs that surrounded the pit, the seminarians must enjoy many off-hours sitting around, discussing their classes, theology, or whatever seminarians discussed.

As she got closer, she saw that the ashes were still warm, smoldering faintly, as if something unseen breathed beneath them. Shredded fragments of burned pages peeked through the soot, their edges curling like dying leaves.

She picked at a few with her thumb and index finger. Several of the larger pieces hadn't burned completely, so she gathered them and took a seat in one of the chairs. Placing the scraps on her lap, she read a collection of disjointed words and phrases: "last meeting," "though it...forever," "sorry but...seminary," and "can...be friends."

Among the fragments lay photographs of a high school couple, the air of first love about them. Studying the scraps, a knowing smile crept across Maureen's lips. It was a much younger Daniel Caruso, with long hair, wearing a tuxedo, and a beautiful girl standing next to him in a prom gown.

"No conspiracy here," she said out loud. Caruso must have been getting rid of his past life, a life he couldn't take with him into the priesthood.

Wiping her hands, she gazed around at the peaceful setting of the school, thinking that solitude, sometimes, can heal a soul. But perhaps, as in these two murders, it can drive one to insanity and murder.

Satisfied that the strange burnings had nothing to do with the murders, she stood to leave, the cool autumn air ruffled her hair. Pulling out her cell phone, she called her cousin. "Well, Daniel Caruso's moved on," she said, relaying what she had discovered in the embers. "Nothing says spiritual renewal like a backyard inferno of old girlfriends."

Despite the ache in her head, she drove straight to the sheriff's department, stubborn resolve pushing her forward. She knew Captain Pollard would likely be waiting, arms crossed, ready to demand why she had ignored her leave and was meddling in another detective's case. But at this point, what was one more interrogation from that toad?

Thankfully, when she parked in the lot, she noted that Pollard's unmarked cruiser was gone. She entered the building and walked directly to Caleb's desk.

"Hey, Maureen. Good to see you." Caleb glanced around conspiratorially. "Pollard just left."

"Good. I've got quite a bit of new info that might help us narrow in on our killer." She relayed what her uncle had told her about the secret room behind the confessional. Pulling out her cell phone, she scrolled to the photo Brendan and Aiden had discovered. She tapped the photo and hit "Print," sending the image to the department's printer. She turned the phone to Caleb, showing him the group of young men with Father Gabriel.

"What's it mean? Who are these guys? The photo looks old. I mean, that guy—isn't that the head of the seminary?—his hair is white now." He pointed to the rector.

"We don't know. My uncle thought this one guy with the initials of M.M."—she pointed to the young man—"looked familiar, but that's all he could say. It's definitely not Matthew Mueller, considering how young Father Gabriel looks in the photo, that's for sure." She pulled up a chair and sat down next to the deputy. "You should take this to the seminary and show it around. Especially to Father Gabriel. Maybe he can explain that secret room and what it's used for." She got up and walked over to the printer. When she returned, she handed Caleb the print, then looked away. "We need to make some headway and soon."

The deputy met her gaze, his expression grave. "I agree, and I thank you for your help. I would have been a fool to turn it down." Then, a smirk tugged at his lips. "And let's be honest. If Pollard's going to breathe fire, I'd rather not be the only one getting burned."

She gave his shoulder a quick, teasing slap. "See? You do have some survival instincts, after all."

She exited the office and walked out to the parking lot, just in time to feel her cell phone vibrating in her jacket. Pulling it out, she felt a flush, seeing it was a text from Simon.

Aiden tried to concentrate on his meal as best he could.

"Hey, Okeyo," said Daniel, poking the young man with his elbow. "You're not eating, and you haven't said a word. What's up?" Daniel moved his fork, pushing aside overcooked peas.

Manuel gave Daniel a sour look. "Leave him alone, Daniel."

"Huh?" Okeyo looked around at the faces of his friends, his reverie broken.

"Are you thinking about murders?" Daniel asked him, reaching for the salt. "This meatloaf tastes like it was made last year."

"Leave the guy alone," repeated Nathan. "We're all on edge, and with exams looming, too." Nathan looked at Okeyo. "We have to let the police do their jobs. Don't worry about it. God will sort it out. Remember"—he looked at his fellow seminarians—"God is a higher pay grade than us poor, miserable seminarians." He focused back on Okeyo. "And none of us thinks you killed anyone, right, guys?"

Okeyo's head jerked up. "What do you mean? Do you seriously think that I did harm to those boys?" His hand went to his heart, as if he were trying to calm it.

As if God answered his question, Aiden spoke. "None of us thinks that, Okeyo," Aiden chimed in. "And Porter Mill's Sheriff's Department may be small, but they're good at solving murders." He grinned. "My cousin's solved a few in her time, so let's all just concentrate on our upcoming exams, okay? As Nathan said, give it to God."

The group mumbled their assent, and the talk turned to the exams, theological discussions, and, of course, sports.

Okeyo pushed the food around his plate. Aiden watched his friend out of the corner of his eye, suspecting Okeyo's appetite had been swallowed by the gnawing dread from the weight of suspicion pressed on him.

Aiden's heart sank as he thought of how *he* might feel if he were the one suspected of murdering two of his classmates. Suddenly, his appetite also left him.

He looked around at each of his friends. Had one of them really committed these crimes? If he were to take a guess...

But if he suspected any of this group to be the murderer, then surely that person would come for him eventually.

A cold shiver traced his spine.

"What do you all have against me?" railed Milo, as he threw his cards down on the rickety table in the utility room.

Brendan placed a card from his hand down. "Martin Luther, perhaps?" He poured himself a glass of Jameson. The whiskey, along with the Cuban cigars, staples at their poker games, were treasured gifts from his parishioners.

Milo laughed. "Listen, it's like I always say, Luther wasn't *really* trying to leave the Catholic Church, he was just redecorating."

"Yeah," answered Brendan as he rearranged his hand, "and like any bad DIY project, it got out of hand."

Ezra piped in. "Come on, guys, get serious. I have a great hand, and I want it to be my turn."

Langdon looked over at the rabbi, who was sitting directly across from him. "Little dude, you ain't s'pose to tell everyone what you got in your hand." His head shook from left to right. "Boy, you ain't got one brain cell under that beanie." He stretched a large hand out and, like a giant claw, snatched two wings from a KFC bucket.

"Look, by the time it's my turn, everyone will have forgotten what I said." He glared at the Baptist minister. "Besides, you just come for the food, the cigars, and the Jameson. You're some Baptist. You're not a serious poker player." He studied his cards. "And if you don't leave me alone, I'm going to tell your congregation what you do with your free time: drinking, smoking cigars, and cavorting with Catholics—"

"Hey!" cried Brendan. "Enough with the Catholic bashing!"

Ritchie Kim groaned and threw his cards down. "I'm out. And would you two stop bickering like an old married couple? Honestly, you guys need a domestic mediator to help you with your relationship problems."

"I'm out, too," said Brendan. "Ezra, the pot's yours."

The stunned rabbi looked around, then smirked triumphantly, raking in the money.

Cards were flung into a heap, and hands grabbed at the assortment of treats Mrs. Morrison had made for them.

"What is it you always say about your housekeeper?" asked Milo, dragging a potato chip through a creamy dip.

Brendan laughed. "I say that Mrs. M. is better than a wife. She cooks, she cleans, then goes home."

"That's cold," said Ritchie, unable to hide his own amusement. "But she does do a good poker spread." He lit his Cuban and inhaled deeply, leaning back in his chair.

"So can we change the subject and talk about the murders at the seminary?" asked Brendan, popping a cherry tomato stuffed with cream cheese in his mouth. "My nephew is freaking out, and my niece is trying to help the deputy who got this case since abandoning her vacation."

"Okay, so tell the guys about that room you and Aiden found." Ezra slapped at Langdon's hand as the man tried to purloin a wing from the rabbi's plate.

Brendan relayed the story about the secret room and the photo to his friends. "I can't say the photo is any kind of clue, but just finding that room with lights on and no dust anywhere—that speaks volumes to me." He gave an involuntary shudder, remembering the eeriness of the room. "The place had a bunch of old theological texts, yellowed letters, and a brittle manuscript with the same prophecy the killer had been following to the letter. That alone was damning," he said. "These weren't some obscure verses stumbled upon in a library. Someone's been using that room to do mischief, and how they found out about it is a mystery to me."

Ritchie and Milo exchanged wide-eyed glances, their mouths slightly open, frozen in stunned silence at the eerie description.

Brendan added, "And one of the guys in the photo seems so familiar. I just need to find out who M.M. is."

"Hey, maybe it's the killer's lair?" asked Ritchie, raising an eyebrow. "And what about all the stuff you found in that mausoleum?" He turned to Milo, laughing. "Does this killer have *two* lairs now? What is he, a Batman villain? One creepy hideout isn't enough? Maybe he keeps one for plotting and one for storing all the weird junk he collects, you know, trophies from his kills, like I hear about on all these murder shows." He paused, the smile fading. "Or maybe the mausoleum's for ritual and the secret room is for reality. Public performance in the mausoleum, private obsession in the room. That's even creepier, isn't it?"

The group suddenly stopped what they were doing and stared at their friend.

"What?" Ritchie asked.

"Since when did you get so morbid?" asked Ezra, staring at the young minister.

Ritchie laughed. "Probably from you guys! You're the ones always inserting yourselves into these murders. I'm just an observer, observing."

"Well, certainly *someone* knows about that room," said Brendan, lightening the mood. "And someone knows what's going on over there and may be protecting the murderer." He let out a groan, "Guess I'm going back there and look around some more." He drew the cigar smoke into his mouth, holding it for a moment, savoring the flavor of the illegal contraband before exhaling slowly. "I'll have to let the rector know what I know. He *must* know about that room, and maybe what's going on inside that mausoleum. He's been there for ages."

"Don't be steppin' on no one's toes, bro," said Langdon. He nodded over at Ezra. "Me and the little dude can help you, you know."

Brendan nodded. "Thanks, guys." He paused, rubbing the stubble on his bearded chin. "I pray it isn't one of the seminarians. A *seminarian*? That's too awful to even think about. These are young men who came because God called them to a higher standard of life. They are literally giving their entire lives to serve God." His shoulders sagged. "It's too awful to think about, but at the moment, the best candidates are the Kenyan kid and Caruso. He's the one with the scratches on his face and neck, claiming they came from shaving."

"How about that weird guy, Marcus something-or-another?" quipped Ezra. "He's more believable as a murderer than one of those boys. And that horrible dog that follows him around all the time." He gave a visible shudder.

"True, but I hadn't really noticed his hands until we went with Mo to his house, which incidentally, got broken into, and he's horribly gnarled from arthritis. He'd have a lot of trouble pulling back the string on a bow or strangle a fit young man, but I guess it could be done—if he really wanted to do it."

The men murmured in agreement, their voices low and unified.

"How about the rector?" inquired Ezra. "He's a bit...odd...and didn't it sound like he didn't care for those two boys? I mean, he *is* old and probably getting a little senile. Maybe he didn't mean to kill them, but one thing led to another, and before he knew it, he was just having a bad day. You know, like when the coffee machine breaks, your favorite TV show gets canceled, and then suddenly, you're knocking people off." Ezra flailed his arms wildly, barely managing to stay in his chair.

Langdon stared at his friend, a piece of chicken wing dangling from his open mouth. "You kiddin' me, little man? He kilt them 'cause he were havin' a bad day?"

Ezra looked over at Brendan, who was trying hard to keep from laughing. "I was just trying to help."

"And you're a big help, Ezra," said Brendan, "but we still have nothing substantial that leads us to a killer."

"Okay, so who are your suspects?" asked Ritchie. "Start with that."

Brendan nodded. "Good thinking, Ritchie." He glanced at Ezra. "Wish we had your murder board here, Rabbi."

Langdon groaned.

Brendan ignored his friend. "Let's see…well, my nephew Aiden is clear, and then—"

"Whoa," cried Milo. "Why are you excluding him? Wasn't he the one who 'found' both bodies?" He made air quotes with his fingers.

"True," acknowledged Brendan, "but I know my nephew."

"Still…" insisted Milo.

"Okay, okay," said Brendan, raising his palms in obeisance. "Aiden's on the list. Then there's Manuel Bautista, the Filipino kid. Maureen told me Joseph used to follow Manuel around, questioning his faith, and now she said the boys told her Manuel's doing the same thing to them. And supposedly he's got no problem holding his own in an argument, but still, I can't see him committing those acts." He raised his eyes to the ceiling. "And Daniel Caruso—he's not a big guy, but out of all of that group, he seems pretty feisty and capable of inflicting pain if the situation arose. And he seems pretty pompous for a seminarian, very self-serving."

"Anyone else?" asked Milo.

"That young man from Kenya. His first name is Okeyo, but I can't remember how to say his last name. He was taken in for questioning after Aiden found Matthew's Bible and a blood-stained handkerchief in his jacket."

"You think *he* did it? Or at least one of the murders?" asked Ritchie, relishing a sip of the Irish whiskey.

Brendan rubbed the tip of his nose. "Hard to say. I mean, so far, he's the one who got caught with the goods. He's not denying it but not exactly confessing either. Did he have something against one or both boys? I can't say. He seems self-deprecating, quiet, and a little standoffish, but I've also heard he's got quite the temper and has gotten into it with some of the other boys. And Marcus Dean did say he was *very* adept with his archery skills."

Brendan paused momentarily, searching his brain. "And that Saint Anna Wang medal...my nephew said he didn't see it on Joseph Lin when he found his body, and that the Kenyan boy and that Wingate kid each sported one. But when Maureen and Caleb questioned them, they each swore that Joseph had given them one. And, of course, Okeyo's from a different culture, so that could be where I'm getting my perception of him. The police questioned him after they found all that stuff in his room but let him go for now."

"So that's it so far," added Ezra, brushing crumbs from the table onto the floor.

Langdon took his shot. "Yeah, an' we gonna pull out the little dude's murder board that he made up for the las' murder we done had." He reached over to pinch the rabbi's bearded cheek. "This little man got real talent when it comes to drawin'."

Ezra slapped the big man's hand away.

"Well, I, for one," said Brendan, "thought it was a huge help, and I think we'll be using it again." He gave Ezra an approving nod. "But let's continue with our list of potential suspects."

The men stopped talking, and the room became silent.

"Okay, winding up our thin line of potential killers...there's Eugene Wingate—a very strange boy—not sure how he got the calling to be a priest, but nothing really ties him to any of the murders, other than his weird personality. And the last potential suspect's name is Nathan something. He's *very* quiet and very unassuming. He appears to be the one always trying to calm the group down when they're arguing about the murders."

"Well, there you go," said Ritchie. "It's the quiet ones who are usually the murderers. Nathan gets my vote."

That caused the group to go into another fit of whiskey-induced laughter, lightening the conversation.

The men then stood, stretched, and headed for the door.

Brendan reached for his cane. "I know these murders won't be solved overnight, but for the souls of these poor boys and their families, I pray it'll be soon."

He swung open the utility room door, and Mary Magdalene darted inside with a yowling Saint Peter hot on her heels. The feline's eyes locked onto a few stray morsels under the rickety table, and he pounced on them with unbridled enthusiasm.

"Dude," screamed Langdon, nearly tripping over the cat, "don't that cat ever settle down? Sweet Jesus, Lord of all, that animal gonna be the death o' me!"

Ezra pushed his friend out of the utility room door with his hip. "Come on, it's a cat and you're as big as Goliath. Stop being so scared of God's creatures. Honestly, a guy your size scared of a cat? Next thing you know, you'll be running from squirrels and demanding an exorcism for a goldfish."

Brendan rounded up his friends, chatting with them as they donned their coats and caps and left the rectory.

As he closed the door, Brendan's mind quickly reverted to the murders. Deciding to leave the mess in the utility room for the following day, he let Mary Magdalene out one last time, then made his way upstairs and to his bedroom.

After a long, hot shower, he slipped into a pair of flannel pajamas, a gift from his older sister, Róisín, the sister who always ensured the gifts she showered her baby brother with were functional rather than frivolous or fun.

He dragged his hand across the fogged-up bathroom mirror, streaking away the condensation. As his reflection emerged, he stared back at himself, searching for something—answers, clarity, or just a face he still recognized.

The staring contest lasted for several minutes as he debated what he would do next. Slowly opening the cabinet, his eyes fell once again on the numerous amber bottles of pills neatly arranged on the shelves inside. Tonight, his eyes rested on the Xanax. He longed to put the murders of the two young men out of his mind and trade his anxiety for a good night's sleep.

He chewed his lower lip until a tooth took a little too much flesh, breaking his thoughts. Giving in, he snatched the vial from its place, unscrewed the cap, and tapped out some pills. They went easily into his mouth as he downed them with a glass of water.

Closing the cabinet door, he felt good about the possibility of finally getting a good night's sleep but also hated himself for his one weakness.

Two more innocent deaths, he thought. What was happening in the small town of Porter Mills? The most the sheriff's department ever usually had to deal with were dog bites and a few drunks on a Saturday night. But now, murders seemed to be on the rise. Senseless murders, but murders with no clear motive, and no viable suspects that stood out.

He left the bathroom and slipped into bed. Calling for Mary Magdalene, he waited, but it was Saint Peter who reached the bedside first, leaping gracefully onto the bedspread. Brendan gently lifted the tiny dog onto the covers and watched as the two animals found their spots and readied themselves for a long, peaceful sleep, for which Brendan envied them.

Reaching for his breviary, he prayed for around half an hour, then grabbed his favorite puzzle book and opened it to the last crossword that had practically given him a migraine. He looked at number thirty-two down and pursed his lips in disgust.

"What's an eleven-letter word describing a leather case or pocket worn by cavalry on the left side, suspended from the sword belt?" He slammed the book shut and flung it across the room. Saint Peter shot off the bed like a missile and vanished down the stairs. "Saint Augustine is easier to understand than that drivel."

Yawning, he found the Xanax blissfully taking effect, his only concern being whether he'd wake in time to celebrate daily Mass.

Sleep claimed Brendan, but peace never followed. He tossed and turned through the night, trapped in the ghosts of Iraq—seeing, hearing, and feeling it all over again. The things he had witnessed during his time as a Marine in the Gulf War continually haunted him, and the things he had done refused to let him go.

CHAPTER 24

Wednesday Morning

Maureen woke before her alarm. She glanced at the clock and grimaced, imagining her friends still asleep after a night of dancing, drinking, and general debauchery, while she was stuck in Porter Mills, helping solve a pair of murders.

Sitting on the edge of the bed, she reached for her phone, checking for a text from Simon. Smiling, she discovered his sweet words and laughed at the emojis. Feeling refreshed and in good spirits, she got up, dressed, and was ready to meet with Caleb and see what new information he had uncovered, praying that he had discovered something that would wrap this case up quickly.

Maureen's happiness was short-lived as she filled her travel mug with coffee. With Marcus Dean eliminated for now, the suspects narrowed to the seminarians present during the times of the murders, along with Father Gabriel. Right now, Okeyo Masamba looked promising, and Daniel Caruso, with his ridiculous tale of shaving accidents, wasn't far behind.

Just another day in paradise, she thought, but then remembered—paradise was thousands of miles away, and she wasn't there.

After morning Mass, Father Gabriel sat at the staff dining table, absently pushing his breakfast around the plate. The weight of the secrets he carried churned in his stomach, making each bite feel impossible.

He scanned the handful of seminarians who remained in the building, glad the majority had gone to help out their home parishes, while others were off on retreat. He wondered if any of the young men could ever imagine the knowledge he possessed regarding Saint Charles, the many years of secrets he had been forced to keep. He prayed they never found out, and that went for the police, too.

This seminary *had* to remain open, but still, these deaths *had* to be resolved, and soon. The archdiocese, along with that infernal archbishop, Malachy O'Clery, had succeeded in closing several churches and schools in the Baltimore area, leaving the faithful angry and brokenhearted simultaneously. Saint Charles could be next on the chopping block, and unless the killer was stopped, it would happen sooner rather than later.

Because the morning's temperature had plummeted, Brendan decided to greet his daily Mass attendees inside the church.

"Father, that was an outstanding sermon today," quipped Frank Angelino as he pumped Brendan's arm. His wife, Edna, tapped her foot impatiently.

"So, Edna, any thoughts on the message today? The woman caught in adultery—'Let he who is without sin cast the first stone.'"

Edna Angelino crossed her arms over her ample chest, her posture as firm as her opinions. "Yes, Father. I have *one* question. Where exactly was the *man* in all this? She didn't commit adultery by herself."

"Here we go again," sighed Frank.

Brendan laughed. "Fair point, Edna. Scripture does leave out a few... interesting details."

"Mmm-hmm. And I noticed the crowd dropped their stones pretty fast. Very touching." She turned and glared at her husband, who was eyeing an attractive younger woman. "Except someone here was gripping *his* like it was the last biscuit at the church picnic."

Frank gave his wife a mock look of hurt. "I was just making sure my aim was good—for spiritual purposes."

"Spiritual, my foot." She uncrossed her arms and pushed a stray hair away from her face. "Anyway, I liked the part where Jesus bent down and wrote in the dust. Probably scribbling the names of *every man in town* who needed to mind their own business."

"Or maybe he was doodling while he waited for people to realize throwing rocks isn't a good hobby," added Frank.

Edna grabbed his arm and dragged him away.

"Hey, you're pulling too hard on my reins. My soul's a little like my car. It runs better with a little grease and a lot of prayer."

Brendan laughed at the couple but was grateful for the faithful few who made the sacrifice each day to come to church and worship God.

After the last parishioner had exited the church, he glanced at his watch. His plans for the morning were to meet with Father Gabriel regarding the secret room, then pick up Langdon and head over to Ezra's house so they could redo Ezra's now famous stick-figure murder board.

"No time for breakfast today, Mrs. M.," cried Brendan as he dashed into the rectory to pick up his jacket and Mary Magdalene.

The housekeeper gave him a lazy glance as she continued drying a glass. "You told me yesterday you were meeting with your former teacher, then going to Rabbi Lieberman's house. So, no breakfast was made."

Brendan slapped a hand to his forehead as if trying to physically erase the absurdity of the moment. "You're right, Mrs. M. I totally forgot I had told you. Sorry." He gave her a sheepish grin. "And I'm not sure how long I'll be or what the rest of my day looks like."

Mrs. Morrison set the glass down on the counter and turned to him. "Did you forget about that outreach program your brother wanted you to help Father Tim with?"

"I didn't forget," said Brendan, emitting an exasperated sigh. "I'm just giving it a well-deserved time out for a bit."

The housekeeper gave a cheery laugh and returned to drying the dishes. "Just the same, I'm making a casserole in case you decide to come back to the roost tonight."

Grabbing a dog leash, he passed by the housekeeper, planting a chaste kiss on her cheek. "Have I ever told you I'm the envy of all Maryland priests because of *you*, Mrs. M.?"

She pushed him away, laughing. "Get out of here, you, and try to behave yourself."

Brendan gave her a mock salute, and after grabbing a chocolate chip cookie from the cookie jar, he and Mary Magdalene made their way out to the car and headed toward the seminary.

As he parked, he watched several seminarians, books in hand, walking about, chatting—the memories stirred by these visions tugged at him, and a slow smile began to form on his face.

He grabbed his cane from the back seat and gave the tiny dog a loving pat along with a stern warning. "Now you behave yourself. I'll be back as soon as I can." He ruffled her fur again, knocking the frilly pink bow off her head.

Locking the door, he made his way to the main building.

"Good morning, Father," greeted the seminarians who passed him.

He was glad he'd kept his clerical garments on after Mass, though he felt the sin of pride creeping in as he basked in the quiet prestige of being a seasoned priest among boys only beginning their journey. As he walked down the hallowed hallways, he chided himself for his vanity and murmured a prayer of humility.

Knocking on the rector's door, he entered, finding the old priest sitting in a chair, gazing out the window.

"Watching the leaves blow off the trees, Father?" quipped Brendan, as he reached out to shake Father Gabriel's proffered hand.

The rector smiled glibly and motioned for Brendan to take the empty seat across from him. "No, just watching the season change, as I've been watching the seasons in my life change." He moved his eyes over to Brendan. "And now, when I should be enjoying the fruits of my labor, I have two murders within these hallowed grounds to contend with." He looked down at his hands, wringing them like a man trying to pray the guilt away. "So what brings you here today, son? You sounded serious over the phone."

Brendan's mood darkened, uncertain as to how to approach the subject, but then he thought the direct way was best, so he hit the rector with what he had discovered, leaving out his nephew's complicity.

He watched his former teacher closely and could've sworn he saw a sudden jerk, barely perceptible, yet impossible to miss, like a wire snapping beneath the surface. Father Gabriel remained stoic.

"My hand hit that lever, and when I moved it around, the back panel suddenly opened."

Still no movement from the rector, yet Brendan watched as the blood drained out of the wizened face.

"That room is still being utilized, Father. We—I—found shelf upon shelf with several rows of vintage books and a box containing old photos of Saint Charles." His eyes drilled into the rector's, assessing his demeanor. "I found this among the photos. It was the only one with people in it."

He thrust the photo in front of the priest. The old man jumped as if a jolt of electricity had just gone through him.

"I know this is you, but who are the other young men, and what was, or *is*, the purpose of that room?" His hand remained holding the photograph, forcing the priest to look at it.

For several painful moments, Father Gabriel stared at the young faces, then ran a finger over the entire image, as though he were trying to bring the scene to life.

"Talk to me, Father," urged Brendan. "I'm here as a friend, not your enemy."

As the rector looked up, Brendan saw tears forming in the old man's rheumy eyes. "These lads were students of mine. A long time ago. They're priests now, and some may even be dead."

"So what are their names?" He pointed to the one who reminded him of someone. "Especially this one. Who's M.M.?"

The rector turned away, sniffing, as he reached into his pocket for a handkerchief. "I can't remember names. There have been so many." He looked up at Brendan, his eyes red. "And as for that room,"—he gave a defeated sigh—"you'll have to remember that the Archdiocese of Baltimore was established in 1808, and it took all that time to get this seminary to become a reality. That was back in 1845, thanks to the Dean family's money. It was designed and built during a time when the tensions that would eventually lead to the Civil War were beginning to simmer. The designers anticipated problems if the country went to war. However, they had no idea of what those problems would entail, but it was agreed upon that a secret passage would be built into the place."

He wiped his nose as Brendan waited, his senses heightened on hearing this extraordinary news.

"Over the years the passage leading off the grounds had collapsed, so right around World War I, the rector at that time thought it prudent to wall it up, leaving just a room, and that maybe that room could be a sort of archives where all our important documents and memorabilia could be stored."

Brendan had so many questions. "So who knows about it? Or should I ask, how many are *supposed* to know about it? Do the students know?"

Father Gabriel slashed the air with an angry hand, his brows furrowing into a dark scowl. "Knock it off, Father. I feel as though you're badgering me. Each rector assigned here just used it to store things, archival-type things. Nothing of great value."

"Well, gosh," Brendan began sarcastically, "two of your seminarians *have* been murdered, and I have a sneaking feeling that that room plays an important part in it." He added, "And I believe that photograph has some kind of meaning, or else why would it still be around?" He sat back in his chair. "Don't forget, I have a nephew who attends here, and I do *not* want him to be the next victim."

"I can't tell you what I don't know. The secret location of that place has only been passed down from rector to rector. No one else should know of it."

"Yet I found it the first time I sat in there," interrupted Brendan. He stood, reaching for his cane. He knew the police would have to be told of this finding, but he kept that to himself. He didn't want to give the rector time to clean up or hide anything that might be considered as evidence. "Father, I think the students will probably be questioned again. Maybe one of them found that lever as easily as I did, and that person just might be our murderer."

Father Gabriel also stood, hanging onto the back of the chair for support. "You think you're so smart! That room is sacrosanct and must not be disturbed!" He shook his free hand at Brendan, clenching it into a fist.

Brendan stopped and turned to face the rector. "Father, if you're with-holding information that could help us catch whoever murdered those boys, then I hope your jail cell comes with stained glass and incense, because it's about to become *your* new 'sacrosanct' place of worship." He exited the room without waiting for a response.

Brendan fumed as he walked to his car. Even Mary Magdalene's joy in seeing her master didn't improve his mood. Slamming the door after he got in, he sat in silence, vowing to share with Maureen what he had discovered so far so she and her fellow deputies could find out what secrets that room held.

Turning the ignition, he drove in silence to Langdon's house, racking his brain as to the clues the room could hold.

Ezra had dragged out his trusty murder board that had served them so well when they were helping Maureen solve Porter Mills previous murders. Balancing it on a kitchen chair, he studied his primitive drawings, his hands resting on his hips.

"They can make fun of me all they want," he groused, remembering how Langdon had tormented him regarding his depictions of each subject. "This board helped crack those cases."

Hearing the doorbell, he quickly ripped the old drawings from the board and threw them into the trash.

"You guys are early," he called out as he opened the door, stunned to see someone other than his two friends. Leah Goldstein stood calmly in the doorway, eyes expectant, as if waiting for him to invite her in. His mouth opened, but for a second, no words came. He glanced around, confused as to where his friends were. He gaped at Leah as she waited for an invitation to enter.

"Rabbi? May I come in? I need to speak with you."

Finally, remembering his manners, Ezra shook his head as if to return him to the present. "I'm sorry, Leah. Yes, please, come in." He gestured with a quick sweep of his arm, still trying to catch up to the surprise of her arrival.

He showed her into the kitchen, where he pulled up a chair and motioned for her to sit. He caught her glancing at the murder board and was embarrassed to see he had forgotten to remove one of his sketches, the one of a woman lying prone, very much deceased.

Steering her away from any uncomfortable questions, he asked, "So what brings you here, Leah?" He added hastily, "And could I offer you something to drink?"

Taking a seat, she tucked a stray hair behind her ear. "Well, my uncle is in the hospital and has pneumonia—the doctor says they're doing their best to get as much fluid out of him as they can, but it doesn't look good—"

"Leah, I'm so sorry," interrupted Ezra. "What can I do to help?"

Leah took in a deep breath. "Rabbi, he's a hundred and two and we're not looking for him to come out of this. I just wanted to give you a heads up and let you know to start preparing for a funeral."

Ezra's face took on a serious demeanor. "Of course, Leah." He thought for a moment, then asked, "Does your uncle have a tallit? If not, we can get him one."

Leah gave a weak laugh. "Rabbi, my uncle must have a dozen. He collected prayer shawls from all his travels. He has several from the Holy Land."

This made Ezra laugh. "Good, good." He slipped back into his rabbinical demeanor. "Then let me know approximately how many family members may be attending and if any of them want to participate in the service. And, of course, when the time comes, our *chevra kadisha* will perform the tahara, cleanse the body, and dress it for burial. Also, if you're planning to sit shiva, I can help you out with that." He made a mental note to gather more information to give to Leah at a later date. "And again, Leah, I hope your uncle had a fulfilling life and that the afterlife, when his time comes, will be even richer for him."

"Thanks, Rabbi Lieberman," said Leah, rising. "I'll keep you posted. He belonged to a synagogue in New Jersey, but the last few years, he's been in a nursing home here in Maryland, so that's why I'd like the funeral to be at our synagogue."

Ezra also rose and led Leah to the door. "That's fine. It will be my honor to perform his funeral when the time comes."

"Thanks. See you soon."

Ezra opened the door to let the woman out. On the other side stood Brendan and Langdon—Langdon's hand frozen midair, poised to knock.

Leah's breath caught, and Ezra quickly put her at ease.

"Leah, these are my friends: Father Brendan O'Clery and Pastor Langdon Boothe." He pointed to the Yorkie that Leah was already making friends with. "And this is Mary Magdalene. Guys, this is Leah Goldstein, one of my congregants."

Everyone acknowledged each other in greeting as Leah slipped past them and left. Brendan and Langdon then pushed their way into the house, heading for the kitchen. Brendan went to the cabinet containing plastic bowls and filled one with water for Mary Magdalene.

Langdon went right for the refrigerator, grabbing a bottled water. "Dang, little man! That the next Miz Lieberman? She all right! You ain't gettin' no younger, so's you better make your move." He unscrewed the cap and took a swig.

Ezra's head tilted, and he placed his hands on his hips, staring at the gigantic Baptist in disbelief. "I don't believe you, you *yutz*. Leah Goldstein?"

Brendan watched them. "Honestly, Ezra," he began, "she's very attractive. Is she single?"

"You two are unbelievable. The poor woman was here to make funeral arrangements."

Langdon poked Brendan with his elbow. "A widow gal! Perfect, little dude. Go on with your bad self." He set the water on the table and took a seat.

Brendan followed suit, leaving Ezra stunned, hands still firmly planted on hips. He didn't even bother to correct them that it was her *uncle* dying, not her husband.

"Unbelievable," repeated Ezra, then pulled out a chair and took his place at the table. "Can we get on with why we're here?"

Langdon reached over the table and patted Ezra's cheek. "Yo, let's dip. Board's ready, right?"

"And if either of you makes fun of it, I'm kicking you both out."

Brendan gave Langdon a wounded look. "Okay, okay, let's just get this over with, and maybe get out of here for lunch."

Ezra turned the board around, ripping off the last sketch and replacing it with more stick figures, these representing the seminarians as well as Father Gabriel.

Langdon couldn't help but let out a snarky laugh.

Ezra's brows knit tightly together. "What did I just say?"

Langdon pressed his lips together, shoulders rising in a quick shrug, his dark eyes wide with barely contained amusement. He looked like he was fighting the urge to burst into laughter.

Ezra chewed on his bottom lip, choosing to ignore his friend.

Brendan quickly changed the tone of the meeting. "So, let's check out Rembrandt Lieberman's sketches here…ah, I see they're pretty much all the same, except this time around the rabbi put names over their heads."

Ezra gave a dismissive *hmph*, arms crossed like a fortress. "Well, those boys all look alike, all dressed in black. Can we just go with what I've got here?"

"I ain't sayin' nuthin'," said Langdon, looking around the room innocently.

"Then let's start with the Kenyan boy, Okeyo." Brendan stood, reaching for his cane. He walked over to the board. "Okeyo had Matthew Mueller's Bible and that bloody handkerchief stuffed into a jacket. Plus, Marcus Dean said that several of the boys would come to his place and shoot arrows, and supposedly, Okeyo was way above average in the sport. And remember, when he was brought in for questioning and confronted with the two murders, he remained calm, and while he never confessed to anything, he said the murders were his responsibility—his words, not mine."

"So what do you think? That he did it? Maureen said the guys all told her the kid has a bad temper." Ezra walked over with a colored marker and wrote what Brendan had just said over the stick figure of Okeyo. When he heard a sarcastic snicker from Langdon, he turned and glared at the man.

Brendan shrugged nonchalantly. "Hard to say. It's still unfathomable to think that a seminarian could kill *anyone*, let alone another seminarian. But human nature *is* human after all. I mean, he never explained how those items got into his room. Did he take them as souvenirs, or were they planted there to obscure the real killer?"

"Good points, bro," quipped Langdon, reaching down to pet Mary Magdalene. "Next."

Brendan laughed at his friend's impatience. "Okay, Eugene Wingate. Aiden said he saw that Anna Wang medal on him, too, like Okeyo. Everyone says he's a little on the strange side, but no one can expound on that. It's 'just a feeling' they say. He supposedly has weird dreams and premonitions. Weird doesn't make you a killer, though."

Ezra laughed. "That's a good thing, otherwise Pastor Boothe here would be in real trouble."

"Go on, little man. You be sleepin' with one eye open t'night."

"NEXT," said Brendan loudly, and pointed to another picture. "Nathan Silk. Aiden says he's another first-year student and appears to be fairly intelligent and is usually the mediator when he sees his fellow students arguing or fighting. He's also known to be quiet and mostly keeps to himself."

"Ain't he the pasty white boy, kinda…" Langdon spread his arms denoting girth. "He be eatin' double portions at his meals."

"Sounds like a murderer to me," said Ezra. "My money's on him."

Brendan continued, ignoring him. "So now we come to Manuel Bautista, the Filipino kid. Also a first-year student, and again, a smart boy, devout, but also likes to spar with his friends and gets into frequent squabbles."

He pointed with his cane to the next sketch. "Daniel Caruso." Brendan sighed. "Aiden says this boy goes looking for a fight, and not always the verbal kind. He's pretty argumentative, and most of the boys try to keep their distance." He stopped for a moment, reached into his pocket and pulled out a handkerchief, just in time to catch a loud sneeze. "Excuse me. And don't forget, he had several scratches on his face and neck. That's usually a telltale sign that someone's been in a scuffle with someone trying to protect themselves." He stuffed the handkerchief back in his pocket. "He's in his second year, and I guess he thinks he's the greatest thing to come through that seminary"—he looked at each of his friends, a smile spreading across his face—"and we all know that title belongs to me."

Ezra and Langdon made loud gagging noises, and Ezra capped it off by lobbing a crumpled paper ball at the priest's head.

"All right, all right," said Brendan, laughing, his palms out in appeasement. "So other than my nephew, there's the staff, but at the top of my list next to Okeyo is Father Vincent Gabriel." Brendan went back to his seat and laid his cane against the table. "He may not be the actual murderer, but it seems like each time I speak with him, he gets more defensive, like he knows more than he's letting on. He's a good man and a devout priest, but he's always been the secretive sort, you know? Like with his love of the drink. And I know he's getting on in age, but my spidey-sense keeps screaming at me. And Okeyo sure does stick up for him, almost like he's got a worship jones."

"You thinkin' that ol' white man kilt them boys and the Kenyan kid helped him, or at least is protecting him?"

Brendan pulled at his beard. "I don't know, Langdon," he said, and relayed to them what happened when he went to confront the rector with the photo and the hidden room. His eyes roamed aimlessly across the ceiling. "He's hell-bent on saving that seminary, and who knows the lengths he'd go to, to keep it open, even though rumor has it the archdiocese wants to shut it down."

"The archdiocese, meaning your brother?" asked Ezra.

"Ezra, he *is* the archdiocese, and if he wants Saint Charles gone, then it's as good as gone." Brendan sighed and added, "Although he'll likely wait until his nephew is ordained and then shut the doors."

For a while, they all sat in silence.

"Hey, what about social media, Bren? I know how you like to snoop around and dig up stuff. Have you looked to see what these boys are up to?" Ezra grinned and gave Langdon a look of superiority.

Brendan laughed. "You know I did! And Aiden, my junior spy, told me that first-year students are supposed to give up all social media, including phones, but as far as I could tell, they all have them. Bautista has a Spotify playlist where some of the songs have pretty strong language. The others were similar, nothing torrid, as far as Aiden could find out." His forehead wrinkled in thought. "He did say that Nathan Silk's page was pretty sad. His older brother committed suicide, and the Wingate kid had several quotes from atheists like Stephen Hawking, Carl Sagan, and Carl Jung. That might spark concern about orthodoxy without being directly heretical, but not much that would point to being a killer. And the kid from Kenya had no social media presence at all, and his cell was clean." He paused for a moment, then said, "What I really need is to get hold of these kids' files, but they're all sitting in the rector's office. I'd need a plan." He looked at his friends, grinning.

"Bren, that would be awesome," exclaimed Ezra. "We could be your decoys." He nodded to Langdon.

"I have some ideas already," said Brendan. "It may not be ethical to bring my niece into it just yet, but my nephew will be a more than willing assistant, and with you guys involved, too, we'll soon have the murderer served up on a silver platter."

Langdon burst into a harsh, guttural laugh. "Hoo-ee! You be gettin' that boy kicked outta that place, for sure!"

"Don't listen to the big guy," said Ezra. "Do what you have to, to solve these murders." He stuck his tongue out at the big Baptist.

"Jes' sayin'," Langdon said, laughing as he extricated himself from his chair and went to the refrigerator, opening the door and scouring the contents. "Didn' that gal leave you no food, little man?"

"I can't believe you're hungry again," groused Ezra. "You said you had eggs, pancakes, and sausage for breakfast."

"Hey, the good Lord done gave me a massive app-tite, and I ain't 'bout to waste it. I don't jes' eat—I *fellowship* with my food." Grumbling about the lack of decent food in Ezra's fridge, he grabbed an orange, gave it a contemptuous glare, and closed the door.

Ezra stared at his friend, purposely waiting for him to take his seat and peel his orange. "Did you bring that riddle with you, Bren? Maybe we can take a look at it again," he said to Brendan.

Brendan reached into his shirt pocket and pulled out a folded paper. "Here," he said, handing it over to the rabbi. "I made several copies. You can put this up on your board as evidence."

After tacking the paper to the board, Ezra read the riddle out loud:

"When the shepherd is blind, the flock shall bleed.
A serpent coils within the house of God, its fangs in the hearts
of the chosen.

Three shall fall before the dawn of reckoning.
One by the hand of judgment, one by the weight of sin, and one
by the fire of truth."

"So who's supposed to be the shepherd and who's the flock? And why does the entire flock have to bleed?" Ezra stared at his friends. "Does that mean the shepherd is the killer and the flock are the seminarians? Yikes."

"That second line be the same. Talks 'bout a serpent in the house o' God—*that's* the killer! And them chosen with fangs in 'em? They be the seminarians!"

Brendan buried his face in his hands. "Yes, and it talks about three falling. I'm thinking of having Maureen get Aiden out of there. He needs to be removed from the seminary for his own safety, away from the killer."

Ezra put a hand on his friend's shoulder. "We'll get this person before they get to Aiden, Bren." He looked at Langdon for help. "We have God on our side, right?" He pushed his glasses up the bridge of his nose.

Just then, Langdon jumped out of his seat, causing Ezra to jump. "Yes, Lord Jesus, Father God! We get this devil-killer 'cause we got Jeeee-zus! He be God all by hisself—don' need no help! I serve a God who spesh-lizes in the impossible! The grave couldn' hold him, no, and the devil cain't stop him!"

Ezra froze at the sight of the huge Baptist dancing about, shouting at the top of his lungs. He gripped Brendan's shoulder hard, causing the priest to laugh.

"Hey, at least he's on board with helping get this maniac. And it could be worse."

Ezra looked at Brendan. "And how could it be worse?" He placed his fists defiantly on his hips.

Brendan leaned in and whispered, "He could have grabbed your yarmulke and thrown it onto your highest cabinet." He laughed when he saw Ezra look up at a cabinet he would never be able to reach.

After Langdon finished his extemporaneous worship and praise session, the three clergy decided they had had enough of murder and decided that with no motive for either boys' murder, they were no further along in finding their killer.

CHAPTER 25

Wednesday Afternoon

The confessional was stifling. Father Gabriel sat, still as a stone except for the glance he cast at his watch. Minutes ticked by like a slow drumbeat, each second dragging on like a sermon gone too long. Something wasn't right. Where was that irritating person?

No sooner had he rechecked his watch than he heard the door creak open. The confessional was finally occupied. Sliding the screen open, he exhaled in relief.

"What took you so long? I can't be seen with you, and I have a staff meeting in half an hour."

The figure on the other side apologized. "So let's get going. I have a schedule, too."

Father Gabriel closed the screen back and deftly toggled the lever that opened the entranceway to the secret corridor. He entered it, then held the panel back for the other person.

"Hurry up," he urged.

"Don't rush me, Father."

The priest turned to them. "You've crossed a line you can't uncross, and now I'm left cleaning up the wreckage. If these murders don't end right now, this seminary will be closed for good, and when that happens, you'll wish you only had God to answer to."

The person hesitated, casting a wary glance over his shoulder, then followed Father Gabriel through the hidden door, vanishing into the dim corridor beyond, swallowed by the shadows.

When they came to the room, Father Gabriel opened the box full of old photographs of the seminary. He gave the figure an icy glare as he set the top of the box aside. "They have that photo and are passing it around. You've gone too far, and I can only think of one way this can end."

WEDNESDAY LUNCHTIME

Brendan's time mulling over potential murder suspects had passed in a blur of friendly banter, underscored by the quiet weight of death lingering at the edge of his thoughts.

After bidding his friends farewell, he got into his battered Honda and headed to his office, going over various ways to extricate the suspect seminarians' folders from Father Gabriel's office.

A few quiet moments slipped by as he passed corn field after corn field, the crops now reduced to ragged stubs, cut down after the harvest by huge farm implements.

Suddenly, his quietude was dissolved as his cell phone rang. Noting the name on the caller ID, Brendan immediately felt a headache coming on.

"I know why you're calling," he answered gruffly. "I haven't had time to—"

"Just shut it for a minute," interrupted the archbishop. "I know you're taking care of our nephew, and I want you to continue, although I can't say I'm happy about you poking your nose into police business—again—but Father Tim is expecting you this afternoon."

"But I never—"

"Shut—*up*. Dear God, but you test my patience. Anyway, I had my assistant call him, and you have a three o'clock appointment with him. And Brendan, you'd better be there, or your entire vocation will be terminated on the spot."

"You can't—" But Brendan found himself speaking to the air. He tossed the phone on the passenger seat, his mood darkened. He needed to check in on Aiden and speak with Maureen to see if she and Caleb had discovered anything new.

After arriving at the rectory's office, he used the facilities, then picked up Mary Magdalene's leash, attaching it to the little dog. He grabbed a bottled water from the fridge and, before leaving, went over to the window, shaking the curtain, yelling for Saint Peter to come down from his climbing. Unfortunately, the cat only let out a wicked meow and scooted further up the curtain.

"Then stay there, you *eejit*," grumbled Brendan, as he picked up Mary Magdalene and left.

Forty-five minutes later, he arrived at Saint Ann's, a parish just outside the Baltimore city limits. After allowing Mary Magdalene a few minutes to relieve herself, he scooped her up and knocked on Father Timothy Mahoney's rectory door. He got no response. He raised his hand and knocked louder. Moments later, he heard heavy footsteps approaching.

The door creaked open, revealing a woman whose rough exterior promised trouble. Her hair hung in greasy, straggled tufts around her face, like it had lost a long battle with a comb, and her small, beady eyes narrowed with suspicion. The dress she wore clung awkwardly to her body, too tight by several sizes, giving her the look of a sausage forced into its casing. She crossed her arms and glared at Brendan, blocking the doorway like a bouncer at a nightclub.

When the woman said nothing, Brendan introduced himself and explained why he was there.

The woman uncrossed her arms. "This way," she grunted, then looked at the Yorkie. "But *that* stays outside."

Brendan looked aghast. "She goes where I go. I can't put her out in this—"

"Wanda," came a weak voice from within, but somehow, it carried, echoing all the way to the front door. "That's Father O'Clery from Saint Margaret Mary's. Let him pass and let that little dog in, too. Honestly," Brendan heard the man mutter, "no need to be so nasty."

Wanda gave Brendan the iciest of glares but led him into a stale-smelling room where the wizened Father Timothy sat in a recliner, reading from a religious tract and chain-smoking.

He set his book down and tried to rise, but Brendan rushed over to him, urging him to stay seated. They shook hands, and the older priest offered him a chair. A harsh, phlegmy cough rattled from his chest.

"Pull it close, Brendan," he said, laughing. "I'm pretty deaf these days."

"Father, it's so good to see you, and you look great," said Brendan.

Father Tim gave a raspy laugh. "Now you're going to have to go to confession for lying. Here, hand me that young lady."

Brendan set Mary Magdalene on the priest's lap, and she immediately began licking his face. The old man laughed, making Brendan feel good about bringing the little dog. It did his heart good to see the old priest smiling. He looked over at the housekeeper who had remained standing, arms crossed again, looking much like an SS storm trooper.

"So, Malachy hoodwinked you into helping me start this outreach program, huh? Sly as an old fox who's been kicked off three farms and still sneaks back for leftovers." He cooed over Mary Magdalene. "I'm sorry he got you involved in this, but I'm glad you're here. I have no idea what that man wants. You know," he said, "I met Malachy decades ago at a retreat I helped organize, and even then, I knew that boy would go far, but I also thought of him as very pompous and self-important."

"That's a fair assessment," mumbled Brendan.

Father Tim laughed again, coughing up something that went directly into a yellowed handkerchief. "Aw, he's not all that bad, he just needs to get that stick from out of where the sun doesn't shine...relax a bit." His face lit up. "He should be a bit more like you, Brendan."

This amused Brendan, but he knew he was here to help this poor old priest who should have been retired a decade ago.

"If wishes were horses, Father...you know that old saying. Anyway," began Brendan, as he pulled several folded sheets of paper from his jacket, "here are some ideas I had for your outreach program." He began reading. "We can do a church thrift store. I'm sure your parishioners would be glad to donate some of their used clothing, and the money you'd make could maybe help with some repairs." He looked around at the shabby rectory and thought they'd need more than thrift store revenue to fix this place up. "And you could do a coffee shop to bring in the teens, and then I'm sure you have some nurses here that could volunteer for prenatal classes. And of course, there's always prayer ministries. Invite some of your other denominational churches over for coffee and light refreshments and talk about how you *all* can serve the community." He stopped and waited for an answer, but Father Tim was using the sputum-filled handkerchief as a tug-toy with Mary Magdalene.

"Father?" he pushed.

"This girl is just the sweetest," he said, burying his wrinkled face into the Yorkie's soft fur, knocking her pink bow askew. He looked at Brendan. "I heard you, son, and they're all good ideas, thanks. And I may have some folks in the parish that could help me with all that. Could you leave that list with me?" He giggled like a schoolgirl when the dog gave his nose a mischievous nip.

"Sure, Father. And when you get some of the people together and decide what you'd like to participate in, give me a call and I'll come talk with them." He stood, eager to escape the gloom pressing in around him.

"Sounds like a plan. And bring this one with you when you come back." He handed the dog back to Brendan. "Maybe I should get me one of them. They'd be a great companion for me."

"Over my dead body," muttered Wanda, her fleshy face contorting into a scowl that looked barely held together.

Father Tim winked at Brendan. "That could be arranged," he whispered, making Brendan laugh.

Then he realized that would only mean another murder.

He shook hands with the old priest and left, heading back to the countryside, leaving the cloying city life to others.

Returning to the rectory, Brendan picked at the pot roast Mrs. Morrison had left warming in the oven for his dinner, but his mind was otherwise occupied. Both murders nagged at him. No obvious motives and the only suspects...? *Everyone* in that seminary...and possibly someone from the outside. If he could come up with a decent motive, he'd be one step closer to narrowing down a suspect, but there was no rhyme or reason for the murders. And that riddle, or the notes left on the bodies...this was a mystery he was not going to be able to unravel, and that made him angry.

He took out the note he had made from his slacks pocket and unfolded it, studying the cryptic words again.

When the shepherd is blind, the flock shall bleed... That's what was found under Joseph's body, and *For pride—humility* was under Matthew's.

He set the note on the table, staring at the words until they tangled in his thoughts, building and churning until his brain felt ready to short-circuit. Pushing his plate away, he stood and retrieved a plastic container for the remains, popping it in the fridge. He then set the plate on the floor as he watched Mary Magdalene devour the scraps. Saint Peter jumped down from the curtain he had been trying to tackle, but by the time he made it over to the dish, the little Yorkie had licked it to a glossy, spotless shine.

Picking up the plate, he brought it to the sink, washed it clean, and set it on the rack to dry. He retrieved a clean glass from the cabinet, found the bottle of pinot a parishioner had given him, and poured himself a generous glass.

By the time he reached the living room, a familiar ache had taken hold of his bad leg. He propped his cane against the chair and lowered himself into the seat, his hand already working over his stiff leg.

Perusing the pile of books he had stacked haphazardly on the stand next to his chair, he passed up Saint Augustine's *Confessions*, Thomas Aquinas's *Summa Theological,* and Pope John Paul II's *In God's Hands*, for the new crossword and anagram book he had purchased the previous week.

Mary Magdalene stared up at him, her head tilted, giving her bow a tipsy look.

"What?" he said to the little dog. "Don't judge me on my choice of entertainment tonight." The Yorkie gave a slight whimper and found a comfortable spot by the chair, plopping down beside him.

After several hours, Brendan had worked out most of his anxieties. He'd finished three crosswords and two anagrams. This new book's puzzles were so much easier, and he only had a few more lines to finish before the fourth crossword was done. Twenty-seven down read: "A cloth merchant, referring to a person importing fabric goods from the Eastern world; merchants or traders that dealt in cloth, typically fine cloth not produced locally, like velvets, and other expensive materials."

"Bingo! I know that one! It's 'mercer'!" he yelled loudly, raising his eyes heavenward, palms together in prayer. "Thanks for your great wisdom, Lord!" His actions caused Mary Magdalene to emit a yip as he grabbed his cane, grazing her in its movement. "Sorry, girl, but now I can go to bed, but after prayers, of course."

Feeling his brain had been adequately exercised, he put the book down and picked up his breviary, praying the ancient prayers that dated back to the eleventh century—prayers that calmed his soul but not his physical pain.

Finally, after having offered his night prayers, he and Mary Magdalene ascended the stairs and began preparing for bed.

Brendan stood beneath scalding water, so hot it felt just shy of boiling. He stayed there for several minutes, letting the heat and steam clear his mind.

Two murdered seminarians, his nephew's safety, Marcus Dean, Father Gabriel, Father Timothy—he felt the familiar twinge of anxiety creeping in, and this time, prayer offered no relief. How would he be able to fix all of this?

He turned off the shower and stepped out, grabbing a towel. Wiping the steam off the medicine cabinet's mirror, he stared at his reflection, seeing the same disappointment as always. He thought of Psalm 51, the one where David proclaimed that his sins were always before him. How he could relate to David!

Lingering on the person before him, he knew only one way to diminish those sins, if only for a night. Opening the cabinet, the nighttime ritual of gazing over the amber bottles stirred something uneasy inside him. He hated himself for being so weak, but the physical and mental agony he suffered could only be quelled by what was in those bottles.

He retrieved a vial, then slammed the cabinet door shut, a grunt of self-loathing escaping him. He filled a glass with water, his hands shaking slightly as he opened a bottle, praying it would dull the ache inside.

CHAPTER 26

Wednesday Evening

Okeyo unwrapped the winter scarf from his neck as he genuflected and moved to kneel in the pew after entering the chapel that evening.

Crossing himself reverently, he bowed his head and began praying, his lips moving quickly to silent prayers. After several moments, he stood and began a slow, penitential walk up to the altar, the red sanctuary light reminding him that Jesus was present in this space. Before the towering crucifix above the altar, Okeyo fell to his knees. His face crumpled and became wet with tears.

"My Jesus," he wailed, "I am responsible for many bad things that have happened here, and I beg you for your help. I cannot carry this burden alone. Please tell me what to do." He wiped at a tear, then continued. "Two men of God are dead, and it is my fault, and my fault alone." He paused, head tilting slightly as a faint sound came from the confessional.

Raising himself, he took a few tentative steps closer to the large structure, stopping, his ears pricked. No more sounds came, yet he felt the impulse to see if someone was in there, or if they needed help.

As he got closer, he felt his heart pounding. With his hand on the handle to the priest's side, he slowly opened the door, praying another dead seminarian wouldn't fall out.

As nothing jumped out at him, he exhaled a breath he had not known he was holding. He checked each side of the confessional and, satisfied that it might have been a mouse that had taken up residence in the old chapel, he returned to prayer, walking back to the altar.

No sooner had he taken his place at the altar, than he heard the chapel door slamming shut. His heart was immediately gripped with fear, but he *had* to know who had been watching him…and possibly waiting to murder him.

He rushed to the entrance and yanked the door open. The evening air brushed over him, raising a chill he couldn't quite shake, but nothing stirred. No one was there.

Trembling, he returned to his pew and snatched up his scarf, determined to leave the space he had come to for solace. None would be found here tonight.

A rising sense of dread shadowed the short walk to the dorm, mere steps away. As he stepped inside, the warmth of the place eased his fear. Several seminarians greeted him as they scurried to the game room to watch a DVD. He acknowledged them, then quickly jogged up the stairway to the dormitory.

The hallway was quiet, the only sound the faint hum of an old radiator and the occasional groan of aged wooden floorboards.

His breath slowed as he entered his room. Light from the hallway crept under his dorm room door, casting a thin line across the floor. He threw himself onto a chair, but the feeling of doom lingered. A thought had crossed his mind earlier. It was only a thought, but if it proved to be helpful, then maybe it would stop any further murders, including his own.

Standing, he moved to his desk and retrieved the photograph the sheriff's deputies had passed out to his fellow students earlier. When the deputies had passed the photo around earlier, none of his classmates recognized the younger men—but Father Gabriel, noticeably younger in the picture, stood out immediately.

He stared at the group of young men. Who were they? Seminarians maybe? He knew the older man with thick, dark hair was Father Gabriel— that much was certain, but the boys? The M.M. in the photo had a certain familiarity. His face darkened, and he prayed that the rector…

But Okeyo refused to allow his mind to go there. Father Gabriel had been kind to him. He couldn't stop staring at the photograph. It was burrowing into his thoughts like a splinter he couldn't remove. Every time he looked away, it clawed its way back into his mind, demanding answers.

Riffling through the papers on his desk, he retrieved a copy of the riddle and studied it, reading it out loud three times, pondering every word:

> *"When the shepherd is blind, the flock shall bleed.*
> *A serpent coils within the house of God, its fangs in the hearts*
> *of the chosen.*
> *Three shall fall before the dawn of reckoning.*
> *One by the hand of judgment, one by the weight of sin, and one*
> *by the fire of truth."*

Okeyo set the riddle down, his mind working overtime. "Father Gabriel has to be the shepherd, and we his flock." He nodded absentmindedly. "The serpent is the killer, and he has chosen three of us that he feels must die." His shoulders sagged. "Everyone has figured *that* much out already."

He glanced at his watch. It was still early enough that everyone was either watching television or playing games. Free time was a luxury none of the seminarians wanted to waste.

"Aiden's family is not the only one who can solve crimes," he said, trying to feel braver than he knew he was. "I will go secretly into my fellow students' rooms and see who may be hiding something." He grinned smugly. "I will uncover the truth and keep Father Gabriel from harm."

Removing his shoes, his socked feet glided easily on the old wood flooring. Opening his door and sneaking a peek at the hallway, he left his room and went to the first seminarian's room.

His nose wrinkled at the smell of old sneakers and heavily soiled gym clothes, but he found nothing incriminating. He was able to get in and out of each room without being discovered but was becoming frustrated at finding nothing helpful. Quietly leaving each room, discouragement was enveloping him until he came to the last room on his list.

He knocked lightly on the door, as he had at each student's room, and when no one answered, he let himself in. The room was amazingly neat and orderly. Textbooks were stacked on the desk as if they had never even been opened.

A small table sat next to the bed. Okeyo saw papers scattered on its top, the only sign of disorder in the entire room. Picking up one of the papers, he saw it was a copy of the riddle. No, he thought, not a copy. It was the same parchment as the original note found on Joseph Lin's body, down to the last curl of aged-looking fiber...except for one small detail. This copy had the last line of the riddle, which had been ripped from the note on Joseph's body. The missing portion read: *Only the faithful shall see the light beyond the veil.*

Okeyo's brow furrowed sharply, a cold sweat prickling his skin as his mouth turned to sand. Shock hit him like a slap on the face. This room housed the killer.

He pulled out his phone and quickly snapped a shot of the parchment and continued searching through the stack of papers. He spotted a sheet with several names on it, two of them being Joseph's and Matthew's, which were crossed through. A third name sent Okeyo reeling. The third person who was to be murdered!

Continuing his search, he came across a yellowed newspaper article. He turned toward the door, his ears pricked, listening for any sounds of footsteps. His eyes scanned the article. After quickly reading it, he folded it carefully, along with the list he had discovered, and slid them into his pocket. He needed to get out of this room before he was discovered. His body trembled, and he needed to tell someone, and soon.

He tried his best to shuffle the papers back into some semblance of order and headed for the door. Peering out, he saw no one, so he made a beeline for the stairway.

Just after Okeyo closed the door and walked away, a figure leaned ever so slightly from the far end of the hallway, silent, patient, and full of dark purpose.

As Okeyo jogged down the stairs, he nearly collided with Aiden, who was on his way up, his arms full of heavy class books.

"Aiden," he panted, catching his breath, "I need to show you something, something very important, but first I must find the rector. Will you meet me in my room in a little while?"

"Sure, Okeyo. Just let me drop these off and I'll meet you there." He paused and studied him. "Everything all right?"

"Just come by my room when you can." He continued down the stairs without answering.

Once on the first floor, Okeyo raced to the rector's office, only to find it locked. Of course, he thought, it was late and the rector would be elsewhere. With no time to spare, he ran back up the stairs and to his room to await Aiden, locking the door behind him.

He took the purloined papers out and smoothed them, placing the photograph of Father Gabriel and the young men next to the faded newspaper article on the bed. Everything was beginning to connect.

A knock startled his thoughts. Aiden, he thought, and, relaxing a bit, went to the door.

With a hesitant hand, he turned the knob and cracked the door open, his thoughts still steeped in dread of what might await him.

It was not Aiden. The door exploded inward, and the attacker loomed over Okeyo, each labored breath warming his skin.

Okeyo's eyes narrowed, but then he laughed nervously, patting his chest with fluttering fingers. "Oh, it's you. Can I help you with something?" He took a tentative step back, his legs hitting the edge of the bed.

The other person glanced at the photo and the papers spread out on the bed. A grin crept across his face, but it quickly twisted into a mocking sneer as he glared demonically at Okeyo.

Okeyo tried to take another step back, fear tightening his chest as he stared at the person before him, but the bed stopped him.

A light clicked on in his brain. Staring suspiciously at the monster he had let in, he whispered hoarsely, "It looks almost like *you* in that photo. But it can't be—unless you're…" His eyes went back to the picture and newspaper article, but when he looked up again, he saw the figure coming at him, his eyes flashing like a demon possessed.

"We need to talk," said the visitor. "About everything. About you…and what you now know."

Okeyo stood rigid, uneasy.

"You should've never gone to my room and snooped around. Those papers weren't yours to take." From his pocket, the person drew a long, black rosary, the crucifix glinting in the dim light. His fingers curled around it tightly.

He lunged at Okeyo, forcing him to fall backward, stumbling onto the bed.

Okeyo barely had time to react before the visitor wrapped the rosary around his neck, the crucifix digging into his throat as he struggled, legs kicking against the floor. He clawed at the beads and his eyes bulged.

But then, just as the room began to blur, the figure hesitated. For a moment, the grip loosened.

Gasping for air, Okeyo looked up, only to see eyes that didn't appear to be human anymore. Instead, they were black and soulless, like the void had come alive and was staring back.

Suddenly, he extricated himself from Okeyo and went to the window, throwing it open and knocking the screen out, watching, as it fell to the ground below.

Okeyo lay helpless as the figure approached again. He struggled to scream, but only a rasp escaped his injured throat. With one hand, the person Okeyo thought he had known grabbed him by the neck, pushing him toward the open window.

As they grappled and stumbled toward the window, dread clawed its way up Okeyo's spine. He knew, deep down, in the marrow of his bones, what was coming.

He fought with everything he had, but this creature had become something else, something monstrous. Okeyo's hands slipped against sweat and cloth, his strength fading fast. The man's grip was relentless, almost inhuman.

Then, with terrifying ease, Okeyo felt himself being hoisted. His feet left the floor as he kicked, thrashed, and gasped at a prayer, but it was useless. He was hauled upward, dragged toward the open window, and moonlight was the last thing he saw.

There was no scream, only the soft grunt of effort, the scrape of fabric against the windowsill, then silence.

Okeyo plummeted into the night like a broken doll, his body swallowed by darkness until it hit the stone walkway below with a sickening, final thud.

The shadowy figure leaned out of the window, peering down to confirm the life below had been extinguished, then turned and headed for the door. After collecting the photo and newspaper article, he carefully wiped the doorknob clean of fingerprints, then pulled it shut. The latch clicked softly into place, and silence returned to the dormitory, heavy, unnatural, like the building itself was holding its breath.

After depositing his books in his room, Aiden backtracked and knocked on Okeyo's door. After a few attempts and getting no answer, Aiden assumed his friend had gone to sleep. He decided to catch up with him at breakfast to learn what was so important that the rector had to be notified, and so, returned to his room.

CHAPTER 27

Thursday Morning

Mrs. Morrison filled Brendan's coffee mug for the fourth time. "Father, you're going to be buzzing, what with all the caffeine you've had this morning, and only a bowl of oatmeal." She gave the priest a loud, theatrical *tsk tsk*, wagging her finger like a schoolmarm.

Brendan lifted his head to meet his housekeeper's eyes. "I think this morning I need the jolt, Mrs. M. My brain is foggy, and as usual, I didn't get much sleep."

The housekeeper's face darkened, and she pulled out a chair and sat next to him at the table.

"Father, I need to say this." She pressed her lips together so tightly they turned white. "I want you to think about seeing someone. I believe your PTSD is getting worse." She placed a motherly hand on his shoulder. "At least tell Maureen. Or your brother. Your family loves you and would want to help you."

Brendan gazed out the window, remembering the sermon he had just preached at daily Mass no more than a half hour ago: *Fear not, for I am with you; be not dismayed, for I am your God; I will strengthen you, I will help you, I will uphold you with my righteous right hand.*

Sure, it sounded good, and it was easy enough to tell others how to handle *their* anxieties and depressions, but to believe in the power of those words? So now, instead of feeling better about himself, he sank deeper into a funk.

He forced a smile and decided to lie to his housekeeper. "You're right, Mrs. M. I really should see someone. Tell you what…I'll google some therapists and see who fits the bill. Okay?"

Mrs. Morrison beamed. "Thank you, Father. You know you're like a son to me, and I want only the best for you." She rose from her chair, and the weight of the lie he had just told her struck Brendan's heart like a knife. She took the half-eaten bowl of oatmeal to the sink. "So what are your plans for the day? I don't see anything on the kitchen calendar."

"I'm taking a break from all this murder and mayhem to pick up my mother, the Celtic storm herself. She's demanding to hear what's going on with her grandson at the seminary."

"Well, give her my love and"—she scurried over to a cake dish—"give her a piece of this coconut cake. She'll enjoy it." She put a slice in a plastic container and handed it to Brendan.

"Mrs. M., you're the best. Ma will love it." He took the container and, with his other hand, leaned down and gave Mary Magdalene's head a gentle ruffle, the little Yorkie letting out a contented sigh. "And I'll look into that… you know." He gave her a sheepish grin and, reaching for his cane, he bade the housekeeper goodbye and headed out to his car.

The seminarians filed into the chapel, their footsteps hushed against the stone floor, as morning light streamed through the stained glass, casting colors across their bowed heads.

Aiden scanned the chapel for Okeyo, but when he didn't see him, a flicker of worry crept into his chest. Maybe he should have knocked harder last night on his friend's door, or maybe even let himself in. Maybe Okeyo was sick and needed help.

His mind raced, and as soon as Mass was over, he ran back to the dorm, taking the stairs to the second floor two at a time until he reached Okeyo's room.

Knocking loudly and calling out his name, Aiden finally decided to enter, praying the door was not locked. It wasn't. He turned the knob and entered the room, hoping he wouldn't find his friend sick, or worse. However, Okeyo was nowhere to be found, and the room was freezing. He looked over at the window and saw it was wide open and the screen missing.

Thinking that was odd, he walked over and leaned out, glancing around the area. His eyes fell on the crumpled body of Okeyo, and a scream tore from his throat before he could stop it. He couldn't believe the unearthly sound came from him.

Crossing himself, he ran out of the room, hollering to anyone who could hear him. Several of the seminarians who had just returned from Mass ran to him.

His words tumbled out as he described finding Okeyo. "Call the police," he said. "*Now.*" He motioned to them, leading them around the side of the building, where Okeyo's lifeless body lay crumpled on the cold ground.

Brendan arrived at Our Lady of Grace, already knowing how his visit would go. He parked the Honda and grabbed the flowers he had picked up, hoping it would put the little banshee in a good mood.

"Good morning, Father," said one of the sisters cheerfully. "Mrs. O'Clery just went back to her place. She'll be glad to see you."

Brendan scoffed. "Well, that would be a first, but thanks, Sister Agatha." He nodded to the young nun and headed toward Eabha's room. He rapped on the door lightly, then walked in.

"*Dia ár sábháil.* Look who finally made it. Sure, and I was beginning to think the Lord was keeping you from me, Father O'Clery." Eabha sat in her recliner, her cane across her lap.

He set the wedge of coconut cake on the counter. "From Mrs. Morrison," he said, pointing to the container.

That brought a rare smile from his mother. He held back a sigh, walked over, and stooped to hug the old woman, planting a kiss on her head, her curls a bold, unnatural red that defied her age.

"And the Lord wasn't keeping me, Ma. I had a few things to take care of. How are you today?"

Eabha gave an unladylike snort. "How do you think I am? I'm stuck in this place with the world's slowest aides. Couldn't even get a proper cup of tea this morning, and the eggs, too runny to eat. And a priest, too busy to visit his poor old ma."

Brendan found a vase in the cabinet and arranged the flowers. "Sorry, Ma. But at least you're in good hands here, aren't you?"

Eabha gave a dramatic laugh. "Good hands? Ha! Sure, and the only thing good around here is the food, and it's tasteless mush. You priests are all the same—too busy with your holy duties to give a second thought to your ma. You should be more like your brother."

And so it begins, thought Brendan, pulling up a chair next to his mother. "Ma, Malachy never comes to see you. I don't know why you always stick up for him. I'm here all the time. I even said a special prayer for you at Mass today, just like I always do."

Eabha waved a bony hand at him. "A prayer? A prayer won't fix this place."

Brendan sighed, knowing the visit wouldn't be improving. "And I thought you liked it here. Anyway, what can I do for you right now? Want to go sit out in the lobby?"

"Now why would I want to go out there and sit with all those old people?" she snapped. "No, son, just sit here and tell me what's going on at that seminary."

I can handle that, thought Brendan, diving headfirst into the chaotic string of events at Saint Charles.

Sheriff's deputies descended on Saint Charles in force, Caleb emerging from the lead vehicle, tense and alert. Cell phone in hand, he ran to where Father Gabriel was pointing.

"Maureen?" he yelled into the phone. "Oh, thank goodness. Look, you're not going to believe it, but—hang on… Okay, Father, please don't touch anything and tell the boys to stand back… Sorry, Maureen. Well, it looks like we've got another one. I think it's time to get these kids and the staff out of here and close this place down until we get to the bottom of these murders. Actually, we probably should have done it earlier, but it should be done soon…before anything else goes south." He gathered his thoughts momentarily then added, "Look, I hate to ask, but can you get over here?" He waited for an answer, then ended the call.

Walking over to the body, he knelt and placed two fingers on Okeyo's carotid artery, feeling for any sign of life.

Looking up, he yelled out, "Get an ambulance here, I think I might have a pulse!" He stood, retrieved his cell phone, and began clicking photos of the scene. He also checked the boy's body for any cryptic notes. At this rate, he thought, this seminary would soon be devoid of any students.

The seminarians had gathered around, all chattering about yet another tragedy. But had Okeyo tried to kill himself, or did somebody else try to end him? Could he have felt guilty for the two murders?

Caleb put his phone in his jacket and rubbed his eyes wearily, gathering his thoughts.

"I want you boys to go back inside. Detectives will want to talk with all of you, and if you know *anything* about what happened here, I'll need to know." He waited until each of the young men acknowledged him, then watched them walk back inside, all looking back at the crumpled body of their fellow seminarian.

"Father, what's going on here? What kind of place are you running?" Caleb looked at the rector, whose face was a ghostly white, and all the man could do was open his arms and shrug.

"The boy is alive then?" he asked Caleb, in a hushed voice.

"Just barely." He looked up at the open window and pointed. "Either he fell, jumped, or someone pushed him." He looked at the rector, who was staring at the curtains blowing in the wind.

A rising wail pierced the air, drawing closer with each second. The siren hit a fever pitch just as the ambulance rounded the corner and pulled up beside the building, where deputies gestured toward the scene.

Two EMTs flew out of the ambulance with equipment in hand. They moved quickly to assess Okeyo's condition, then, after inserting an IV and placing an oxygen mask over his nose, they lifted him onto a gurney and into the waiting ambulance.

"How's he look?" asked Caleb.

The driver of the ambulance, an athletic-looking young man with tattoos illustrating both arms, shrugged. "Could go either way, but I have to tell you—if he makes it, it'll be a miracle. He's broken quite a few bones and has multiple contusions and probably a concussion." He didn't wait around for Caleb to comment. The ambulance sped away, with Maureen passing it on her way in.

The Jeep fishtailed slightly as Maureen swung it into the lot, skidding to a stop next to the flashing squad cars, her pulse racing to match the sirens. Jumping out, she ran to where Caleb was standing, attempting to calm Father Gabriel.

"Is he...?" she asked, the question trailing off.

Caleb shrugged stiffly, his shoulders tight with unease. "Doesn't look good, but I'll check in on him later. Right now, I need to get to the bottom of what's going on here." He gave Maureen a pathetic look. "Sure could use your help."

She gave him an easy smile and told him that, of course, she'd help. "I'm scared my cousin may be next, so whatever it takes, count me in."

They headed for the building, Father Gabriel tagging along as if in a trance.

Once inside, Maureen searched for Aiden. He was huddled together with what was left of the seminarians.

Aiden, come over here, she mouthed, waving her arm frantically.

Aiden excused himself from the group and practically ran to her. "Maureen, it was horrible. Okeyo was my friend, and he's—he's the third one to die." His eyes teared up as he looked away.

"Well, the EMTs said he was still alive and if he—"

"He's still alive?" Aiden said excitedly. "That's great!" He crossed himself.

Maureen patted the air with her palms. "He's alive, but there's a good chance he won't make it. That was a long fall he had." She looked at her cousin, her eyes narrowing. "You know anything about this?"

Aiden scratched his neck nervously. "I don't know. Last night, he caught me on the way up to my room. He looked frantic, and he was running downstairs to look for Father Gabriel. He asked me if I could meet him in his room, and I said sure. But when I knocked, I got no answer, so I figured he was asleep." He shook his head shook slowly. "If only I had known..."

Maureen's heart broke. "Aiden, there was nothing you could have done." She needed to ask the hard question. "Do you think he jumped? I mean, I know this is a stressful place, so maybe—"

Aiden's head jerked up. "What? No! Absolutely not! There's no way he'd do that!"

Maureen gripped his shoulders with quiet strength, anchoring him in the moment. "Okay, then what do you think happened? Did you hear or see anything last night?"

Aiden shook his head frantically, words spilling fast. "He just wanted me to stop by. He seemed really upset. Said he had something to show me. No one was in the hallway. Most of the guys were in the game room." His breath hitched, eyes darting, the panic in them saying more than his voice ever could.

She looked at Caleb. "Was there a note anywhere around him?"

The detective shook his head. "No, no note." He grunted in exasperation. "And we've got nothing. No motives for *any* of these killings." He crossed his arms and began pacing. "And the only clues are that riddle, the cryptic notes found on the boys, that rosary used to strangle the first boy, and the arrow found in the second boy." He uncrossed his arms and raked his fingers roughly through his hair. "And that handyman seems to have a great alibi—arthritis."

Maureen glanced at her cousin and saw he was practically hyperventilating. "Aiden, go back to your friends. I'll check in with you later."

Nodding gratefully, the young man didn't need to be told twice.

"Look, while we're here," Maureen said, "let's take a look at that mauso-leum my uncle and his friends got into. Maybe there's something in there."

Caleb frowned. "I'm not going to any place where dead people are. I don't mind working with live ones, but dead ones? Uh uh."

Maureen laughed and grabbed the arm of his jacket, dragging him out of the building and toward the old cemetery.

"You're gonna owe me, McNeely," he said, fighting her all the way to the huge stone edifice.

Maureen gave the mausoleum a once-over before entering. "The Dean family, how quaint. It's as run down as his house." She took a step past the open door and into the darkness. Pulling out a small flashlight, she turned, and seeing Caleb, hands on hips, feet dug in, she grabbed his jacket sleeve again and yanked him into the darkness.

"Yuck, a spider web!" Caleb yelped, swatting at the clinging strands like they were on fire. "Get it off!"

Maureen's lips curled into a smirk. "Don't make me repeat what I'm seeing to the other deputies."

"I couldn't care less," he said, wiping the web material on his slacks. "Yuck."

Maureen shined the light down the stairway to the crypt. Motioning for a reluctant Caleb to follow, they wound their way down to the dank bottom. Sweeping her flashlight over the area, she eyed the three half-empty bottles of wine her uncle had described. She pulled a latex glove from her tote and picked up each of the bottles, inspecting them and smelling the contents.

"Smells fairly fresh," she said. She placed the bottles down, then flashed the light on a dark corner, where a swatch of fabric, around a yard in length, hung loosely.

"What the heck is this for?" she said. "Why would anyone hang a piece of fabric in a mausoleum?" She stepped to the wall and, with a gloved fin-ger, lifted a corner of the fabric that had been duct-taped to the cold stone. "What a weird way to hang fabric. Could this be the tape that caused the sticky mess we found on the chapel floor?" And then, "Oh, no, look, Caleb, it's that same photo, and it's tacked onto some kind of cork board." She pulled out her cell and took a picture of it. "Check it out." She motioned to Caleb to take a look.

"Stranger and stranger," he said, still picking off fragments of the spider's web from his face.

Maureen studied the photo again and this time saw a name over the young man that had looked so familiar to her uncle. "Look, Caleb. There's a name over his picture. Myron M." She looked at her partner. "Now that's a new name, but we now know it's not Matthew Mueller. Wonder who it is and why his photo's here in the Dean crypt."

She shoved the photo into her jacket pocket. "Come on, let's get out of here. I definitely want to have a word with the rector about this." She looked down at her watch. "Maybe we can set up a meeting with him at the chapel and speak with him afterward." She turned to go, shining her light on Caleb, still fidgeting about.

Grabbing his wrist, she dragged him up the stairs and out into the cool fall air.

From behind one of the weathered outbuildings, a shadowy figure observed the two detectives leaving the mausoleum, eyes narrowed, breath still. There was no fear, only a cold calculation, and a growing certainty that if they got too close to the truth buried within the seminary, they, too, would have to be silenced.

Aiden walked numbly to the common room, his mind reeling after what he had witnessed. As he entered, the seminarians were milling around the room, their anxiety palpable. Spotting Eugene, Nathan, Manuel, and Daniel, he made his way over to his friends.

"Two deaths and a possible third," Manuel was saying. "What if we're all targets?"

Aiden's eyes studied Daniel Caruso. He stood leaning against the wall, cool and calm, picking off a thread from the T-shirt he had been sleeping in when awakened by the commotion.

"We all have sins to atone for, don't we?" Daniel commented.

Manuel jumped, his face drawing close to Daniel's, spittle flying from his mouth. "What is that supposed to mean? Are you saying we *deserve* this? That Joseph, Matthew, and Okeyo *deserved* this?"

Eugene flinched, taking a step back. Aiden feared a fight was about to erupt.

Manuel continued. "Tell me how men—*good* men—studying for the priesthood, deserve to be murdered in such horrific ways?"

Daniel, unmoved by Manuel's histrionics, replied calmly. "I'm saying none of us are innocent."

Before Manuel had a chance to reply, Aiden stepped forward, pushing his way between the two.

"This isn't the time for blame, guys," he said, praying his words would be a balm to hot tempers. "We need to stay united." He looked at each one, then, his courage slipping, cast his eyes downward.

Manuel turned his anger toward Aiden, his eyes flashing with anger. "You're the one who keeps finding the bodies. You might not have killed them, but maybe you know who did and where the bodies were, and that's how you were always the first one to find them."

Aiden's face grew flaming hot. "Well, remember, Manuel...*you* were with me when we found Matthew's body."

The room fell silent. Daniel snickered and sauntered away from the group. Manuel turned and stormed off in the opposite direction. Nathan stared at Aiden, gave a shrug, and walked off, too, while Eugene slunk away without a word.

Aiden squeezed his fists together, then released them, his frustration mounting. With nothing more to be said or done, he returned to his room.

CHAPTER 28

Thursday Afternoon

Brendan sat with Ezra and Langdon, lingering over a half-eaten lunch at their favorite spot, Mom and Pop's, Porter Mill's answer to comfort food and cholesterol, served with a side of nostalgia and gossip.

"...so that's how that came to be. Pretty cool, huh?" Ezra glanced over at Brendan. "Hey, did you hear me?"

Brendan jerked his head up and looked from one friend to the other. "Huh? I'm sorry, Ezra. My mind is elsewhere." He relayed the latest tragedy to his friends.

Ezra reached across the table and gave Brendan's arm a friendly pat. "Your poor nephew! And now another young man? This is getting scary."

Brendan let out a long, tired breath and slowly straightened in his chair, every movement weighted with exhaustion. Checking his watch, he said, "Father Gabriel's supposed to speak with the boys after lunch. He told me I could attend the meeting when I spoke to him earlier. I didn't ask if I could bring guests, but if you guys aren't busy this afternoon, I'd love to hear your thoughts on what he says."

Langdon, who had been using a toothpick on a stubborn piece of something stuck between two teeth, said, "Hey, it's better to beg for forgiveness than to ax for permission!" He grinned widely, his lips peeling back to reveal a row of large, slightly crooked teeth.

Brendan gave a weak laugh. "I believe you're right, Pastor Boothe. So let's get in that Caddy of yours and scurry off. I'll leave my car here." He flagged down their waitress and gave her a gift card and a few dollar bills.

"Egads," said Ezra, "is that from yet *another* of your parishioners? Do they think you eat out *that* much?"

"Hey, Mrs. M. is only there certain hours and can't keep me fed all the time." He reached into his wallet and pulled out a handful of cards. "These keep me going."

Ezra slapped his forehead. "*Oy gevalt!* My congregation needs to take a lesson from yours!"

The men left the restaurant and piled into Aretha and headed for the seminary.

Brendan, Ezra, and Langdon had entered the chapel seconds before the rector began. They took their places in the back of the chapel and waited for the din to settle down.

The seminarians settled and sat in tense silence as Father Gabriel stood at the pulpit, his face pale and drawn. Brendan noted some new seminarians in attendance, probably those who had been at the week-long retreat. They sat in on the gathering, wide-eyed, hanging on every word regarding the murders they had not been privy to.

Scanning the chapel, Brendan saw Maureen and Caleb off to one side. He kept his gaze fixed on her until, at last, her eyes met his. She smiled lightly and gave him a simple nod.

Father Gabriel finally addressed the seminarians. "I called you all here to the chapel for an emergency meeting." Father Gabriel cleared his throat, his eyes scanning his audience, his face grim, as if to underscore the seriousness of the situation. "We've been under attack since the first tragedy. Evil has entered our sanctuary, and it feeds on fear and division. But we must not falter in our faith."

Manuel Bautista stood up and looked around the chapel. "Excuse me, Father, but with all due respect, faith isn't stopping our friends from being systematically murdered."

Brendan perused the group of young men, now chatting excitedly amongst themselves.

"Men, *please*," yelled Father Gabriel, his arms raised in a weak attempt to quiet the crowd. "Please, listen to me. Losing faith will only ensure more do."

Aiden, who had come in after Brendan and had chosen to sit with him, poked him with his elbow and nodded to where Daniel Caruso was sitting. He was scribbling something in his notebook, one hand idly tugging at the scratch on his neck where a scab had formed.

Father Gabriel continued. "As rector, I am instituting stricter rules, or I will be forced to close this place down. No one is to wander alone after dark or leave the seminary grounds. Confessions will be held daily, and I expect everyone to participate. I know exams will soon be upon you, but this is a time for reflection and repentance."

Again, voices were raised in objection, but Father Gabriel would not budge.

"This is my final word. Let this be a lesson in the vow of obedience you will all be taking as future priests." The rector gave the small group a perfunctory look, then said, "Now go to your afternoon classes."

The mumbling continued for a while, then one by one, the young men exited the chapel, none looking happy about the rector's orders or the possibility of their school closing.

As Aiden stood to leave, Brendan pulled him back. "I need your help, but you can't tell your cousin."

Aiden stared at him, but then a sly smile began to grow. "You got it, Uncle Brendan! What's the plan?"

Brendan turned to Ezra and Langdon. "I'll text you when I'm done with 'you know what'"—he used air quotes—"and let you know where to meet me." His friends nodded their compliance.

Moments later, Aiden stood outside the rector's office, while Brendan slipped stealthily inside, sidling up to the tall filing cabinets. Pulling each drawer out, he searched for the personnel files for the seminarians whom he considered as possible suspects.

He hurried his search as quickly as he could, his heart racing. He knew that, if anyone approached his nephew, they'd have seniority over him and he'd have to let them pass, but for now, he continued rifling through the folders.

Finally, coming across the first one, Manuel Bautista, he grabbed it and continued his search.

Before he could locate a second folder, he heard voices in the hallway, one being his nephew's.

Brendan saw a stocky young Hispanic man dressed in black clerical garb entered the office, casting a wary, hard-edged glance at Brendan bent over the bottom drawer of the rector's filing cabinet.

"And who are you?" he asked pointedly in a thick accent, his eyes focusing on the folder Brendan clenched in his hand.

Brendan Francis O'Clery's analytical brain, the one that never failed him during wartime, snapped into gear. He stood slowly.

"I'm Father Timothy Mahoney, from Saint Ann's," he lied seamlessly, "and I'm perusing student folders, looking for some sharp seminarians that can assist me next month at my Christmas Masses." He gave the man a hard look and asked, "And you?"

The young man cleared his throat and shifted from one foot to the other. "Oh, I'm sorry, Father Mahoney. I didn't...well, I'm Deacon Juarez. Juan Juarez. Please forgive me, Father. I was looking for Father Gabriel. You startled me." He gave Brendan a weak smile.

Brendan rewarded him with his most warm, welcoming smile. "Deacon Juarez, how very nice to meet you. Let me just grab a few promising lads here and I'll be out of your hair." He stooped back over the bottom drawer and fingered through the folders that were arranged alphabetically, quickly picking the ones he needed.

Standing again, he tucked the folders under his arm and reached for the cane that had been resting by the rector's chair. As he passed by the deacon, he smiled again at him. "*Es un placer conocerlo*, Deacon Juarez. I trust our paths will meet again soon." He dipped his head and exited the room.

The deacon's mouth fell open. "And you, too, Father Mahoney. Nice to meet you."

"Father *Mahoney?*" asked Aiden when the two were away from the rector's office.

"Long story, son," quipped Brendan. "Now let's go find your cousin. And remember," he said, nodding to the folders he was hiding in his jacket, "not a word."

Aiden gave a silent and solemn nod.

Brendan stopped long enough to text Ezra and Langdon, letting them know where they were headed.

Maureen elbowed Caleb, and they dashed to the front of the main building, blocking the rector as he entered.

"Father Gabriel, Detective Martinez and I found something in one of the mausoleums in the old cemetery. Would you be so kind as to help us out with something?" She snuck a conspiratorial look at Caleb.

"A *mausoleum?*" he screamed. "What were you doing in that sacred place?" The old man began shaking. "This is too—"

Maureen interrupted him, placing a palm inches from his face. "Look, Father," she began, "you can allow us access now to any part of this seminary or we get a warrant. Either way, we're getting to the bottom of whatever's going on here."

Father Gabriel puffed his cheeks but acquiesced. "You're right, Detective. These murders need to be solved, and quickly, and I want to help in any way I can." His shoulders sagged, the fight draining out of him. He gave a small, reluctant nod. "We can go to my office and discuss how we can relocate these boys to other institutions where they'll be safe."

When they all looked up and saw Brendan and Aiden approaching with his ragtag crew of clerics, Maureen saw the rector's face brighten. No one seemed to notice the bulge in Brendan's jacket.

"Father O'Clery, and with my seminarian! I want you to know that your help here is appreciated, even if I didn't originally show it." He gawked at the two incongruous figures with him. "And who are these two?"

"Father, please," said Maureen, ignoring his questions. "I have something important to ask you." She retrieved the photo from her pocket and showed it to the man. "This is that photo that's been circulating, and now we've discovered it in the Dean family mausoleum. There's a name written over the head of the young man in the photo that some seem to think looks familiar. Can you tell me who Myron M. is?"

"Myron M.?" echoed Brendan, his voice tinged with curiosity.

Father Gabriel grabbed the photo from Maureen's hands and stared at it. Maureen watched his face go from crimson to a ghostly white.

"You recognize him, don't you, Father?"

The priest thrust the photo back, forcing Maureen to take it. "I have no idea who that is. That was taken decades ago. So many students come through this seminary each year. I only wish I could remember them all." He gave Maureen a wistful look.

"Father," said Maureen, amused, "I doubt that many young men come through every fall, and besides, these boys are here at least four years, and some as many as eight. Plenty of time for bonding. I think if you look hard enough, you'll see that you know him." She held the photo out again, but the priest didn't take it. She shook it at him. "Myron M.? Who is he, Father? This is a police investigation, and if you're concealing infor—"

"I'm not concealing *anything*! I'm an old man and my memory isn't what it used to be." He looked away. "Look here, I said I'd help in any way I could, but I simply can*not* remember every boy that comes through here."

Maureen caught the subtle twitch in his body, the restless energy betraying his nerves.

"Now, if you don't mind, I have work to do. I suggest you allow me access into my seminar and go on about your business and find out who's killing these boys, and soon, so I won't have to evacuate the place." He turned on his heels, brushed rudely past them and stomped into the building.

"Hoo-ee, what a *couyon*!" cried Langdon in a strange accent. "That ol' white dude be headed for a nervous breakdown."

"What's a *couyon*?" asked Caleb.

Maureen rolled her eyes. "Don't get him started, Caleb."

"Now, li'l girl, don't be like that! Son, that's Cajun for you is like a *crazy* person! It means that dude's hangin' on by a thread thinner than Aunt Lulabelle's church panny-hose. He be 'bout two steps from hollerin' at squirrels."

Langdon clapped Caleb on the back with a hearty thump, nearly jostling the deputy off balance.

"Come on, let's get out of here," said Maureen, ignoring her uncle's friends. She looked at Brendan. "You coming?"

Brendan thought for a moment, then said, "Let's go over to the chapel," and strode off, his companions trying to keep up with him.

As they walked inside the chapel, Brendan's eyes drifted toward the altar where he observed Eugene kneeling in the pew, head bowed, hands folded.

"Go on, Mo. The guys and I are going to stay here for a while." He held up a hand. "Wait. How about you meet us back at Ezra's? He's got his murder board up again—stop it, don't laugh—anyway, we can compare what you and Caleb have so far, okay?" He looked at Caleb. "You're invited, too, Caleb."

Maureen's gaze followed his to Eugene Wingate. "I guess that would work. I need a good laugh." She grinned at the little rabbi, then nodded to Caleb, and the two left, leaving the clerics behind.

"Stay here, guys," said Brendan. "I want a word with that kid. He's an odd duck, sure, but I've got a feeling."

"Sure, Bren. The big heathen and I will wait here for you." Langdon swished his fingers around in the holy water font, then turned to Brendan, a pleading look in his eyes. "But please hurry."

Brendan reached for his cane and strode quietly down to the pew occupied by Eugene Wingate. When he reached it, he eased in, sitting next to the young man.

"Your rector's preaching unity, but all I see are cracks forming."

Eugene's head came up, but his hands remained folded. He looked at Brendan, his face sad. "It's not just the murders. This place...it's like the walls are closing in." He looked up at the crucifix over the altar and then back at Brendan.

Brendan cocked an eyebrow. "And what about you, Eugene? Do you know anything about these murders? Are you keeping something from the police?"

"I—I don't know what you're talking about, Father. And I'm not implying anything. I'm just saying that secrets don't stay hidden forever, especially in a place like this."

Eugene stood suddenly, casting a cold glare at Brendan. He picked up a worn missal and stomped out of the chapel, clearly unnerved by Brendan's pointed questions.

Brendan sat stunned for a time, then returned to his friends.

"Strange kid, huh, Bren?" asked Ezra.

"Strange doesn't even begin to cover it, Rabbi."

Ezra slid his glasses high onto his nose as he set his now-infamous murder board on a chair, tilting it slightly to balance it. "You said Maureen and her deputy friend are on their way?"

"Yeah, just Mo," Brendan told him. "Caleb opted out. Family stuff."

"Are you going to tell her about the folders?"

"You must be *meshugah*, Rabbi. Not until I read through them first."

Ezra laughed and nodded. "Smart man." He placed a bowl of chips and a small container of dip on the table with a warning to the Baptist preacher. "If you take more than your allotted share, you're out on your butt."

Langdon's eyes got small. "You gonna make me, little man?"

The rabbi rolled his eyes and went to the refrigerator and pulled out a pitcher of iced tea.

The doorbell rang, and Brendan got up to let his niece in.

"Okay, let's talk," she said, pushing past him, setting her tote bag on the counter. "These murders have me stymied. You know I can't stand to leave a puzzle unfinished."

Brendan laughed and pulled out his pocket-sized crossword and anagram book. "Hey, you're preaching to the Catholic choir here."

Maureen grabbed a seat. "So let's get this show on the road."

Ezra took the cue and grabbed a marker, and walked over to his murder board and stood, gazing out at his audience.

Brendan looked at his niece. "We've got a few things. How about you?"

Maureen's lips curled, and she picked at a fingernail. "Same," she said, the word tinged with discouragement. She looked around at the men seated at the table.

They all looked at each other.

Then Brendan spoke. "So let's just go over what we've got. Maybe something will jump out at us. Let's start with the facts, what we know to be true."

Maureen threw her hands up. "All right then. We have two murders, one strangulation and one shot with an arrow and suffocated," she said sarcastically. "Not to mention Okeyo's fall—or push—from that window. The smudged fingerprint on the parchment was blurred, too blurred to be of any use. There's no DNA anywhere to be found, and no motives for these murders and no decent suspects. All we have are a few cryptic notes and a riddle." She turned to Brendan. "So what else can *you* add, Unc?"

"Hey, that's a start," said Ezra, drawing two stick hands around another stick figure's neck, labeled as "Joseph Lin."

Maureen shot a look at Brendan, clearly trying not to laugh at the rabbi's primitive representations.

As Ezra finished drawing an arrow coming out of another stick figure, Brendan cleared his throat. "I've got lots to add." He looked at Ezra. "Get your marker ready, Rabbi."

He stood and took his place next to Ezra. Pointing to the two deceased stick figures, he began. "First, let's start with who knew who in that seminary. According to my young intelligence operative, Aiden, who I've questioned extensively, Joseph Lin and Matthew Mueller were known to several of the boys. Other than the out-of-staters, most of the Maryland guys know each other to some extent—Maureen knows all of this. They all came up through the same Catholic schools in the area." He pointed to the drawing that represented Daniel Caruso. "Daniel knew both boys from Saint Thomas

Aquinas High School over the line in Pennsylvania. And Aiden said that Daniel had loaned Joseph thirty-five hundred dollars for medicines for his grandmother back in China, and that Joseph wasn't paying Daniel back fast enough."

Ezra jumped in quickly. "But didn't Aiden also lend money to Joseph?"

"Yes, but only about a hundred dollars, and I wasn't happy about that when he told me," offered Brendan, "but it was from his summer job, so it was his to lend. So thirty-five hundred dollars is a pretty good motive for murder. And remember, Daniel had those scratches on his face and neck. So let's say Daniel tried to get the money out of Joseph, but Joseph didn't have it, and Daniel lost his temper. Easy enough for hands to find their way around a throat if you're angry enough."

"Tell me about it," Maureen said, glaring at Brendan. She pulled out her notepad and flipped through the pages. "And I went up to the schools and got quite a bit of information from some of the teachers who remembered the boys." She looked at her notes. "Evidently, before receiving his priestly vocation, Daniel was quite the ladies' man." She laughed. "Remember, he was burning old love letters and photos from his misspent youth. And from what Aiden told me, Matthew was constantly criticizing Daniel for his—how do I put it delicately?—conquests." She looked up from her pad, smirking. "A great motive for murder. Daniel needed to put an end to the carnal accusations that must have followed him into the seminary."

"Okay, so Daniel Caruso looks good for both murders. Next," announced Ezra.

Maureen spoke up. "Let's look at Manuel Bautista."

Langdon, who had remained quiet, spoke up. "Ah, Filipino food...heavenly...pork menudo, chick'n adobo, pork belly sisig..." He drifted off in a world made entirely of food, a smile spreading across his face.

Ezra pursed his lips. He reached out, flicking his fingers at Langdon's head. "Can you, for just one minute, stop thinking of food? We're in the middle of two murders, possibly three, depending on how that poor Kenyan kid is doing."

The Baptist minister sat up straight and looked around. "A man gotta have his dream, little dude, and mine is food."

Maureen grimaced. "Here we go again…look, let's continue. I want to hear your theories, not audition tapes for *Saturday Night Live.*"

Langdon raised both palms. "Go on," he said apologetically, "I'm puttin' my dreams on hold."

Maureen flashed him an icy glare before smoothing it over with a brittle smile. "All right then, back to Manuel. He also attended Aquinas but didn't really mingle with Joseph or Matthew until the seminary, so the school couldn't help there, but according to Aiden—"

"That kid's turning into quite the detective, huh, guys?" said Brendan proudly.

Maureen gave him a sour look. "Please don't encourage him to snoop around like you guys do. Let him concentrate on becoming a priest."

"Just saying," said Brendan, lifting his shoulders.

"Then don't say anything," snapped Maureen. "Anyway, if I can continue, Aiden said that he'd hear Matthew Mueller make fun of anything Filipino"—she looked over at Langdon, who had talked himself into making a sandwich from items found in Ezra's fridge—"especially Filipino *food*, saying it was made from pig's faces, and that they ate fried grasshoppers—"

"That's apan-apan," interrupted Langdon, "and they made with garlic 'n' onyuns and lots of good spices. And don't forget balut," he added.

"Say what?" asked Ezra.

"Balut," repeated Langdon. "You get one of them fertilized duck eggs that got a sort of developed embryo, you boil the sucker, then scoop it up in the shell and *de*-vour it." He smacked his lips.

Ezra stared at his friend. "Where on earth did you ever get the nerve to eat all that stuff? It sounds horrible."

Langdon grinned. "Brother Terrence married one of them women from over there, an' they have me over for dinner now 'n' then." He grinned even wider. "I sure eats good when I go there. Diff'rent stuff, ya know?"

"Well, I'm going to gag," said Ezra, mimicking vomiting.

Maureen sighed audibly. "Guys…"

"Go on, Mo," said Brendan. "Ignore them."

"Anyway, Aiden said those two would get into it. Maybe Manuel just had enough. I mean, Matthew was insulting his heritage, and the kid had just begun his studies there. Not very priestly."

The men nodded in agreement.

"Okay, so moving on to Nathan Silk. He attended a public school but knew Joseph and Matthew from other stuff, like Nathan's family's physician was Mueller's father, Dr. Theodore Mueller. He also knew the Mueller family through Matthew's uncle, a...let's see"—she thumbed through her notes—"a Norm Kowalski. He was the gym teacher at Nathan's school, and he was pretty rough on the kid." She added, "Nathan was also in Eagle Scouts with Joseph."

"So no bad blood between any of them?" asked Brendan, flicking off a crumb left by Langdon's sandwich.

"None that anyone told me. So, no motive there. Moving on...Eugene Wingate."

"Hoo-ee," said Langdon. "Everythin' 'bout that boy is jes a li'l bit sideways, like a picture frame that you cain't quite get to hang straight, no matter how much you nudge it."

"But is he *harmless*? Maybe just *acting* like he's a bumbler? That's the question," said Maureen. "Aiden told Uncle Brendan that Matthew gave a mock sermon in a class about 'running the good race,' and he compared faith to a race where, and I quote, 'only the strong and focused stay on course, not the ones who are always lagging behind or stumbling around like lost sheep,' and he was looking straight at Eugene, grinning."

"Ouch," said Ezra, "that had to hurt the boy."

Brendan piped in. "Aiden said Eugene told him he was so humiliated. He knew Matthew was making fun of his physical and mental acuity, and that he could just 'kill him'—his words, not mine." He reached for the bottle of water Ezra had set on the table. "I know the boy's a bit strange, but he actually has a high IQ and knows Scripture backward and forward."

"So how's 'bout my young African brother in the hospital?" asked Langdon. "How bad do the docs say he be lookin'?"

"I haven't checked in yet. Caleb was going over to the hospital." Maureen turned to Brendan. "Did your junior detective say anything about *that* relationship?"

"Don't get your pantyhose in a wad, niece. Since arriving in August, my *junior detective*, Aiden, and Okeyo seemed to have forged a friendship.

I guess they've sort of been each other's anchor through the challenges of their first few months at the seminary, and believe me, a friend like that is a lifelong treasure in the priesthood."

"So no issues with Joseph Lin or Matthew Mueller?" Maureen grabbed a water and mouthed a *thank you* to Ezra.

"I didn't say that, dear niece. Aiden said Okeyo thought Matthew was a racist because he was always comparing him to African Americans who, shall we say, have less than stellar reputations, like that R. Kelly guy, and Kanye West, just to name a few. Okeyo took that as a huge insult. Of course," he went on, "that could have been Matthew's way of teasing, and not meaning any harm."

"*I'd* take oh-fense to it," sneered Langdon. "Them bad gangstas make us saints look mighty bad."

Ezra piped in. "But they still found all that evidence in his room, and he did say he was responsible for the murders, whatever that meant."

Maureen sat back in her chair, throwing her notepad on the table. "Well, that's it. Do those sound like reasons to murder someone? And to add to it all, every one of these boys said they were alone in their rooms, so no one to alibi them."

"We still have that secret room and that weird photograph," offered Brendan. "I wonder if the police found anything else interesting in it. There's also the stuff we saw in the mausoleum. I wish I could tie them all together to these murders." He pursed his lips, his head shaking, adding, "And maybe the murders were just that and had nothing to do with all these strange things we've added into the mix."

"And Marcus Dean is likely out, right, Bren?" asked Ezra. "What a creepy guy." He gave an involuntary shudder.

"As far as I'm concerned, for now anyway. But as for Father Gabriel—"

"He's on your radar?" Maureen asked.

Brendan stretched out his jaw and played with the stubble that he called a beard. "He's not off of it, that's for sure. That old man is hiding something. I don't think he actually killed anyone, but he knows more than he's letting on, and playing the geezer card. He's as wily as a Baptist preacher at a poker game."

"Hey!" yelled Langdon. "That ain't nice." He settled back down in his chair, grabbed a bag of chips, and tore it open with a satisfying rip, shoving his hand inside like he hadn't eaten in days.

Ezra finished writing what they had discussed on his board and turned to the group. "So we're back to square one then, even with all this new info?"

"Not necessarily," opined Maureen. "If the Kenyan boy lives and can tell us who pushed him—if indeed that's what happened—then that'll cinch it, and the killer will be caught." She crossed her arms. "Caleb's there with Deputy Hayes now, just in case anyone tries to ensure he won't be able to speak."

"Then let's pray he pulls through," Brendan said, his head bowing under the weight of sorrow.

After a stretch of silence, Maureen stood, gathered her notepad and bag. "Got to bounce." She shook her head, a sadness in her eyes.

Langdon and Brendan stood, and after Maureen left, Ezra began cleaning the table.

"I'd love to chat more, guys, but I've got a bar mitzvah class full of twelve-year-olds who think Moses invented TikTok. Pray for me."

Brendan stood, zipping his jacket and grabbing his cane. "I'm hearing the youth group's confessions tonight for the teen Mass on Sunday, and if I hear one more girl tell me they stole their sister's boyfriend, I might need confession myself. And I want to delve into those folders. Should be some good reading." He watched Langdon grab a handful of chocolate kisses from a candy bowl and stuff them into his coat pocket. "How about you, Pastor Boothe? Any plans?"

"Y'all be lucky. I got me three casseroles, two committee meetin's, and a group of ladies mad at the color I picked for the church carpet." He reached into his jacket and pulled out a knit cap.

Ezra chuckled. "Sounds like a holy trinity of trouble."

Brendan clapped him on the shoulder with a grin. "At least you get bagels, Ezra. I just get teen guilt and angst."

Langdon pulled the cap over his head as he headed for the door. "And I get potluck and heartburn."

Brendan turned to head out, then looked back at his friends, his face a question mark. "Hey, guys. After we get done with our church stuff, how would you like to come with me tonight to check out that mausoleum again?"

The two clergy looked at each other, and Brendan knew they didn't relish the idea.

"Sure, Bren," squeaked Ezra, looking at Langdon. "We'd love to come with you, huh, Langdon?"

Langdon's eyes grew wide, and he began buttoning his coat nervously. "Sure, I guess so. Hey, I ain't 'fraid, if that's what you be thinkin'."

"Good," Brendan said, rubbing his hands together. "Meet me at the rectory around eight tonight." He waggled his eyebrows in a way that was meant to be ominous but came off more like a cartoon villain. "And don't be late."

"Sure thing," Ezra said, his voice catching, as he cast a wary glance at the imposing Baptist beside him.

"We be there." Langdon scowled, and Brendan offered a self-assured smirk.

Langdon and Brendan left Ezra's, saying their goodbyes as the biting wind hurried them along. Brendan unlocked his Honda, threw his cane in the back, and got in.

The moment he hit the icy seat, he gasped and reached for the heat switch like a man about to meet his maker.

"Dear God, why is this November so cold when you've been heating up our world with global warming?"

Just as the car finally started to thaw, his cell phone shrieked to life, making him jump.

"Hold for the archbishop…" was all he heard when he answered.

Emitting a disgruntled sigh, he pulled out of the rabbi's driveway, fuming. Minutes later, Brendan heard his brother's voice.

"Why can't you make your own phone calls? Are you that high and mighty? Practicing to be the next American pope?"

"*Bí ciúin*," said Malachy, telling him to be quiet in Irish. Then he snorted. "Sure, and don't I sound like Ma when we were kids?"

Brendan found no humor in his brother. "Why did you call me, Mal? Ma had better be dying. I'm busy."

"*Tsk, tsk,*" Malachy clucked. "Such disrespect for your archbishop, and your old ma."

Brendan heaved a sigh as he pulled into the rectory's driveway. "You were my big brother before you were the pompous archbishop of the Baltimore diocese." He added, "So you want to go all Irish? Then you're a big fat *liúdramán*. And if you need a translation, go see Ma—like you ever would."

Brendan caught a rare laugh from his brother, a sound so unusual, it surprised him.

"Look, Bren, I just wanted to see how it was going with Father Tim and the outreach program. And also how Aiden's doing. I know you and Maureen are deep in it with these murders, and before you say something you'll need confession for, I just want you to know that I'm very grateful that you're looking in on the boy. You've helped ease Finn and Mary Virginia's minds. So," he said, drawing out the word, "you have my eternal gratitude."

Brendan laughed. "Eternal, huh? Well, I'll take it, Mal. And of *course*, I'll keep an eye on Aiden. We need all the priests we can muster in the O'Clery clan, huh?"

"Thanks, Bren. And keep me updated on Father Tim. Please, do whatever you can for him before it's too late. He *is* in his eighties, you know."

"And still has a parish...that's sad, Mal. You need to let him retire."

"He doesn't want to, and to be honest, he may be a little deaf, but his brain is still sharp, and his parish loves him."

"Aye, aye. Now give me a good old archbishop-type blessing before you go."

Brendan heard more Irish than a leprechaun on Saint Patrick's Day, none of which could be repeated in polite company, and then the line went dead.

CHAPTER 29

Thursday Night

Maureen sat on her sofa, staring sadly at her half-filled suitcases. She began unpacking her clothes, thinking that, by now, her girlfriends would have familiarized themselves with the lay of the land, found all the party places, and probably had already forgotten all about her.

Her phone rang, and the caller ID announced that it was Caleb.

"He's still intubated, and there's no change in him. They've done an MRI and are waiting to see if he improves." Maureen heard the sadness and frustration in his voice. "The hospital's put a call in to his folks, but Kenya's a long way off, and they may not have the money to just jump on a plane and fly over here."

Maureen pressed her eyes together, her heart aching for the boy who had possibly come face-to-face with the killer of two of his friends. She wondered if his parents would be able to make the flight over to say goodbye to their son or would they have to suffer the agony of receiving no closure upon his death?

"Okay, Caleb, keep me posted. And you can give the hospital my number, too, if you want to go home and get some sleep."

Just as she ended her call with Caleb, the phone rang again, and this time she felt a faint smile growing on her lips.

"Hello, Detective Archer. How are things in western Maryland?"

"Boring and cold without you, Detective McNeely."

The sound of Simon's voice warmed the chill she had felt after hearing about Okeyo's condition.

"Anything new on your seminary murders? And will you ever get to leave town for warmer climates?"

Maureen wanted desperately to laugh, but the unsolved murders and the attack of another young man had her stymied. She refused to let this puzzle go without a solution. She caught Simon up on the latest in the investigation, which had produced no progress, and then the talk turned to more interesting topics.

"Look," he offered, "I'll tell you what. When this is all over, I'll fly you down to whatever island you want, and we'll have our own vacation."

Maureen's lips twitched. On one hand, his suggestion sent a pleasant jolt through her body, but she wasn't sure she was ready for a week away with a man she had just started dating. A nervous laugh escaped her. "Let me get through this investigation first, then we'll talk about a vacation." She closed her eyes, wishing she could let herself fall in love again, like a mad schoolgirl.

They chatted for almost an hour. After ending the call, Maureen silently cursed herself for being so afraid of a relationship. A detective and sheriff's deputy for almost two decades, frightened of love.

But she could no more change her fears than she could un-live the pain that caused them. She threw the phone down onto the sofa and went into the kitchen, looking for a wine glass and something to put in it.

CHAPTER 30

Friday Midmorning

After Mass and breakfast, Eugene sat alone in the dimly lit common room. His rosary slipped between his fingers, the beads clicking softly, but his lips never moved in prayer. His mind was a storm, torn between doubt and guilt, spiraling into a deepening abyss. His faith, once a sanctuary, now felt like a prison, and the visions and nightmares were increasing. The weight of the murders pressed on his chest like an iron shroud, and with every passing moment, it felt as though Satan's grip was tightening.

He suddenly stood, pacing the length of the room. His muttering was low and disjointed, as if his thoughts were spilling out in fragments. The tension coiled tighter within him.

Then he froze, his head snapping up as though struck by divine inspiration, or desperation.

"Confession!" he muttered, his voice growing louder with conviction. "Father Gabriel said he wants us to go to confession."

He checked his watch and realized the chapel would soon be open, with priests waiting to hear confessions. A wave of urgency washed over him. These were the men he had once trusted with his innermost secrets, the guardians of his spiritual struggles. Perhaps now they could help him claw his way out of the darkness of why these murders were occurring.

He hurried through the corridors of the seminary and out into the faint chill of fall. The chapel doors creaked slightly as he pushed them open, and he hesitated for a moment at the threshold, his breath visible in the cold air. The stillness of the empty chapel, the flickering candlelight dancing across the statues of saints.

Finding no other students inside, Eugene quickly entered the old confessional stall, the crime scene tape having been removed. He closed the door behind him, the enclosed space feeling both comforting and oppressive. Taking a deep breath, he made the sign of the cross. His voice was unsteady, trembling with the weight of unspoken burdens.

"Bless me, Father, for I have sinned. It has been...too long since my last confession."

A soft voice responded through the screen, its tone gentle and almost hypnotic. "Speak your sins, child."

The warmth of the voice soothed Eugene's frayed nerves, though he couldn't place it. A visiting priest, possibly. The priest's identity didn't matter, he told himself. What mattered was the chance to purge his soul.

After a pause, he began haltingly. "Recently, I guess, ever since these murders started happening, I've doubted my faith. I've questioned my place here and why God has allowed these murders to happen. And...I've been afraid. Like maybe I'll be next, or maybe I'm the one who committed them while I was in some sort of trance. And I know I shouldn't fear death. I should welcome it with open arms."

The voice on the other side was soft, its cadence calm and unhurried. "We all fear what we cannot control. But tell me, child—do you fear what you cannot forgive?"

Eugene's heart stumbled, his breath catching in his throat. The question unsettled him in a way he couldn't explain. "I... I don't understand, Father. What do you mean?"

The voice replied, its tone a shade darker. "Even the purest heart carries guilt. Yours is no exception."

Confusion caused Eugene to frown. He leaned closer to the screen, squinting to make out the figure behind it. The shadows obscured the priest completely, leaving only the faint outline of a head. A cold shiver crawled up Eugene's spine. "What are you saying, Father? I don't know what you're alluding to. Do you think it's possible *I* murdered those boys?"

The words had barely left his lips before the sound of a door opening on the other side startled him. The abrupt creak shattered the uneasy stillness, and Eugene flinched.

He pushed the stall door on his side open and stepped into the chapel, his eyes darting around. He saw no one.

He pulled open the middle door. The interior space where the priest would sit was dark and unoccupied. He checked the third door to find no one in the other penitent's stall either.

The chapel seemed to breathe around him, the flickering candlelight casting shifting shadows that made the statues appear to move. Eugene's pulse pounded in his ears as he stood frozen, his unease now a full-blown terror.

There was no sign of the priest. No sign of anyone at all.

Brendan made it through daily Mass, but during the customary Adoration of the Blessed Sacrament that followed Friday's Mass, he silently begged God to forgive his aloofness.

He retreated into the sacristy where, while changing into what he referred to as his "civilian" clothes, Billy, his altar server for the day, followed him in.

"Hey, Father B," said the boy, running a sleeved arm across his runny nose, "I just wanted to let you know those soccer tips you gave us really helped last week. We creamed those boys from Porter Mill's Middle!" He pulled off his garb, revealing ragged jeans and a Saint Margaret Mary's team sweatshirt. Mary Magdalene pranced over to him, and he bent to roughhouse with the Yorkie.

Brendan gave the boy a warm smile and ruffled his carrot-topped head, orange curls framing an animated face. "Glad to be of help, Billy. I'm think-ing I've got a few more tips up my sleeve if you guys invite me over to the gym for another practice."

Billy's face lit up. "Gee, Father, that would be cool. Wait'll I tell the guys. We all like hearing about your soccer days as a kid in Ireland."

Brendan's thoughts of Ireland as a kid were few, but Billy didn't have to hear all about his abusive alcoholic father and how his mother had gathered the seven kids one night and left while her husband was in a stupor. He was happily ensconced here at Saint Margaret Mary's with a small but wonderful parish, and he hoped his brother would allow him to remain there.

"Well, son, I've got stories, so let me know when your next practice is."

"Gee, thanks." Billy ran a hand through his hair and turned, fleeing his duties as altar server. "See ya, Father B!" He gave a quick wave as he ran off.

Shaking his head and laughing at the boy's spirited nature, Brendan hung his vestments up and walked over to the rectory and grabbed a muffin to go. He got into his Honda and headed for Father Timothy's.

Eugene slipped back into the common room and quietly took a seat in the corner, well apart from the cluster of seminarians laughing and chatting among themselves. His eyes were heavy with exhaustion, and his untouched breakfast plate had been a silent testament to his unease. Aiden, noticing his fellow student's solitary demeanor at the morning meal, excused himself from his group and walked over.

"You okay?" Aiden asked, pulling out the chair beside him.

Eugene hesitated before speaking, his voice low and strained. Eugene relayed his ordeal at the confessional to Aiden.

"I didn't recognize the priest's voice. At first, it was calm, reassuring. But then it got...strange. And when I finally left the confessional, there was no priest, no one in the chapel. I looked everywhere. He just...vanished."

Aiden's brow furrowed, knowing full well where the priest, or whoever had been in that confessional went. "That's bizarre. Would you mind if I called my cousin? I think she'd want to know about this. She and my uncle,

Father O'Clery, they're like experts at solving weird mysteries, and I'm sure they'll have it solved soon and find out who's killing us."

Eugene poked at a dirt spot on his clerical slacks. "Sure. Whatever. I'm a mess right now. I'm scared, confused, angry. It's like everything's coming at me at once." He glanced up, his voice softening. "I'll take any help I can get. Thanks, Aiden. You're a good friend."

Aiden patted Eugene's shoulder and rose to make the call.

Brendan rang Father Timothy's doorbell and adjusted his clerical trousers. *Must be losing weight,* he thought, and was just about to tighten his belt a notch when the dreadful housekeeper flung open the door, scowling like she'd caught him robbing the place.

"Is Father Ti—"

"I know why you're here. Get in already." She grabbed his wrist, yanking him roughly through the open front door and into the old row home's parlor.

He stumbled as she released her grip and fell into a worn armchair.

"Stay here. He'll come out when he's ready." She turned and left, Brendan feeling very much violated.

Several minutes later, the old priest hobbled out into the living room, wearing a cheery smile. "Brendan, my boy, how are you? Would you like some lunch?" Father Timothy attempted to sit—three times—until his frail frame rested comfortably in the chair opposite Brendan. "The folks that volunteered for the outreach program will be here shortly, but"—he leaned in toward Brendan, then stretched his neck out, looking for his housekeeper—"tell me all about these murders I hear you're working on."

Brendan reached over the arm of his chair to retrieve the cane he had dropped after Wanda had manhandled him into the living room. "How did you hear—" he began, but was cut off by a phlegmatic laugh.

"One of your brother's lackeys, Father Pittinger." He laughed, then coughed, the sound scraping up from deep in his lungs. "He overheard you two talking, and trust me, Pittinger loves to spread his own gospel, if you get my meaning. If the archbishop knew he'd spilled the story to me, his old seminary buddy, he'd be defrocked." Another rasp rattled out of him. "I knew Malachy back when he was just a young seminarian, wetting his pants every time an instructor called on him."

Brendan had no doubt. Father Tim was no fan of his brother. "You're so right, Father," said Brendan knowingly, peeking at his watch.

The old priest continued. "But getting back to the murders, that Vincent Gabriel is sly, and you mark my word, when this is all said and done, you'll find that he's behind these deaths." He nodded his head vigorously.

Brendan's head tilted. "Father Gabriel? You think he murdered those boys? But why would he do that?"

Father Timothy pounded the arm of his chair with his bony hand. "No, no, he'd never *murder* anyone, boy. He's a secretive old bat, but he's no murderer." He picked at a scab on his hand. "He'll be hiding something, trust me. Oh, he's a good administrator—the best—but when it comes to his precious seminary, and the possibility that your brother may close it down"—he gave a brittle laugh—"trust me, he'll do whatever it takes to hide anything that might cause a scandal."

Brendan was intrigued. "Like what?"

Father Timothy tapped the side of his nose and laughed again, a laugh that ended up as a coughing spell. He lit a cigarette. "We have an outreach program to birth, and that doorbell just rang. That means the volunteers are starting to come in." He raised himself with great effort, the cigarette dangling from his lower lip, ashes falling to the floor. "Come on into the dining room. We can sit around the table and get to know each other."

Brendan glanced at his watch again. Had the thing stopped completely, or was time just going that slowly?

He wished he was anywhere but here.

After the outreach meeting, Brendan drove back to the rectory, his eyes glazed over. The consortium of people Father Timothy had gathered from his church and the surrounding community was truly an eye-opening event. Oh, they were nice enough, but what a menagerie! However, he was satisfied. It was over with, and he had promised Father Timothy that he'd check in on him soon, hopefully after these murders were solved.

As soon as he opened the rectory door, Mary Magdalene exploded in a fit of joyful yaps, her tiny paws drumming the floor like a wind-up toy gone mad.

"I kept telling her you'd soon be home, Father," said Mrs. Morrison, as she put a container of milk in the fridge.

Brendan scooped up the little dog, his scruffy beard quickly dampened by a flurry of eager licks. "Someone needs a walk. I've got a ton of work to do, and I need to wear you out so you'll sleep for a few hours."

"Good luck with that," groused the housekeeper. "She and Saint Peter have been chasing each other around the place for hours, and neither has wound down at all." She placed her hands firmly on her hips. "They should both be asleep, but no, they've been running all around my feet, getting in my way."

"But look at this cute face, Mrs. M.," said Brendan, cooing. "How can you be mad at this little girl?"

The housekeeper rolled her eyes and walked to where the leash was hanging on a hook. She grabbed it and thrust it at Brendan. "Here, you go. Wear her out then. I'm off. I'll see you on Monday. There's a honey ham in the oven." She walked over to the coat rack and retrieved her jacket.

"By the way, Mrs. M., Ma called me within a half hour of sampling your coconut cake. She hollered at me for not bringing her a larger piece! Honestly, I get yelled at no matter *what* I do!" He attached the leash and led a prancing Mary Magdalene toward the door.

His housekeeper's face glow as she buttoned her jacket. "I'm glad she liked it, Father. I'll make another one next week, and you can take half of it to her."

"You're the best, Mrs. M."

"Don't I know it, Father. And never forget it." She opened the door and walked out into the afternoon chill.

"I don't know what I did to get such a wonderful housekeeper," said Brendan to the Yorkie, "but I'm hoping she never realizes she's far too good for this circus."

He opened the back door and stepped outside, setting the tiny dog down as they began their slow trek into the biting wind.

CHAPTER 31

Friday Late Afternoon

Brendan had been hungrier than he thought, or maybe it was Mrs. Morrison's cooking skills, but he ate twice as much of the ham as he knew he should.

He lowered the remains on the plate to the floor, and right on cue, Mary Magdalene began her usual evening task, licking it clean with the focus of a nun polishing silver for Sunday Mass.

After straightening up the kitchen, he lumbered into the living room and sank into his recliner, anxious to dive into the folders he had purloined of each of the seminarians. A satisfied Mary Magdalene circled his ankles and, when she found just the right spot, dropped down and commenced napping.

Opening the first folder, he began reading. It contained very vanilla information. He closed it and went to the next. His lips moved silently as he devoured each word, learning more than he ever expected about the young men who had vowed to serve their God.

He found these boys to be highly intelligent. All were top-of-their-class students, some outstanding athletes, and all had been involved in church activities and organizations from an early age.

He kept coming back to Father Gabriel, and even entertained the thought that Marcus Dean, crippled as he was, was involved somehow, or maybe the two of them together were in it.

Expelling a long breath, Brendan let the folder droop in his hands, his eyes glazing over as the words marched on without mercy.

After leaning over the chair to check on Mary Magdalene, he picked up the last folder. These boys were squeaky clean. Their only sin was stress and living with so much testosterone.

He began reading the last folder, his lips once again moving numbly across the words, until he came to something that practically stopped his heart. He sat up straight in his chair, his eyes now fully engaged.

He took in every word. So, he thought. Nine years ago is when everything had all started, and now it was coming to fruition, and from someone he never expected.

He slammed the folder closed, nearly leaping out of his chair in his haste. His leg, however, slowed him down. Grabbing his cane, he limped out to the kitchen, where he had left his phone. He left an urgent voicemail for Maureen then texted his friends to meet him at the seminary.

Eugene knocked on Aiden's door. "Want to walk together for rosary and evening prayers?"

Aiden expelled a quiet breath. "You bet I do. My cousin told me we should all stick together and not be alone if it's possible. Let me grab my coat." He went into his closet and pulled out a thick woolen coat. "Let's go," said Aiden, closing his door. "And let's say extra prayers tonight that this ends soon, and with no one else getting killed."

Eugene nodded. "Amen, to that."

They scurried down the stairs, heading toward the front door. Several more seminarians joined them, along with the ones who had returned from their retreat.

As the group grew, Eugene and Aiden got separated from each other, but Aiden felt safe, since there were almost a dozen seminarians bustling toward the chapel.

"Hey, Aiden," called out Nathan, as he caught up to him. "I want to show you something."

Aiden glanced around but kept walking. "We have to get to the chapel."

"It'll only take a minute. And it's something that'll help your cousin solve these murders." He motioned for him to follow, but Aiden remained glued to the spot. Nathan huffed. "I thought you wanted to help your cousin get this killer. You'd be the hero."

Aiden's resolve began to weaken. If he could help Maureen solve these brutal killings, his family would be so proud. He looked around, seeing the group melt into the night.

"Okay, you win, but let's make this quick. I want to get in there before prayers start."

Nathan grabbed at his sleeve. "Then hurry up. I promise, this will only take a minute." He led the way, and the two of them vanishing into the night, heading for the old cemetery.

"Can't this boat go any faster?" Ezra clung to the armrest as the huge Caddy took a sharp turn.

"Don't you be insultin' Miz Aretha here or you gonna be walkin' the rest of the way." Langdon floored the accelerator, and Ezra fell out of his seat and onto the floorboard of the car, his yarmulke falling off.

Coming from the other side of Porter Mills, Brendan's old Honda sped wildly as he answered his cell phone. He poured out to Maureen what he'd uncovered in the files.

"Get as many deputies as you can muster."

He ended the call and braced himself for the fifteen-minute drive to the seminary—fifteen minutes of quiet agony.

Aiden kept looking back toward the chapel. "We're going to be late." He noted that Nathan was steering him toward the old cemetery. "We're not going into the cemetery, are we? I don't think I want to go."

He slowed down, but Nathan grabbed his wrist.

"We're almost there. I *promise*, it'll be worth it."

Aiden followed the rustling of the fabric of Nathan's cassock. "We really shouldn't be here at all." He raised his voice, surprised at the surge of anger swelling inside him. So unfamiliar, yet suddenly overwhelming. "I want to go back."

"We're here. Look," Nathan said, pointing to the mausoleum, "it's the place your uncle has been checking out."

The old mausoleum stood like a dead sentinel beneath the trees, cracked stone lit silver under the moonlight. Aiden's anger subsided momentarily as he gazed at the name—Dean—in the dim moonlight. Suddenly, it became apparent what Nathan had wanted to share.

He grinned at his friend, eager to proceed. Wind scraped dry leaves across the threshold as Aiden stepped inside. The door groaned shut behind him.

"So it was Marcus Dean after all, huh?" He gave Nathan's back a sharp slap. "My uncle didn't seem to care for the man. So, show me what you've found to prove his guilt. This is way cool, Nathan. Thanks for dragging me here. Sorry I balked."

"That's okay. Come on down to the crypt. That's where it is." He reached into his coat pocket, pulled out his cell phone and turned on the flashlight, shining it down the narrow steps. "Guests first."

Aiden, now fully engaged in the expedition, nodded and stepped gingerly down the concrete steps.

"Boy, it sure is dark in here," said Aiden, his nose crinkling at the musty smell of the dank space. He watched as Nathan handed his cell phone to Aiden, then struck a match and lit a tapered candle, retrieving his phone. "So Marcus Dean's parents and family are buried here. Creepy."

When they reached the bottom, he ran his hands over the top of one tomb. He was surprised to see the one next to it covered with several wine bottles. "Why are these here? I guess Marcus comes to visit with his parents and tie one on. What do you think?"

Nathan had turned off his flashlight so Aiden could barely make him out as he fooled around with something behind one of the tombs.

"Nathan? What do you have?" He reached for his own cell, turning on the flashlight, as his fingers trailed along the damp wall.

Nathan made no sound.

Aiden held his hand out, feeling his companion's head. He laughed. "There you are! What are you doing?" He stared down at the stone floor but couldn't see what Nathan was doing.

Finally, standing up, Nathan pointed toward the floor. "Look at this. Tell me what you see." He had turned the flashlight on again and aimed it in front of Aiden.

As Aiden stooped to see what Nathan wanted him so urgently to look at, he squinted, trying to force his eyes to see what Nathan saw. The dank, musty space made Aiden sneeze.

"I don't see any—"

The words died on his lips as Nathan reached out, slamming a thick, rusted candlestick into the side of Aiden's head. Metal met bone with a sickening crack.

Aiden dropped like a rag doll. Everything went black, and he crumpled to the ground, pain exploding in his skull.

Aiden awoke—moments? hours?—later. Disoriented. Cold. His head pounded as he lay on the concrete floor. The air smelled of damp stone and decaying materials.

Nathan stood over him, eyes glittering. His cassock was now ripped and filthy.

"You should've stayed out of this," Nathan growled. "But no, your nosy uncle had to come back here and foul all my plans and get you to help him." His breath, warm and oppressive, washed over Aiden's face.

Aiden tried to move. Pain exploded behind his eyes, and his body wasn't able to move. "Nathan...please..."

Nathan kicked him in the ribs. "Don't beg, Aiden. Not you. Not Saint Aiden."

Aiden rolled, gasping. Blood ran from his scalp down onto the concrete. "Nathan...what did I ever...do to you?"

"You existed!" Nathan spat. "My brother hung himself in this very seminary because of what Joseph Lin and Matthew Mueller's families did to him. Their families' treatment of him killed him. You think I could forget that?"

He forced Aiden to his knees, muscles knotting as he heaved his limp body onto the tomb in one violent motion.

The cold marble kissed the back of Aiden's neck as Nathan pressed the knife to his throat. He wanted to scream for help but found his thoughts hazy.

"Father Gabriel was supposed to be the third death, but you'll do." His breath was hot on Aiden's face. "You're going to die in here," Nathan spat. "Like he did. Alone. Forgotten."

The air hung heavy and damp, thick with the scent of mildew. The candle flickered nearby, casting twitching silhouettes on the cracked stone mausoleum walls. Shadows crawled across the crumbling stone as Nathan loomed over Aiden, sprawled atop the marble tomb, half-conscious, his breath shallow, blood trickling from the cut on his forehead.

Nathan grabbed a roll of duct tape and secured Aiden's wrists and ankles with the tape.

Nathan stood over him, his back to the crypt's entranceway, breathing hard, as he picked up a gleaming dagger that trembled in his hand. The glint of the knife caught the candlelight, throwing it across the walls like lightning. His lips whispered fragments of Latin and broken prayers.

Suddenly, with a voice that shook with fury, he gazed down at Aiden. "You don't even know what you are, do you? You're just a symbol. A vessel for the rot you and the others left behind."

Aiden stirred slightly and let out a broken groan, his body barely able to move.

Nathan ignored him, his voice rising and breaking in a frenzy of lunacy. "Those two needed to be destroyed. Their families obliterated mine. My parents died and didn't get the justice they deserved after their families killed my brother."

He lowered the knife momentarily as he leaned over Aiden, brushing a hand over his forehead with a twisted tenderness.

"But I was *called*. And I *answered*."

He rose to his feet, knife clenched in both hands, a wild fury blazing in his eyes as his insanity grew. His eyes glistened, not with tears, but with something far darker. He began chanting softly in Latin—broken, clumsy—but fervent.

"*Libera me, Domine... de morte aeterna...*"

Aiden's eyes fluttered. When they met Nathan's, he whispered desperately, "Nathan, please...what are...doing...?"

Nathan's hands shook as he pressed the point of the blade to Aiden's chest. "This is mercy. This is *sacrifice*." He raised his eyes upward and mouthed, *Only the faithful shall see the light beyond the veil.*

He stared down again at Aiden. "You think *you're* innocent? None of you are innocent! Your friends' families destroyed my brother's life and mine, and you walk around this place like you're some kind of saint! You're no better than they are." He raised the blade with both hands, eyes wild.

Just then Aiden heard noises coming toward the crypt.

"Nathan," came a voice, both gentle and apprehensive. Uncle Brendan! Feeling safe, Aiden let darkness take over.

Nathan didn't turn, but the sound of Brendan's voice stopped the downward motion of the knife.

Nathan's hands remained still, poised over Aiden. A sardonic grin appeared on his face as he slowly turned and saw Brendan standing in the entrance, the fear on his face surely noticeable.

"Put it down, Nathan." Brendan kept his voice calm and deliberate. He leaned hard on his cane, sweat glistening on his brow, his breath visible in the chill.

"Well, well, Father O'Clery. "You shouldn't be here. This...this has nothing to do with you." His voice was ragged, barely holding back his rage. He turned back to Aiden, blade flashing again.

"It has *everything* to do with me. Aiden is my nephew and is innocent." He took a breath and continued softly. "I read your file, the secret one Father Gabriel kept hidden. Nathan, you're about to throw your life away."

Nathan turned again to confront Brendan, his eyes wild and glassy. He let out a demonic laugh. "My life ended after my brother died. You can't hurt me any more than I've already been hurt."

Brendan ignored the rant and continued. "I said, put it down, Nathan. It's over. The police are coming." He nodded toward the sounds of sirens and tires gnashing into gravel.

Nathan refused to be silenced. "They threw my brother away like garbage. Mrs. Lin and Mr. Mueller—good Catholic families—*respectable.* They bullied him, tortured him. And when he cried out for help, nobody listened." He stepped back toward Aiden again, the knife twitching in anxious hands. "And now *this* one—nephew of the priest trying to crucify *me*, gets to waltz through life untouched, wearing the same smile that *they* did."

"Aiden has nothing to do with this, and you know it. You just want to murder for the sake of revenge, and as you should know, since you claim to be a good Catholic boy, vengeance belongs to God and God alone."

Nathan's face twisted into an ugly mask. "My brother's suicide killed my parents. My mother died from a heart attack three weeks later, and my father ended up drinking himself into his grave. I was eleven. I had to go into foster care."

Brendan took a slow, tentative step forward, hands raised. "Look, Nathan, I'm sorry for what happened to your brother. I *am*. And I won't pretend to know that kind of pain. But this"—he nodded toward the knife—"this isn't justice. It's another tragedy. And it ends with you being taken away in chains."

Nathan blinked rapidly, the knife wavering.

Brendan's pulse pounded in his ears as he locked eyes with his nephew's would-be killer. He prayed for the police to arrive soon.

His voice trembled but carried the weight of desperation. "Please, Nathan. Aiden has never harmed you. He's just a good, gentle lad, who came here with nothing but a calling to serve God. I'm *begging* you, don't spill another drop of blood. He has a family who cherishes him, who would be shattered if he didn't come home. Just as Christ loves you, they love him." His throat felt parched, his mouth dry as dust. "Whatever hurt is festering in your heart, let me help you carry it. Let me help you find a way back from this. I'm pleading with you, son, please, for the love of God."

He took a slow, deliberate step forward, arms outstretched in an open, unguarded plea, his bad leg throbbing mercilessly.

Brendan saw the boy's body slacken, but not enough to ease the fear he felt for his nephew's safety.

Nathan's voice was low and monotone. "I heard some of the seminarians who are now priests laugh at my brother's funeral when they thought I wasn't listening." His breath caught in his throat. "They actually made jokes at the repast. Said my brother was too sensitive to be a real man of God."

Sirens wailed in the distance, growing louder. The blue and red lights begin to strobe through the doorway.

Brendan turned toward the sound, having almost forgotten about Ezra and Langdon, who stood as still as statues away from the fray.

He turned back and rushed the conversation, his voice softer and more intimate. "And what would your brother want you to do, Nathan? Slaughter someone in a mausoleum? Would he want *this* to be your legacy?"

Nathan studied Aiden's barely conscious form, his hand shaking harder now.

"Please," begged Brendan. "You're *not* a killer."

Silence filled the crypt, the sirens now inside the cemetery.

Nathan's voice was low and flat. "Maybe I am now." He raised the knife again.

This time, Brendan was sure it would be plunged into his nephew's heart. He needed to think, and time had just run out.

Suddenly, Brendan let out a scream worthy of any Irish banshee. He lifted the cane from his side and hurled it like a spear with surprising strength. It sailed through the flickering candlelight, spinning end-over-end, in what seemed like slow motion, until it struck Nathan hard in the side of the neck with a sickening crack.

Nathan stumbled back, gasping and clutching his throat, the dagger skittering to the floor. Then Nathan jolted, turning as Brendan barreled toward him, his breath ragged.

Out of the corner of his eye, Brendan saw Aiden attempt to turn his head, watching silently as Brendan threw himself onto the crazed seminarian, pinning him to the ground with a strength that surprised him.

He drew back a fist and aimed it at the boy's face, pausing momentarily to think about what he was preparing to do.

Nathan stared into Brendan's face, grinning with the satisfaction of Satan himself. "Go on, Father. Do it."

Brendan's fist remained in the air, but his heart sickened. What was he about to do? He was no better than this young man.

He lowered his fist but kept Nathan pinned until he heard footsteps racing down the concrete steps.

But in a turnabout, Nathan lifted his elbow, slamming it into Brendan's jaw. All of Brendan's military training came flooding back into his brain, and he was once again that young Marine in Iraq. He retaliated with a knee to Nathan's gut. Nathan punched blindly.

Then, in a savage action, Brendan bit down on Nathan's shoulder, tasting blood and cloth, shocking himself with the animal-like attack.

They rolled across the stone floor, covered in blood, sweat, and dirt, crashing into the sarcophagus, fists flying.

Nathan seized a shard of broken marble.

Just then Aiden made a feeble tempt to warn Brendan. "Watch out!"

Nathan slashed at Brendan's chest. He grabbed Nathan's wrist and twisted until it cracked. Ignoring the pain, Nathan stretched out his other arm and made a grab for the knife, and when he had it, held it inches above Brendan's face.

Just then, a light burst through the mausoleum door as the glow of approaching blue-and-red lights hung in the air.

"Get away from him!" came Maureen's voice, thunderous with fury. Nathan turned at the sound of her voice, and as he did, Brendan grabbed his wrist and pinned his arm to the ground, causing the knife to fall from his hand. He was then able to flip the boy over and roll away from the danger.

Dazed, Nathan tried to crawl toward the knife, reaching a hand toward it. Maureen kicked it out of his reach, then dropped to one knee beside Brendan, holding his head gently.

Caleb stood over Nathan, whose chest heaved, eyes blazing wildly. "It's over, Nathan."

Sirens wailed louder. Deputies flooded the mausoleum, guns drawn.

Brendan heard Aiden's barely conscious voice from above. "Is Nathan… is he dead?" he rasped.

Maureen shook her head. "No, Cuz. But you're alive. And that's all that matters."

Brendan watched as Nathan collected himself and stood. He tried to shove his way past the sea of deputies, but his plan was thwarted. Caleb grabbed the seminarian and, for several seconds, the two struggled, until Caleb punched Nathan in the face and he went down, dazed.

One of the uniformed deputies lifted him roughly to his feet. They cuffed his hands behind his back, reading him his rights as he spat blood and hurled curses.

Brendan, still sprawled on the cold floor, let out a sigh of relief as he watched another deputy cut through the duct tape on Aiden's hands and feet.

"I was chosen!" screamed Nathan, thrashing, as blood flowed from the corner of his mouth. "You'll see. I did this to avenge my brother! They deserved to die, and I'm not sorry!"

"No, Nathan—or should I call you *Julien*," Branden said bitterly.

Maureen, helping him to his feet, shot him a startled look at the unfamiliar name.

"You let your pain fester into hatred. This wasn't justice. It was revenge. And it ends here." Brendan struggled to stand, as Maureen helped him. He reached for his cane and limped over to where his nephew sat, trying to take in all that was happening. He put his arm around the boy in a tight embrace. He turned to the deputy attending Aiden's head wound but dared not interrupt his ministrations.

Nathan, breathless and snarling, went limp as two deputies dragged him toward the steps, his shouts echoing off the crypt walls before fading into silence.

He laughed in a dry, bitter sound. "Enjoy your little victory, Father O'Clery," he said, turning back to Brendan.

Brendan stiffened at the comment. "You're lucky you'll spend the rest of your life in a cell instead of meeting the God you claimed to serve."

A cruel smirk twisted on Nathan's mouth. He whispered, "I never wanted to be a priest, Father. I changed my name years ago and professed my unending love for God." His eyes raised to heaven mockingly... "I entered this wreck of a seminary for the main purpose of seeking justice for my brother." He gave a cruel laugh. "But I'll be in every chapel, Father. Every silent prayer."

Brendan remained stoic, but his grip on Aiden's cold hand tightened. "And I'll be there to remind everyone that you were just a coward with a knife."

The deputies dragged Nathan up the steps and out into the night, his muttering fading as they led him to the waiting cruisers.

A single candle fought the darkness, sputtering in the mausoleum's cold silence, while red and blue lights from patrol cars slashed across the walls, throwing grotesque silhouettes that seemed almost alive.

Just then Maureen spotted the dagger at his feet. She reached in her pocket and pulled out a glove, picking it up, as she looked over at Aiden.

"Uncle Brendan? Are you okay?" was as much as Aiden could muster.

"I'm good, and you're safe now, Aiden. It's all over."

Aiden groaned and tried to sit up. Brendan motioned for Maureen, and along with the attending deputy, they gently lifted him, just as the EMTs swarmed in. They wrapped a blanket around his shoulders and began monitoring his vitals.

Aiden clutched Brendan's sleeve. "What...happened to his brother? I was only able to catch bits of what was going on."

Maureen looked at her uncle. "I'd like to hear that story myself, and how you came up with the name Julien."

Brendan gave his niece and nephew a weak smile, weariness etched into every line of his face. "It's a long story, guys. It'll be told soon enough, but right now"—he looked at Aiden—"you have to go to the hospital."

Maureen gave Aiden a gentle hug. She looked at Brendan. "And I'm going to find Father Gabriel *now* and have a nice long chat with him. He knows way more than he's told us." She gave her cousin a gentle kiss on the top of his damaged head and turned to go.

"Good luck, then," said Brendan, giving her a sly smile. "I'll be praying for you."

Maureen gave him a wink and walked through the sea of uniforms as she searched for Father Gabriel.

Maureen studied the old priest's face after they had retreated to his office, wondering how he could have let things go so far. And she was about to find out.

The rector sat at his desk, hands folded, almost as though he had been expecting this grilling.

As Maureen entered the office, she dropped the Nathan Silk file, the one her uncle had at last coughed up, onto the rector's desk with a satisfying smack. "Father, we need to talk. You knew Nathan wasn't who he claimed to be, didn't you? How long have you been hiding the truth?"

Father Gabriel looked up at Maureen with tired eyes. "I knew Nathan was actually Julien Mercer the moment he set foot in the seminary. I knew he had changed his name years ago, but I thought...I *hoped* I could save him. But I see now that I failed him, just as I failed so many others." The old rector ran a wrinkled hand over his face. "I had no idea he was a killer—*the* killer. You've got to believe me. I truly thought, and prayed, it was an outsider, a serial killer perhaps." Shaking his head sadly, he continued, his voice soft. "What have I done?"

"You didn't just fail, Father," said Maureen accusingly. "You *enabled* this. You allowed the sins of the past to fester until they consumed everything."

"What would you have me do, Detective?" The rector's voice cracked as it escalated. "Destroy the seminary? The Church? It's all I've ever known, and I do *not* want to see it closed down."

Maureen leaned forward. "Sometimes destruction is the only path to redemption."

Father Gabriel looked at her, as if searching for forgiveness. He shifted uneasily in his chair and began clicking a pen. "I knew Julien Mercer had been a troubled young man, ever since his brother had killed himself in the Dean mausoleum, but I never dreamed he'd take it this far and become a killer. I thought he had come here to fulfill his brother's desire to become a priest, but I know now that was not the case."

Maureen remained silent, forcing the man to continue.

"Detective, I've made mistakes, but I did not aid a murderer."

"But you've been covering for him," she countered. "Why?"

Father Gabriel stopped clicking the pen and laid it down. He looked up at Maureen, sighing deeply. "Because the Church has failed too many already. I thought I could help him. I never thought I was covering for a killer, believe me. Had I known what he truly harbored in his soul, I would have turned him in. I knew he had an unstable home life and I spent hours talking with him, praying with him." His head hung low. "I never saw the hatred and the anger. Never."

Maureen frowned and looked away. Maybe this man truly hadn't been aware of what Na—Julien Mercer—had been planning to do. "So you knew he was Myron Mercer's brother all along."

Father Gabriel pursed his lips. "I knew. I thought I'd be a good mentor and thought his only issues were a sad family life. How could I know he was so angry, so duplicitous? I believed in forgiveness and redemption."

"Redemption?" cried Maureen. "You're either naive or complicit. And right now, I'm leaning toward complicit."

Father Gabriel's eyes met hers, his expression pained. "I had Myron Mercer here as a first-year student nine years ago. He was a good student, but"—his words faltered—"he would never have made a good priest." The rector's eyes seemed to be searching for the right words. "I...I mean," he stuttered, "he...he wasn't good at interpersonal relationships. He could never connect with people. The boy had the personality of a dead carp."

"So why do you think Julien murdered these two boys?" asked Maureen.

Father Gabriel wrung his hands. "This is only my suspicion, based on what he confided in me. Joseph Lin's mother worked in the cafeteria at Myron's high school. The boy was overweight, and Mrs. Lin not only made fun of the boy when he went through the lunch line, she encouraged the other kids to do the same. It was cruel, and Julien probably wanted revenge on the people who caused his brother pain. Killing Joseph may have been Julien's way of causing Joseph's folks pain."

Maureen thought of the pain he must have endured for years. "And the Mueller boy?"

The rector expelled a tired sigh. "Again, from what Julien told me, Matthew's father was a doctor. Myron had crushed his ankle and shin bone during a high school gym class, and Matthew's father was the doctor who set his leg." He grimaced as he continued. "The pain must have been excruciating, because he had pins in his leg for over two months, and the bones must have healed incorrectly because he walked with a limp after that."

"So, why kill Matthew Mueller for *that*?"

The rector raised his hand. "I'm getting there, Detective." He took a breath and continued. "The pain was so bad, and he complained so often, that Dr. Mueller began prescribing oxycodone for the pain. Well"—he spread his arms over his desk—"needless to say, Myron became addicted. He entered this seminary as an addict."

Maureen frowned, sitting up in her chair. "So you let him in like that?"

"Again," he said, "I thought, with the proper atmosphere and understanding, he'd work his way through it. One day, no one could find him for the entire day, so we searched the grounds, and one of the boys found him... hanging there, in that dreary mausoleum. I knew then that my prayers had not been answered."

Maureen relaxed, feeling this was all she'd get from the old priest. She'd find out more when she went to the station to sit in on the questioning of Julien Mercer. She also wanted to ask her uncle how he had come up with the correct suspect—again. A smile was creeping onto her face, but first, she needed to end this interview.

"Detective Martinez will be back later to question you when he's finished with Mercer." She saw the panicked look on his face. She reached out and put a hand over his. "Don't worry, Father. I believe you couldn't have known this would have happened. The detective will just want some background information, that's all."

Father Gabriel put his head in his hands. "You think this is easy for me, Detective? The Church isn't perfect, but everything I've done was to protect this institution."

Maureen took her hand away from his. "Protect the institution? People are dead, Father. If you'd been honest from the start, perhaps we could've stopped this."

Father Gabriel looked down at his clasped hands, silent for a moment.

"And you buried it. All of it. Just like the files we found."

The rector nodded slowly. "Julien came here with vengeance in his heart. I never saw it. I thought...perhaps this place could heal him."

"Heal him? You let a ticking time bomb into a school full of innocent young men."

Father Gabriel's head jerked up in defiance. "The sins of the past have to be reckoned with. I just prayed it wouldn't come to this."

Maureen stood abruptly, the chair making a loud noise as she shoved it back. "You may not be a murderer, Father, but I hope—no, I *pray*—that, after the dust clears on this debacle, you highly consider retirement." She turned to go but addressed him one more time. "Remember, my *other* uncle is the archbishop." And with that, she left, making her way back to the station, and some answers.

On her way back to the office, Maureen called her uncle. "You at the scene still?"

"Yeah, why?"

"I'm heading back to sit in with Caleb and the Mercer boy. I have an ice cream headache after speaking with that rector." She paused. "So can you go to the hospital and sit with Aiden? And maybe get checked out yourself?"

Brendan laughed. "I'm good, Mo, just a little beat up. Anyway, that was our plan. The guys and I will be leaving here shortly, as soon as we give our statements."

"Good," she replied, as she flew through the night in the Jeep. "I'll meet you there when I'm done."

The Jeep skidded into the parking lot of the sheriff's department. Within seconds, Maureen had bounded through the front door, taking the steps down to the basement two at a time.

She collected herself before entering the interrogation room, not wanting to disturb Caleb's process.

"And that's when you decided to enter the seminary?" asked Caleb, as he gave her a nod of recognition.

Maureen watched as the young man, now known to be Julien Mercer, twisted his wrists around uncomfortably in the handcuffs.

"I always knew I had to finish what he started," he said, looking everywhere but at Caleb's eyes.

"But your brother wanted to become a priest. *You* wanted to murder people."

Julien gave a weak shrug. "The more I thought about the pain everyone had caused him, the more I figured they needed to be wiped off the face of the earth, like they had forced my brother to be."

Caleb sat back in his chair, tapping his pen. He looked over at Maureen, his lips twisted into an I'm-getting-nothing-from-this-guy look.

"So tell me about the people who picked on your brother."

Julien stretched his neck, his eyes searching for something unknown on the ceiling. "Let's see…well, Mrs. Lin—and believe me, she was no looker either—would heap extra portions of food on my brother's plate and tell him she was only helping him to earn the title of being the fattest boy in school, and that maybe he'd win a prize. She'd tell him, in front of others, that no girl would ever want him unless he lost some weight and got a personality, and that plastic surgery wouldn't even help." His head dropped, and finally, he met the detective's eyes. "Now, do you think that was a nice thing for a school employee to do to an impressionable high school kid?" He gave a rude snort. "I wanted to kill her then and there when Myron would come home crying and tell me what she had said. But"—he rubbed his wrists, slipping his fingers between the cuffs—"after Myron killed himself, and the more I thought about it, the more I knew it would be better to take something away from *her*, something she really loved. So I heard Joseph wanted to be a priest and had applied to Saint Charles, and that's when the idea came to me."

"So you never really wanted to become a priest?"

Julien gave him a wide grin. "No way, Detective. Not on your life. I just needed to get into that seminary." He scratched at his nose.

"And what about the Muellers?"

Julien laughed, lifting both cuffed hands to rub tired eyes. "Dr. Mueller…what a charmer. When the school insisted everyone take gym classes, Myron did his best, but that was never good enough for his gym teacher, Norm Kowalski. So, when Myron got tackled in a football practice game, a sport he loathed, his ankle and shin got crushed, and he needed pins in his leg for a few months, and he was in a boot cast for another month. The injury never quite healed right, and Myron would be in tears at night. So, our mom takes him back to good old Dr. Mueller, who does what? Writes him a quick prescription for oxycodone, and when that runs out, he writes another one. Needless to say, my brother became an addict."

"So he still got accepted into Saint Charles?" asked Caleb, urging the boy on. He shot a glance at Maureen, where she sat taking notes.

"He got in, yes," said Julien. "He was a brilliant guy, and Mom and Dad begged and cajoled the bishop at the time, and Father Gabriel let him in. And Myron was happy there for a while."

Caleb jotted something down, then looked up and asked, "So what happened?" He watched the young man rub his eyes for several seconds.

Julien hung his head. "Myron's depression seemed to totally engulf him, and quickly. His weight kept skyrocketing, no matter what he did, so he told me he might as well eat what he wanted and whenever he wanted. And fighting his addiction to the opioids also consumed him. Trying to stay away from them was as hard as being an addict." He dragged a fingertip along the side of his nose, a slow, distracted motion that matched the heavy slump of his shoulders. "Father Gabriel called my parents and said Myron was struggling, not just with his grades, but socially, emotionally, and spiritually."

"What did your parents do?"

Julien shrugged. "What could they do? They figured if Myron wanted to drop out, he could, and if his grades plummeted that much, he'd be kicked out anyway. It didn't really matter to them one way or another." His face darkened, and his eyebrows sank. "That's when the bad stuff began to happen."

Caleb's eyes widened. "Bad stuff?"

Julien began coughing, and Caleb signaled for a deputy to bring in a bottle of water. After the coughing spell, Julien was able to continue.

"He'd call me, depressed, saying that he was struggling to stay clean and that the depression from being overweight and the taunting he received in high school had followed him into the seminary. He also used to tell me that he held the Lins and the Muellers responsible for shattering his trust in people, and believed their callousness had driven him past the point of recovery and sent him spiraling into a dark, irreversible tailspin. He said the pressure was getting too much for him and that he wanted to end it. I asked him what he meant by that, and he told me, flat out, he wanted to kill himself."

Caleb shot another glance at Maureen. "And what did you and your family do?"

A tear was forming in Julien's eye, and he sniffed. "Before we could come up with a plan, the seminary called and said he had hanged himself." He banged his cuffed fists on the table. "And I soon found myself despising Father Gabriel, not just for what had happened, but for standing by and letting it happen at all. He should have seen my brother was in distress and gotten him some real help. And that's when *my* plan was born." He sniffed again, raising his hands to wipe his nose.

"To kill Joseph Lin and Matthew Mueller, right?"

"Yes, to take away someone *they* loved...and they deserved it. I'm not sorry they're dead, and if I have to spend the rest of my life in jail, then so be it. My family is gone, and I have nothing left." He shot Caleb a defiant look. "I knew those two had always wanted to become priests, and my plan was to follow them into the seminary and end them. So I waited until both of them were here together to enter. I studied hard and told our parish priest I had a vocation. I passed all the interviews and got all the right signatures. The rest is history. *My* history."

Caleb's brows knit together, a flicker of confusion crossing his face as he leaned in, ready to press for answers. "So why all the theatrics, Julien? The parchment with the riddle, the cryptic notes? Why not just kill the two boys?"

Julien allowed a small smirk. "Just me improvising and having some fun. To throw everyone off." His eyes drilled into Caleb's. "To make you all work for this."

Maureen spoke up. "Why did you feel the need to kill my cousin? The only one who never did you any harm?" She folded her arms across her chest, waiting for an answer.

Julien let out a low, wicked chuckle, the sound curling with menace and delight. "Aiden? Well, I did need three killings, like the riddle said, and the third was going to be Father Gabriel, but unfortunately, your cousin just happened to be in the way before I could get to the rector." He spread his palms out. "Nothing personal, Detective."

Caleb exchanged glances with Maureen and laid his pen down, nodding to the deputy, signaling the interview was over. "Get him processed, then take him to a cell," he ordered.

Maureen watched the deputy lift the young man by the arm and escort him out. When the room had cleared, she took a seat next to Caleb.

"I bet you're glad that's over with," she said, gripping his forearm.

Caleb laughed, shaking his head. "You have no idea! So how did your uncle come up with Julien Mercer as the suspect?"

It was Maureen's turn to laugh. "You'll have to ask him that." She checked her watch. "Hey, I'm going to the hospital to check on my cousin and the Kenyan boy. My uncle's there. He can tell you all about it."

"Deal!" He stood, grabbed his jacket, and tucked his pen and notepad into a pocket. "I can finish up here later. It'll take time to get Mercer fingerprinted and all the paperwork completed. Let's go."

By the time they reached the hospital, it was almost midnight. They flashed their badges and asked where Aiden O'Clery was being treated.

To their gratitude, Aiden had been discharged from the emergency room, but he, Brendan, Ezra, and Langdon, were nowhere to be seen. Maureen returned to the desk to see where they might have gone.

One of the nurses overheard the conversation and came over to them. "You'll find the boy in room 304, third floor." The smile on her face told Maureen there was something more. "You'll see when you get there, but rest assured, your cousin is fine." She gave Maureen a wink and returned to her duties.

Maureen looked at Caleb. "So, let's go to room 304."

They got on the empty elevator, riding in exhausted silence. When they exited, they checked for room numbers until they came to it. As they got closer, they heard talking and laughing, and it sounded more like a party than a hospital.

Maureen stepped into the room first and stopped cold. Her mouth dropped open at the sight of Aiden, seated beside the hospital bed, where a cheery Okeyo sat, a lopsided grin going from ear to ear, looking healthier than she'd dared hope. Brendan, Ezra, and Langdon stood nearby, grinning happily.

She walked over to the bed, first gingerly hugging her cousin, who displayed a bandaged head. "Glad you're okay, Cuz," she said, rubbing his back. She looked over at Okeyo and reached for his hand, gently patting it. "And really glad *you're* doing so well." Releasing his hand, she stood back.

"We'll have to question you later, but it can wait until you're feeling better." She gave him her warmest smile.

"Yes, I am good, Detective. I had God Himself watching over me, as well as Mother Mary. I knew I would be in no great danger." His grin was contagious as he looked fondly at his friend Aiden.

Maureen turned to Caleb and nodded. She hugged Aiden one more time. "Then we'll be in touch, Okeyo. I see you're in good hands." She glanced over at her uncle and his friends, giving them a thumbs-up and a broad smile.

Maureen and Caleb turned to go.

Once out of the room, Maureen let out an unladylike groan. "Oh boy, am I glad those kids are okay. They've both been through a lot and may need counseling when this is all over."

Caleb laughed. "Hey, *I* may need counseling! This has been some case." He stopped Maureen as they waited for the elevator. "Listen, Maureen, I just want to thank you for helping me. I know you missed out on your vacation."

Maureen punched his upper arm. "Nonsense, my friend. I've got another week of leave to use up. I guess a 'stay-cation' is better than no vacation, right?"

The elevator opened, and two nurses exited.

Stepping in, Caleb laughed. The door closed. "Have fun on that stay-cation, okay? Sounds like tons of fun."

Maureen stuck her tongue out at him.

CHAPTER 32

Saturday Night

Brendan lay in his bed, one arm propped behind his head. He had been unable to get to sleep. He was glad his nephew had come away from that horrific scene with nothing but minor injuries, but he knew the delicate boy would be changed forever by what Julien Mercer had done to him.

Mary Magdalene lay quietly snoring at his right side, while an unusually docile Saint Peter was snuggled next to the Yorkie. Brendan closed his eyes, hoping to take some time to process the events of the past two weeks.

Brendan's thoughts went to his medicine cabinet and to the amber pill bottles that he knew would give him the rest and peace he needed, but tonight, he was determined to forgo them, his heart turning to prayer instead of pills. And maybe he would, he thought, take Mrs. Morrison's advice and see a professional.

The thought of his Savior, Jesus, hanging on the cross for him, gave him strength; if Christ could endure that, he could make it through one night without the pills.

Closing his eyes, he began to pray, his lips moving silently. Time slipped away, and at last, peace came, and with it, blessed sleep.

SUNDAY MORNING

After being able to sleep for five or six blissful hours, Brendan awoke to a hungry cat pawing at his chin.

A quick coffee and dog walk later, Brendan fed both animals and headed next door to Saint Margaret's to say his morning prayers before the parishioners came in for the first Mass, which was at eight o'clock.

After Mass, he returned to the rectory and picked up the landline in his office to call Aiden, eager to check in. Brendan was anxious to hear how he was holding up.

Just as he was dialing the number, his cell phone's ringtone rang out with the Rolling Stones' song, "Sympathy for the Devil," and his mood shifted with the knowledge that the grand archbishop was calling.

"And here I thought I was going to have a peaceful Sunday," Brendan sighed, taking a seat and resting his cane on the arm of the chair.

"Don't be smart with me. I can have you transferred out of that cushy parish in a New York second," growled Malachy O'Clery.

"Then it's a good thing we're not in New York. So what is it *this* time, brother dear?"

Brendan heard a *hmph*, then, "I only wanted to ask how Aiden's doing. I'm going to have to call Vince soon and ask him for his retirement papers, and that's a job I'm not going to enjoy."

"Isn't that what you have your flunkies for?" He reached down to rub Mary Magdalene's fluffy ears.

Malachy chose to ignore the comment. "So? How's the lad? Any news?"

Brendan settled back in the chair. "I was about to give him a ring when you—great timing as usual—called me. But I'm sure he'll come through this okay. He has a family who loves him. I promise to call you back after I've spoken with him."

"Grand," replied the archbishop. "And Brendan...don't forget about Father Tim."

Brenda pressed his lips together. "He has his program chairpeople, Mal, so I don't have to babysit the man. I told him to ring me if he has any issues. I'll not be driving back and forth into Baltimore unless he has a problem.

But, Mal, the man can barely walk, see, or hear, and those cigarettes are killing him. Don't you think it's time to put him out to pasture? Poor guy!"

"I would, so, but he says he doesn't want to leave, so with the priest shortage, I'll keep him there—that is, if *you're* okay with that."

Brendan let an audible sigh escape. "Goodbye, dear brother."

"Goodbye, dear brother." And with that, the archbishop was gone.

Brendan checked his watch. One Mass to go, then he had to pay his penance and take his ma to lunch. A phone call from his brother was preferable to what he had to look forward to.

CHAPTER 33

A week later, a poker night had officially been declared, and the five cleri-cal comrades squeezed around the rickety table in the rectory's humble utility room—half storage closet, half sanctuary of snacks and banter.

Brendan stared at his cards, then pushed two nickels into the pile. He gave Milo a sanctimonious grin.

Milo lowered his head and glared at Brendan. "Don't make me nail ninety-five reasons why that bet's a heresy."

The group laughed while Milo, the seldom-winning Lutheran, emitted a hissing sigh, throwing his cards down in frustration. "I call. As usual."

Brendan placed his cards down, showing his winning hand and raking in the minute pile of nickels. "This will all go into the poor box."

Langdon reached for the bottle of Jameson. "That ain't even gonna get no poor folks a meal at McDonald's."

"Probably not," said Brendan, reaching for a chicken salad slider, pre-pared by Mrs. Morrison, "but when I take *everyone's* money tonight, the poor will have a banquet."

Langdon growled as he reached for a slider resting on Ezra's plate. The little rabbi slapped the big man's hand.

"So, bro, tell us how you done come up with that name, and how you figgered out who the murderer were."

Ritchie Kim puffed away on his Cuban. "Yeah, I haven't heard the entire story yet. Boy, you sure get yourself into some stuff, Brendan." He laid the cigar down in a glass ashtray and began filling his plate with the sliders, chips, and a generous glob of dip.

Brendan gestured to Langdon to pass the Jameson, and as he filled his glass, he began.

"Well, you guys know the gist of the story, but as for figuring out the real name of Julien Mercer, I owe it all to my love of crosswords and anagrams." He leaned back, letting the golden whiskey roll over his tongue, savoring every burn and warmth it left behind. "I knew one of those boys had to be the murderer—"

"After you eliminated that guy, Marcus Dean, right, Bren?" asked Ezra. Brendan set his glass down. "Right."

"That white boy looked right good at first, huh?" said Langdon.

"He did," continued Brendan, "but I kept thinking it *had* to be one of the boys. But seminarians? It goes against everything we Catholics believe in, so I knew that one of them had to be an imposter, or a truly wicked person—"

"Or both," added Milo.

"True dat," exclaimed Langdon, raising his glass.

"I had my nephew Aiden wait outside while I searched through the folders in the rector's office. Even though those boys all swore they were in their rooms during the murders, I eventually uncovered information from Father Gabriel's hidden papers."

"So get to the name," cried Ezra, as Langdon *shushed* him.

"Well, one night I was doing a fairly easy crossword and the clue was, 'a six-letter word meaning a dealer in textile fabrics, especially silks, velvets, and other fine materials,' or something like that. Anyway, the word 'silk' jumped out at me, and my brain immediately went to Nathan Silk. And, that six-letter word, mercer, for some reason, made me remember that incident where the seminarian hanged himself. His name was Mercer—Myron Mercer, the cryptic M.M. initials on that blasted photograph. That was in Father Gabriel's *secret* stash of files."

"Wow, what a brain," said Ritchie Kim. "How do you even come up with these things?"

"He got his nose in all them puzzle books, that's how," said Langdon, shoving an entire slider into his mouth.

"Well, all those words do help," admitted Brendan, "but mostly it was dumb luck."

"Ain't nuthin' dumb about it, man," said Langdon. "You got it goin' on, brother." He held his hand up for a high-five, and Brendan gave it a hard slap. "And how's about that there riddle? Whaddya think it meant?"

Brendan laughed. "I asked Mo to ask Mercer when she questioned him. I was itching to get that one figured out. She told me he just wanted to put the fear of the Lord in the other seminarians and maybe have them turn on each other so he'd be able to get away with…murder. Oh, and also to muck up the police investigation, which it did."

"So what about that Kenyan boy?" asked Milo. "Didn't he cop to the murders in the beginning?"

"He did," said Brendan, "but that's only because he began to think that maybe his beloved rector was the murderer, and God bless him, he was willing to take the blame just to protect that old guy."

"Gee," said Langdon, "that there's layin' down your life for your bro, for sure."

Ezra stood, stretching his arms over his head. "Hey, you never told us the story about Marcus Dean, how he went from seminarian to groundskeeper."

Brendan nodded and rubbed his hands together. "Yeah, well, Marcus should be telling it, but I guess you guys aren't going to venture a trip out there, so I may as well spill. Marcus was several years ahead of me. We had lots of help in the kitchen back then since there were more seminarians, and there was this one woman, almost fourteen years Marcus's senior. Anyway, she took a shine to him and reeled him in, or at least that's the way we all watched it go down. We tried to tell him she was looking for someone with money, and she knew the Dean family had it. So, she lures him with the biggest temptation we have here on earth, and before you know it, she's pregnant. Well, Marcus got kicked out, his family disinherited him, and he was forced to marry that woman. After the baby was born and the woman knew there was no money to be had, she left him and he never saw either one again." Brendan paused, recollecting the events. "He would have made a great priest, but he fell for what that woman was selling and has had to live with that shame all these years."

The utility room grew silent until Ezra piped in. "Gee, now I feel sorry for the guy."

"Man," said Langdon, "that boy gotta be more like me. I ain't got *no* problem saying no to any of them females. They be like them she-devils that suck the life right outta a man."

Milo laughed. "Hey, I'd settle for one of them any day. Better than what I have now, which is an empty house."

Langdon frowned. "Then you be one lucky man, bro."

Just then, Brendan's cell rang. He picked it up, grinning. "It's Mo!" He answered the phone and then put it on speaker. "We're all here, so watch that language. It's poker night and, so far, I'm winning. How's the Bahamas?"

"It's everything I imagined, Unc," she said, "and I'm so glad you insisted I take a later flight to catch up with my girlfriends, if only for a few days."

Brendan could tell she was relaxed and enjoying herself. He could hear music and some of his niece's friends laughing and chatting away. "Glad to hear it, Mo. You've earned this one. Stay safe and we'll see you soon."

"You got it. I'm really enjoying doing nothing but eating, drinking adult beverages, and working on my tan. Life is good."

Just then, he heard a shrill scream in the background and what sounded like a fight.

"Mo, what's going on?"

After a few seconds of silence, Maureen answered. "Got to go, Uncle Brendan. One of the female customers got her purse grabbed, and they're calling the Bahamian police. And I see the perp, and where's he's running to. Got to run—literally." And the phone went dead.

The five men looked at each other, stunned.

"Please tell me she's not going to chase that guy. That's *meshugah*," said Ezra, looking at Brendan in a panic.

Brendan felt like he'd been hit with a stun gun. "Lord, I hope not, but it did sound like she was giving chase, huh?" He looked at his friends.

Langdon's lips stretched into a slow, crooked smile, his smooth dark skin glowing under the light, and his eyes danced like he was holding back a secret joke. "Anyone wanna go to the islands? May be a good case for *us*."

Laughter filled the tiny utility room as the clerics tossed cards at the towering Baptist. Brendan held Mary Magdalene on his lap, her tiny tongue brushing his hand, and for a moment, the world felt right. Life would bring its trials, he knew, but here—now—he felt God's presence in every laugh, every touch, every heartbeat. Peace, he realized, was not the absence of trouble, but the warmth of love carrying them through. And for now, that was more than enough.

ACKNOWLEDGEMENTS

This story would never have been possible without the help and support of so many talented and generous people.

First and foremost, I give thanks to God, the One who blessed me with this wild, creative, never-sleeping brain and the passion to use it.

Also, my deepest gratitude goes to Father Michael Roach, my "forever" parish priest, who teaches Church History at Mount Saint Mary's Seminary in Emmitsburg, Maryland. His friendship and insight planted the seed that grew into this story, and his knowledge and encouragement propelled me forward every step of the way. This book owes much to his invaluable insight into seminary life, and his help and guidance meant a great deal to me. I'm deeply thankful for the spark that helped bring this book to life. He inspired its heart, its spirit, and its humor. And may he never have seminarians like the ones in this book!

A huge thank-you to my developmental editor, Jennifer Donovan, whose thoughtful guidance helped shape unforgettable characters and a plot full of twists and humor.

To my copy editor, Shannon Cave—you've been with me through all four books, and I can't imagine entrusting them to anyone else. Your steady hand and keen eye make every story stronger.

To my gifted and endlessly patient illustrator, Kerry Ellis, thank you for capturing the heart of my stories time and again. You've created yet another perfect cover that says it all. It's like you're in my head...

My proofreader, Stacy Goitia, has become a long-distance friend whom I have grown to treasure, and I anticipate a long and prosperous relationship.

And, my dear friend and beta reader, fellow author Richard Caldwell, for his sharp feedback, honesty, wit, and constant encouragement. (*The Empress*, and *Fletcher's Pursuit*, available on Amazon)

And as always, to my wonderfully devoted husband, Ron Stout—thank you for giving me the time and space to bring one more book to life. You always come home to find me typing away in the dark as I call out, *"Just give me one more minute!"* You are my rock, my best friend, and the first to cheer me on when the words finally find their way to the page.

Finally, to all of my readers who have been so faithful—thank you for helping me turn inspiration into story and faith into laughter.

www.ingramcontent.com/pod-product-compliance
Lightning Source LLC
Chambersburg PA
CBHW020633260626
47157CB00008B/2725